ESSENTIALS OF DEATH

BOOK 2 IN THE AROMATHERAPY APOTHECARY
MYSTERY SERIES

KIM DAVIS

ISBN: 978-1-963705-84-3

Published in the United States of America by Harbor Lane Books, LLC.

www.harborlanebooks.com

"What are you waiting for? Hurry up and put the boxes on the back counter." Lacie Simmons' harsh voice filled the conference hall as she reached the event booth adjacent to mine. Apparently, the uniformed teen boy hadn't given her low-cut blouse and leopard-print miniskirt enough attention. "Where are the platters? Why aren't they out yet?"

"I...I don't know. My boss only told me to help you bring in the cookies." The teen's voice broke, and his cheeks flushed bright red as he struggled to balance an armload of bakery boxes before precariously perching them on the counter.

"Well, why are you just standing there? Go get the rest of the cookies and find out where the platters are." Lacie used the tips of her bright-red nails—which matched her four-inch, fire-engine red stilettos—to motion the kid into action. She saw me. "What are you staring at, Carissa? I can't believe they'd let a jailbird participate in such an important event."

Her voice sounded like fingernails clawing down a chalkboard as Lacie's barb struck close to home. I had tried so hard to put the arrest behind me but there was always someone to remind me of the scandal. I sucked in a lungful of air, ready to give her a piece of my mind, but snapped it closed when the event manager, Lionel Schmidt, scurried our way.

Turning my attention back to the display in my aromatherapy booth, I worked on the finishing touches for the opening festivities for Oak Creek Valley's annual Playwright Conference and Festival. Every summer, famous, not so famous, and wannabe playwrights, along with actors and actresses, descended upon our town. They participated in seminars and workshops, which culminated in several plays earning a chance to be performed on stage at the end of the event.

"Ms. Simmons, I understand you're looking for the cookie platters?" Lionel's mouth was turned downward.

"Why aren't they already set out for me? I hope you don't think I'm going to do the resort's job for them." Her tone clearly implied the man standing in front of her deserved all the disdain she could muster. "How do you expect me to be ready on time if I have to do everything you should have done already?"

Lacie made it apparent she didn't realize she was dealing with the manager, who, despite his ineffectual appearance—from his bad combover to his reedy voice to his geek-inspired glasses—had a will of steel. He hadn't lasted as manager of the prestigious Oak Creek Valley Inn and Resort for over ten years by being a wimpy pushover. I shuddered to think of the number of stressed-out corporate managers, bridezillas, and mamazillas he'd had to placate. Lacie didn't stand a chance.

"Your contract clearly stated you were to be here two hours prior to the beginning of the event." He raised his hand to stop her from interrupting, then glanced at his watch. "Now I understand emergencies arise, but to waltz in twenty-five minutes before the event and demand us to magically make your booth ready to go will not work."

"Let me talk to the manager. Obviously, you have no idea how to run an event of this magnitude." Lacie turned away from Lionel and began opening the pink bakery boxes.

"Ms. Simmons, I am the manager. Now, if you'll get rid of your superior attitude and get to work, I'm sure you'll be able to prepare your display in time for the opening."

"Well!" Lacie huffed and narrowed her eyes. "There's no need to get snippy with me. Just get the platters here, and I'll do it myself."

"If you had bothered to read the contract, the platters have been stored in the cabinet beneath this counter." He rapped on the space, separating himself from Lacie. "We wanted to make sure they remained clean. If there's nothing else you need, I'll let you get to work."

"Fine, but make sure bell service delivers the rest of my cookies as soon as possible." Lacie didn't sound the least bit sorry she'd been so rude.

I might have uttered a curse or two beneath my breath. Why did Jasper Whitby, the delicious owner of Jean-Luc Patisserie, have to get sick? Instead of spending time together working the kickoff event, I would have to put up with my high school frenemy turned full-on enemy. I muttered when I knocked over several vials of lavender essential oil. Fortunately, the glass didn't break. Otherwise I would have to track down a clean tablecloth and waste time I didn't have to finish up my display.

Most of the vendors were ready and chatted with their neighbors. Lacie had been the last vendor to arrive, and I wondered why she'd been so late. Most likely, she'd spent too much time on her hair and makeup instead of making sure Jasper's patisserie was well-represented. I turned my back and tried to ignore her but it proved difficult since her booth, unfortunately, sat right next to mine. It had been an ideal arrangement when Jasper and I had registered but with Lacie now occupying the space, it had disaster written all over it.

I refocused on the finishing touches on my spa-themed booth for my shop, Aromatherapy Apothecary, and made sure my sign offering five-minute reflexology sessions was prominently visible. There were still twenty minutes before opening so I checked out the other participants. The hotel replicated each of the vendors' logos and displayed them on easels in front of each booth. Some of the booths, such as Jasper's patisserie booth—I refused to call it Lacie's—had a counter in the front to serve the baked goods to attendees. The inside walls of the booth were painted to resemble a quintessential movie Paris café, with pink and black striped wallpaper covering the walls and a painted window that looked out at the Eiffel Tower. Two wrought-iron bistro tables and chairs were positioned in front of the booth for patrons to sit.

Next to the patisserie sat Madame Bonsail's tarot card reading booth. Luxurious brocades and velvet curtains framed the opening, while lace with dangling fringe, rich purple silk, brass candelabras, and skulls graced the interior. Madame Bonsail saw me and motioned me to step all the way in. A raven, perched in the corner, caught my attention. Its black beady eyes watched my every move and goose bumps broke out on my arms.

"Good afternoon, Ms. Carmichael. Come sit. I'll read for you." Madame Bonsail's voice sounded sing-song and almost musical. She wore a long scarlet satin dress, and gold embroidered zodiac signs dotted the bodice. The sleeves of the dress were long and full, which made me think of medieval times. A matching red satin hood and cape covered her short iron-gray hair and flowed down her back.

I had no idea how old Madame Bonsail was. Her hair had gone completely gray, yet her face appeared unlined, and her light blue eyes were clear and bright. Her skin didn't have the pulled look of someone who used a plastic surgeon, so perhaps she colored her hair to appear older or perhaps she used a copious amount of Botox.

"I only wanted to admire the way the hotel decorated the booths. I'd hate to intrude if you're busy." Besides, I wasn't sure I believed in tarot reading, but I didn't want to hurt her feelings. My dad, a pragmatist, didn't place any credence in the practice, but my grandmother, on the other hand, had enjoyed having her cards read.

"Please come in and have a seat. I've been waiting for you to show up." Madame Bonsail gestured around her. "They've done a fabulous job, haven't they? It was sheer genius to host a competition and bring in set designer students to create the booths. Although it'll be difficult for the judges to determine who the winner is. They're all brilliant."

"It seems a shame to put so much work into each set for this one event." By my guesstimate, at least twenty vendors were represented, so a lot of time and money had been invested.

"I heard they were going to use some sets for the final play productions next week. Are you going to be able to attend any of the performances?"

"Jasper said he'd get tickets for Friday night." My ears grew warm. Jasper and I had gone out on a few dates, but it wasn't like we were seriously dating. Anytime our friendship moved toward romance, Lacie had a way of inserting herself and derailing any progress. She'd been doing that to me ever since high school. "How about you? Any plans to see a performance?"

"No. I have conflicting plans I can't change." She gestured toward the plush red velvet chair. "Sit. I've been wanting to read your cards for several months."

Great. Ever since I'd found a neighboring shop owner's body and solved the crime, people had become curious about me. It didn't help that everyone, and I do mean everyone, in our small town also knew about my scandalous arrest in San Francisco the previous year. But I did as Madame Bonsail requested.

"Before I start, I want to tell you I have a strong premonition that your dad will soon experience a life-changing event." She fingered the tarot cards but didn't say anything.

"Is it a good change, or is it something we should be worrying about?"

Madame Bonsail cocked her head to the side, and the raven mimicked the movement. "I'm not getting the feeling that there's danger involved, so I wouldn't worry if I were you. Sometimes, these premonitions are foggy, but if the message becomes clearer, I'll be sure to let you know."

I wasn't sure why she had shared her premonition with me. But I nodded and pointedly glanced at my watch. I didn't have all day to sit here.

"Don't worry. This won't take long, so relax and let the cards speak." Her voice took on a sing-song quality. She shuffled the deck of cards three times, then divided them into three piles face down. "Turn the top card over from each pile and lay each one out in the middle of the table."

I tried to tune out Lacie's snippy voice, bawling out the

poor bell service kid and did as she instructed. While I might not know much about tarot cards, I was pretty certain the first card I'd turned wasn't good if the look on Madame Bonsail's face gave me any indication. It read the Five of Pentacles. The next card, the Ten of Swords, seemed even scarier, especially when a deep furrow appeared between Madame's brows. My hand froze in place as I clutched the third card. Death stared back at me.

CHAPTER TWO

A screech and the sound of breaking glass released me from Death's grip. Lacie's shrill voice could be heard berating some unfortunate victim. I threw the skeleton card down and jumped up from the chair.

"Wait! You need to sit down so we can resolve your cards." Madame Bonsail's gaze fixated on the three cards I had chosen.

"Maybe another time." I rushed out of her booth and hoped it meant I had left my bad fortune behind as well.

It had been a terrible idea to tempt fate, especially since my shop and life seemed to be settling in, and both had thrived once the murder in the spring had been solved. As I sprinted toward my booth, focused on getting away from Death, I forgot to look as I ran. When I crashed headlong into Lacie, she tripped on her stilettos and the crystal platter of cookies she held, flew into the air. The shriek I'd heard earlier sounded again, this time right in my ear, and the same sounds of crashing glass replayed.

"You imbecile! Look what you did. Jasper's going to kill you." Lacie's face turned beet-red, and dark purple stains dotted her silk blouse along with bits of cookie crumbs. It appeared projectile blackberry jam-filled cookies had blasted her when the platters had dropped.

"I'm really sorry. I ran to find out who'd screamed since it sounded like someone needed help." It was all a lie. I wasn't sorry in the least. Well, I did feel bad that Jasper's delectable cookies were destroyed, but there should be plenty left in the stacks of bakery boxes perched on the bell service cart.

Lionel Schmidt rushed up to us. "I have housekeeping on the way to clean up. We have seven minutes until we open the doors. What needs to be done so you're ready, Ms. Simmons?"

"It's all your fault. These morons you hired created this mess, and I need to go home to change." Lacie jabbed her index finger at the manager and bared her teeth. "I'll be sending you my dry-cleaning bill and the receipt for a new pair of Louboutin shoes."

I peered down at her feet, and sure enough, one of the heels had cracked and appeared ready to fall off. No matter how much Lacie might protest, her shoes were designer knockoffs, not the real deal.

"That's impossible. The booth has to be ready to open in six minutes." The manager placed his hands on his hips. "You can't leave now. I'll have my assistant find you a clean blouse."

"Get one of your staff to open the booth. It doesn't take a brain surgeon to put the cookies on a plate." Lacie hobbled over to the counter and snatched up her clutch. "I'll be back when I can."

"I'm warning you. You're jeopardizing the contract." Lionel raised his voice loud enough so everyone in the conference room could've heard the exchange.

"Whatever." Lacie pushed past Lionel.

"I'll be talking to Jasper about this, and if you think you'll have a job come tomorrow, think again."

Lacie turned and glared at the manager. "Let me make this clear. Jasper will never believe a word you say about this, and I'll make sure you never get even one tiny crumb from his patisserie ever again if you try."

Poor Jasper. His patisserie could potentially suffer because of Lacie's arrogance. He never saw the damage Lacie left in her wake and wondered why people complained about her. She had mistreated his customers so egregiously when she first started working at the patisserie, whenever he wasn't around, that I'd finally suggested he put security cameras inside the shop to keep tabs on his staff. Lacie's attitude had immediately changed, and she became the ideal employee. Now it appeared her insolence had reemerged whenever she felt Jasper wouldn't find out. Or, more likely, she wanted to make me look bad any and every opportunity she could. Lacie Simmons wasn't a nice person.

As a group, we watched Lacie stomp off as best she could on the damaged heel, our mouths hanging wide open. Lionel called his office and asked his assistant to come to the rescue. The housekeeping staff descended and, within moments, the broken glass, cookies, and blackberry jam splatters were disposed of.

I returned to my booth to make sure I was ready for the doors to open. In addition to my essential oils display and samples, I would provide attendees with a five-minute-mini-reflexology session. The resort had thoughtfully provided a pedicure chair so I could soak the guests' feet before performing aromatherapy reflexology. Given the number of attendees, I anticipated a nonstop flow of clients and knew I'd be exhausted by the end of the evening.

With five minutes remaining until the doors opened, I made sure a fresh plastic liner had been inserted into the soaking tub. I'd change the liner out with each new customer. With several drops of tea tree oil, a natural anti-septic, added to the warm water, I felt assured their feet would be clean before I worked on their reflexology session.

I turned the battery-operated candles on and started the spa music playlist from my iPhone. Speakers were placed directly behind the pedicure chair, and the music would be just loud enough for the clients to hear but not so loud as to disturb any other booths. With everything in place, I stepped out of the booth and looked at the patisserie.

A woman rapidly placed cookies on platters. Her coral-painted nails flashed in the spotlight illuminating the counter. Her ash-blonde hair, cut in a bob that accentuated her high cheekbones, showcased her china-blue eyes, which were enhanced with dramatic blue mascara. Dressed in a navy-blue wool skirt suit, she looked efficient and not at all flustered as I would have been, especially with the piles of empty bakery boxes littering the front of the booth.

"Let me help you." We had a scant minute before the doors opened, and I wanted to make sure Jasper's booth was perfect. I nodded to the woman and started breaking down the bakery boxes and laid them on the counter. When all the boxes had been flattened, I scooped them up and stashed them beneath the counter, out of sight.

"Thanks. I tried to work as fast as I could to get the cookies out before the hordes descend, but I'm not sure what to do with the boxes." She extended her hand. "I'm Delaney Allman, Lionel's assistant."

"It's so nice to finally meet you in person. I'm Carissa Carmichael." I shook Delaney's hand. I'd talked to her multiple times on the phone in the weeks leading up to the event. "I appreciate you stepping in and helping the patisserie out. Jasper came down with a bug and, well, his assistant is kind of flaky."

Delaney's laugh filled the room and her southern drawl became apparent. "Honey, I am well aware of who and what Lacie Simmons is. Why Jasper would put up with her shenanigans is anybody's guess."

About to make some smart-alecky response, I cut it off when the doors were thrown open and the room filled with the sounds of people ready to enjoy themselves. I hustled back to my booth, ready to provide soothing attention to the attendees. Except no one showed up at my booth. I stepped out and peered down the aisle. There were hordes of people gathered at the far end of the room, and a few young teens trickled down to sample Jasper's cookies. Delaney must've seen my concern.

"Don't worry. They'll make their way down here." She chuckled. "They always hit the wine-tasting booth, then the desserts, then check out the other vendors. Except for the minors. They mostly hang out at the dessert booths the entire time."

A high-school-aged girl placed three cookies on a napkin. She nudged her friend. "Come on, I want to visit the tarot card reader. I want to find out if Trig is gonna ask me out.'

"Ah, to be young and foolish again." Delaney winked at me as the girl ran toward Madame Bonsail's booth. "And to be able to eat all day long without having to watch my figure."

I laughed. Delaney, still slender, appeared as though she worked out to maintain her figure. Even though I guessed her to be about ten years older than me, she was in better shape in her late thirties.

CHAPTER THREE

A trickle of guests took advantage of my services as the first thirty minutes flew by. A lull hit my booth until a woman stood in front of me. She appeared to be in her late fifties to early sixties. Her short hair, dyed a bright magenta-red color, did nothing for her sallow, wrinkled skin that sagged around her jowls. The name badge, hanging from a beaded lanyard around her neck, showed her name: Rachel Walton.

"Are you giving reflexology sessions?" She peered over my shoulder at the pedicure chair.

"Yes, and it's your lucky day. There's no waiting." I directed her to sit in the chair and started the foot bath after using hand sanitizer and donning fresh disposable gloves. "I'm Carissa, and I'll be providing your reflexology session today. Do you have any concerns or food or plant allergies?"

Rachel waved a hand dismissively. "I'm always tired, and the weight keeps creeping up on me. My doctor says it's to be expected by a woman of my age."

While I dried her feet, I immediately saw that despite a warm foot bath with tea tree oil, her feet were cold, and the skin on the soles was thickened, dry, and scaly. And it wasn't because of neglect because she'd clearly had a recent pedicure. The hot pink polish looked fresh, and her cuticles had been attended to.

I tried not to frown. "Let me guess. Your doctor is male and over the age of fifty?"

"Yeah. How'd you know?"

"Rachel, I don't mean to pry, but has he ordered blood tests for you? Specifically, to check your thyroid functions?"

"No. He checked my cholesterol a few years ago but it was well below normal. But nothing recently." She hesitated. "My insurance changed and doesn't cover tests like they used to. I think he's being cautious about the test fees even though I don't mind paying out of pocket."

Somehow, I was certain his preconceived ideas of women of a certain age experiencing issues had contributed to the doctor's neglect. I didn't agree with his opinion, but instead of arguing, I nodded. "Let me give you a relaxing foot massage. Do you like the scent of lavender?"

"Oh yes. It's such a peaceful fragrance."

I used a generous amount of lavender essential oil blended with sweet almond oil on Rachel's feet, since her dry skin soaked it up like a sponge. I started at the base of her big toe and walked my thumb from the outside of her foot toward her second toe, applying gentle pressure. I repeated on her other foot. Next, I applied more oil and gently drug my thumb from the outside of her foot about an inch below her big toe along the sesamoid bone, then followed it until it ended with a hook shape in the middle of the ball of her foot. Rachel had her eyes closed and appeared to be relaxing.

I repeated the same movements but applied more pressure this time. Rachel's eyes flew up, and her eyebrows lifted. I backed off the pressure and felt her relax. Switching to her second foot, I continued the same movements with gentle strokes, applying more moisturizing oil as needed.

"I hope you know you have a felon touching you." Lacie's screechy voice cut through the quiet tranquility as she barged into my booth.

Startled, I jumped and must've applied too much pressure to the sesamoid bone because Rachel yelped, glowered at me, and pulled her feet away from my grasp. "What the heck? You didn't have to hurt me like that."

"I am so, so sorry Rachel." I offered her a warm towel to wipe her feet. Even though there were people waiting for their turn in my chair, I needed to tell Rachel the importance of getting her thyroid tested. The tender reflexology pressure points that made her jump backed up the physical evidence I'd seen on her feet and skin. "We really need to talk but I have to take care of a problem first."

I marched over to Lacie and none too gently grabbed her arm and led her to the patisserie's booth. When she stumbled on her new four-inch stilettos, I pulled her close to me and yelled. "What is wrong with you? Whatever issues you have with me can wait. Right now, there are a lot of people who paid a lot of money to have a great time. Do not, and I mean it Lacie, do not jeopardize Jasper's patisserie's standing in this community or I'll make sure you're sorry. Now, get into your booth and do the job you were paid to do."

She stumbled again when I shoved her toward Delaney. And then I froze. Next to Delaney stood a tall man with thinning blond hair. The skin around his hazel eyes crinkled as his wide mouth broke into a smile when he saw me. He wore a baby-blue button-down long-sleeved shirt with khaki trousers, but what caught my attention was the paunch that had developed around his middle section. His buttons strained against his shirt and he hadn't aged well. Brett. My high school ex-boyfriend and Lacie's ex-husband. I didn't return the smile. Despite the years since I'd seen him, our breakup had broken my heart, and he'd never apologized for believing Lacie's lies about me.

I nodded to him and then, without another backward glance, marched back to my booth. I'd have to think about Brett later. I'd never told Lacie off like that. While I may have thought about what I'd like to say to her, I'd never vocalized any of it. Instead, I'd held it in and, as a result, made myself seem weak in her eyes. No wonder she preyed on my vulnerabilities. I found Rachel putting her shoes back on. She scowled at me. A new person had taken Rachel's spot, waiting for his turn. He would have to wait a little longer.

"Rachel, I am so sorry you experienced pain. It wasn't my intention."

"No? Well, if what that woman says is true, then I guess I shouldn't expect much from a felon."

"I'm not a felon and the hotel will vouch for me. Lacie has issues so let's just leave it at that." I placed my hand on her arm and drew her into the corner of the booth, away from eavesdropping ears. "Let me explain the pain you felt. The area I pressed on is related to your thyroid. If it functioned as it should, you wouldn't have felt any pain at all. The issues you mentioned about weight, fatigue, and the fact that your feet are so dry and cold lead me to believe your thyroid needs to be checked. Your doctor should have done a simple blood test when you last saw him. Get it done and with some medication, it will help relieve your symptoms."

"Really? You could tell all that just from my feet?"

I nodded. "Yes. It's one of the reasons I believe in reflexology and aromatherapy."

"You just reminded me that my sister has thyroid issues. It's under-functioning, and she has to take a supplement every day." She shrugged. "Guess it runs in the family."

Rachel thanked me and went on her way. I went back to my next customer and stared at the line waiting for a turn. I hurried to sanitize my hands, don new gloves, and went back to work. Most of my clients wanted to close their eyes and relax for the five minutes of reflexology, so my mind wandered freely. I listened to the buzz of voices outside my booth, catching snippets of conversation. Apparently, Madame Bonsail had made an impression, especially amongst the teen girl attendees, while the teen boys were more enthusiastic about the virtual off-trail mountain biking being offered by North Valley Trading Company.

Lacie's sharp voice drowned out the murmurs of voices coming from the conference room floor, and I couldn't help but listen to her conversation. "You can't do that to me, Brett. How am I supposed to pay rent?"

"Business is awful, so I'm not making any money." Brett hissed out the words. "There's nothing I can do, and I'd appreciate it if you'd stop harassing me."

"Well, if you don't cough up the cash I need you're going to find out what real harassment is."

Brett must've lowered his voice because his words were muffled, and I couldn't make out what he was saying.

Lacie, on the other hand, didn't bother to mute her voice. "You'll be sorry for cheating me out of the money I deserve. Just you wait and see."

My client shifted in the chair, and when I looked up, she gazed pointedly at my timer, which had gone off. I'd been so fixated on the argument between Lacie and Brett that I'd completely missed the chime at the end of the five-minute session. I quickly moved on to the new client and, from then on, feverishly worked for the next two and a half hours before the crowds drifted to their welcoming banquet.

Once the conference hall doors were closed, I collapsed on the pedicure chair and turned on the massage function. Ibuprofen would be a necessity before bed. My back ached from bending over feet, and my thumbs were almost numb from applying near constant pressure.

Delaney came in and handed me a cold bottle of water. "That was some turnout. Our biggest group yet."

I groaned. "I might have to rethink three hours of reflexology next year. I don't think my thumbs are ever going to recover."

"Rachel Walton told me about her experience with you. That's pretty amazing." Delaney scratched her nose. "I'll call and make an appointment with you at your shop next week. I've been converted."

"I'm not a doctor, so don't make any medical decisions based on my comments. I hope she understands she needs to see a medical professional."

"She knows and will call tomorrow to make an appointment."

"Have you met her at previous conferences?" My curiosity burned. Rachel seemed to have shared a lot of information with Delaney.

"How can you not know who Rachel Walton is?" Delaney gave me a look that implied I'd lost my mind.

"Um, because I'm too busy working to pay attention to celebrities and entertainment gossip?"

"Well, my dear, you just made best friends with a very famous female playwright. She's won a Tony, and several of her off-Broadway shows have been nominated for other major awards."

My jaw must've dropped open. Could we be talking about the same woman? She didn't strike me as someone famous.

Delaney's eyes sparkled. "Yes, you made a new friend, and I think Lacie made a mortal enemy."

"That's not hard for Lacie to do." I snorted. "What did she do now?"

"You won't believe it." She waited to see if I'd guess. When I kept quiet, she continued her story. "Rachel marched over to the patisserie's booth to give Lacie a talking to about interrupting your session and spreading rumors about your so-called felon background. Lacie couldn't have cared less and tried to tell Rachel about your, uh, checkered past from high school shenanigans to your recent run-in with law enforcement types. Rachel finally had enough, picked up a handful of cookies, and walked away."

"Uh, oh. Lacie didn't. Did she?" I cringed hearing the words Lacie had used to taunt kids since school days. She'd even taunted me since I'd returned home from San Francisco and drowned my shame in food for the first few months.

"Oh, she did." Delaney's face had turned a shade of green. "She called Rachel..."

"Please don't say it." I raised my hands, palms facing out, and tried to stop Delaney from finishing the sentence. But it was too late.

"...a fatso. Word for word, she said, 'Hey, Fatso. If you'd stop stuffing your face with cookies and exercise like a normal person, you wouldn't have to talk to quacks like Carissa on how to lose weight.'"

"Ugh. I can't believe she actually said that."

"I know. I'm still feeling kinda sick to my stomach just thinking about it." Delaney rubbed her stomach. "If looks could kill, Lacie would be dead already. You don't want to cross a woman like Rachel."

"I hope Lacie didn't cause any more trouble."

"Well..." Delaney glanced around to see if anyone besides us were within listening distance. There wasn't.

"Oh dear. Who else did she piss off?"

"Let's just say Madame Bonsail is now another member of Lacie's 'You're a Quack' club. She managed to disrupt several card reading sessions for clients when Lacie barged in and started spouting off-the-wall predictions." Delaney sighed. "Lionel is going to have to ban Lacie from any future events, both as a vendor and attendee. I hope Jasper hires someone more reliable after this fiasco."

"I don't get why she has to be nasty to everyone she comes in contact with." That is everyone except handsome or wealthy men who received her charms. They never saw the real Lacie, including Jasper.

"Personally, despite how irritating she is, I kind of feel sorry for her. She seems to have an inferiority complex and it's her way of making herself feel better." Delaney gave a humorless chuckle. "The guy who came with her finally pulled her back into the booth and gave her a stern talking-to. Apparently, he threatened to withhold her alimony if she didn't behave. Is he the ex?"

Small towns. Everyone knew everyone's business and gossip spread like wildfire. That must've been the part of the argument I'd overheard, but to me, it sounded like Brett had done more than threaten to withhold money. "I think they've been divorced for a few years, so I'm not sure why he showed up with her."

"He left a short while after that, but Lacie seems to have

gotten the message." She peered down at me over the bridge of her nose. "Why does she harass you like that?"

"I have no idea. She's had it in for me ever since I've known her from grade school." I shuddered and hoped Lacie wasn't eavesdropping in the booth next door. "Where is she, by the way?"

"She left the second the guests did. In fact, I think she made it out the door before they had a chance."

I raised an eyebrow. "Did she clean up her booth?"

Delaney shook her head. "She said Jasper told her you'd take care of it."

Oh-em-gee. The nerve of that woman. I sighed. "Guess I'd better start packing up my space, and then I'll get to the patisserie's booth."

"I boxed up most of it. There weren't any cookies left since everyone loves Jasper's treats. You don't have much to take."

"Thanks." I sighed again. It would be a long night, and I was grateful that Ashley, my best friend and full-time employee, had offered to take my apricot-colored rescue pup, Pixie, home so I didn't have to worry about her.

CHAPTER FOUR

With the help of Delaney, I got my supplies boxed and loaded in my new-to-me, used Ford SUV. I drove to my shop to drop off the boxes of supplies. I'd unpack them in the morning and deliver the patisserie's box when I stopped for my morning coffee and treat. Stepping out of my vehicle, I noticed that the patisserie's lights practically lit up the entire block. The shop should have been dark. Maybe Jasper felt better and wanted to get a head start for tomorrow's baking.

I grabbed the bakery's supplies, set the alarm on the SUV, and trudged toward Jasper's shop. The downtown post office's historic bell pealed eight chimes. My stomach rumbled, reminding me I hadn't eaten anything since eleven that morning. I peeked into the window, stunned to see Lacie standing behind the counter with tears streaming down her face. I didn't want to feel sorry for her, but somehow Delaney's comment struck home. Only a miserable person could lash out at others, so I had to guess Lacie must've been a truly miserable person. I gently tapped on the glass door and pulled it open. A bell chimed, and Lacie's face went from pathetically sad to instantly angry.

"Did you come to rub my face in my faux pas?" She swiped her cheek with the palm of her hand. "Why didn't you warn me who that woman was?"

"I don't know what you're talking about. I'm dropping off the box of things you left at the booth." The box clattered when I dropped it onto a table. I hadn't bothered to look through the things Delaney had boxed up, and I hoped nothing broke. I didn't need this kind of drama. Everything was always someone else's fault in Lacie's world, and I, too, often, took the brunt of it. I turned to leave, but she walked from behind the counter and grabbed my arm.

"You've got to help me, Carissa. Jasper's still sick, and he says I have to bake the cookies and muffins for opening tomorrow." She'd finally taken off the stilettos and now had to look up at me. "Brett's stopped my alimony, and I can't afford to lose this job."

"So, bake them." Maybe I shouldn't feel that sorry for her. My feet and back ached, and my stomach rumbled. "I've got my own work to do tonight."

"What don't you get? I have no idea how to use his stupid commercial ovens or even where he keeps his ingredients or pans." Lacie tried to look pathetic by gazing at me through half-closed eyes and batting her mascara-globbed lashes. It only made her look demented. When I didn't answer, she lobbed her best shot at dragging me into helping her. "Fine. I'll swear I'll never harass or insult you again in public if you help me this time."

Now, that was an offer I couldn't pass up. "Put your promise in writing with your signature, and you've got yourself a deal."

"Really, Carissa? Can't you just take my word for it?" Lacie pouted.

"Absolutely not. I'm going to unload my SUV and grab something to eat, and then I'll help you as long as you give me your promise in writing."

"How long are you going to be? I don't want to be here all night," she whined.

"Thirty minutes, maybe forty-five minutes tops."

"What am I supposed to do while I'm waiting for you?"

"Do something useful like setting out all the ingredients and baking pans you think we might need." I puffed out a long breath. What I didn't tell her is that I'd supervise her to make sure she knew how to take care of the baking herself should the need ever arise again. Plus, this would be for Jasper, not Lacie. He could fire her for all I cared. In fact, I preferred Jasper out of her claws.

After lugging the boxes of supplies in from my vehicle and carefully placing them on the table in my tiny office, I rummaged through the refrigerator to see if I could forage some dinner. I found a wrinkled apple, a small jar of questionable peanut butter, a moldy piece of cheese, and a Pepsi, which I assumed belonged to Dillon, my part-time employee. Ashley didn't drink sugary drinks unless she had a margarita during our girls' night get-togethers.

I grabbed my keys and purse before heading to HiHo Burgers, a recently re-opened landmark. Once the greasy, but delicious, cheeseburger and French fries were stuffed into my mouth, I decided to put Lacie out of her misery and help her out.

As I yanked open the glass door, the lights were still blazing from the patisserie's windows. Once again, the bell chimed, but I didn't see Lacie. "Hello? Lacie?"

She didn't answer. Maybe she'd gotten mad because I

didn't offer to bring her dinner. Naw. She didn't eat greasy junk food even though she knew I did. I crossed my fingers and hoped she'd gone back to the kitchen to make headway on the baking during the forty minutes I'd been gone. I sniffed the air but didn't smell the sweet fragrance of cookies or muffins. Lacie clearly planned on me doing all the work.

I marched through the swinging doors and into the kitchen. Still no Lacie. Where could she be? Had she gotten fed up waiting for me and quit? I spied the walk-in refrigerator door half-way open. I'd kill her if she'd left it open and ruined all of Jasper's ingredients before quitting. I hoped she hadn't taken our feud to that level by sabotaging his business. I pulled the door fully open to check on the temperature to make sure it hadn't risen to dangerous levels. Looking up to see the thermometer sitting on the top shelf next to the door, I stumbled as I walked into the chilly space. I reached out to steady myself before looking down to see what I had tripped on.

Goosebumps sprouted all over my skin and it wasn't because of the refrigeration. I'd tripped on Lacie. She laid prone, face down, with knives sticking out of her back.

CHAPTER FIVE

"No. No. Just no." My shrill voice echoed around the refrigerator's walls. Even though I dreaded touching Lacie, I stooped down and put my index and middle finger on her wrist. Her skin was already cool and I couldn't find a pulse.

I jerked my hand back and groped for the cell phone I'd stuck into my pocket. I couldn't help but notice that the grouping of small knives on her back hadn't created any blood from the wounds, and I shivered when I counted ten of them. Running from the chilly space and away from the gruesome sight, I called nine-one-one.

"What's your emergency?" Toby answered the call with his usual seriousness. The image of the studious man, with his black-framed glasses filled my head. In his mid-thirties, he took the late shifts because he wasn't married, and he liked to take college classes in the morning before sleeping. He aimed for a law degree and I admired him for his tenacity.

"Hi Toby, it's Carissa. Can you send a unit and the coroner to Jasper's patisserie?"

"Are you okay? Do you need an ambulance?"

"I'm alive, but, unfortunately, Lacie Simmons isn't. I need to call my dad and Jasper." I shivered and wrapped my free arm around my midriff.

Toby's fingers tapping on a keyboard sounded in my ear, and then responding squawks came from his desktop radio. "Units are on their way, and I'll call the coroner for you. Uh, good luck with your dad."

I guess that's one of the benefits of being the daughter of Robert Carmichael, Oak Creek Valley's Chief of Police. When I need help, it's all hands on deck. I called my dad's cell phone.

"Where ya at, Carissa?" My dad had already been informed I was in trouble. Again. He even had the siren going.

"Jasper's patisserie."

"I'll be there in a minute. Make sure you're safe, and if at all possible, don't contaminate the crime scene." He hung up on me, and silence filled my ears.

Before I could call Jasper, a cadre of sirens split the night air. Strobe lights of blue and red filled the windows of the bakery. It didn't take long for the sound of stomping boots running down the sidewalk to reach me, and the glass door of the patisserie flung open. The bell jingled, and I wondered how to disconnect it before it drove me crazy every time the door opened.

I pointed the way to the walk-in refrigerator and my dad's right-hand man, Officer Bryon Zabor, stepped into the kitchen. I followed him but kept my distance while he carefully checked Lacie without disturbing any evidence. He backed out of the refrigerator and closed the door as far as it would go without hitting her.

"Did you touch anything when you found her?" Bryon pulled a notebook from his pocket.

"I checked for a pulse but was careful not to disturb anything." Unfortunately, I'd been through this routine before and knew the drill. "I did notice there wasn't any blood from the knives. Do you think she died before someone stabbed her?"

"Where's Jasper?" Bryon ignored my question. He looked around the kitchen, and a furrow appeared between his brows. "He didn't leave the scene of the crime, did he?"

"No. He's been upstairs sick all day long. I haven't had a chance to call him yet, although I'm sure this racket and the flashing lights have alerted him that something is up."

"Speak of the devil." Bryon's words were so quiet I barely heard them.

I turned and saw Jasper's wane face. He hunched over at the waist and used the doorjamb for support. "Jasper! Sit down before you fall."

"What's going on? Why are all the police here?" His voice croaked, and it looked like it took every ounce of energy to say those few words. His strawberry-blond hair, normally springy with curls, lay limp on his head.

"Mr. Whitby, please have a seat. I'd hate for you to injure yourself while we ask you some questions."

Jasper allowed himself to be led to a bistro table, and he all but collapsed. The officer who had assisted him tried to casually pull a small bottle of hand sanitizer from his pocket and slather his hands with a generous dollop. I sidled up to him and held out my hand. Whatever Jasper had, I didn't want to catch.

"Bryon, wouldn't it be better if Jasper were allowed to go back to bed and lay down?" I had seen the effort it took for Jasper to sit there. He started to shiver and droplets of sweat rolled down his face. His green eyes were glassy, and the whites were bloodshot. The poor guy had a raging fever. "He needs some ibuprofen and possibly medical attention if his fever doesn't go down soon."

Bryon finally took a good look at Jasper and gave his assent. He motioned for two officers standing near the door to help the patisserie owner back in bed. Their faces held twin looks of horror as if they were going to their deaths. Fortunately for them, paramedics arrived at the same time my dad did.

Chief Carmichael bent over and took a long look at Jasper's face. "How long have you been sick?"

"I caught a cold three weeks ago. The fever started a few days ago." Jasper's voice rasped, and he could barely be heard across the room.

My dad used the back of his hand to check Jasper's forehead. "How high is your fever?"

"I got it down to one-oh-two after taking a few ibuprofen, but that was three hours ago." He slumped down in his seat, and his eyes were half-mast.

Dad motioned for the paramedics. "He needs to go to the emergency room. I'll check in on him later tonight."

They loaded him on a stretcher, put him in the ambulance, and carted him away. The bottle of hand sanitizer made the rounds again, and I used a double squirt this time.

My dad headed to the kitchen to take a look at Lacie and secure the crime scene. When he returned to the public seating area of the patisserie, he shook his head. "I'm sorry to see you in this position again, Cari-girl. Are you okay?"

His nickname for me started the water flow, and he rushed to wrap me in a hug. I sobbed into his uniformed chest. I hadn't liked Lacie, but I'd finally realized she'd become a sad, miserable person who deserved some human compassion. She didn't deserve to die, especially by ten knives. I gasped. Ten knives after I'd drawn the Ten of Swords card earlier today.

Dad pulled away from me and handed me a hanky he'd dug out of his pocket. I dried my eyes.

I lowered my voice to barely above a whisper. "Dad, the knives in Lacie's back. I think I know what it means."

He must've noticed the men standing in the room with us had leaned forward to hear my words. "Let's not speculate right now. Bryon will take your statement at the office tonight while I wait for the crime scene investigators. A detective is being sent from Thousand Oaks, and I want you to talk to him in the morning."

This could only mean one thing. My dad had excused himself from the investigation because his only child had become involved in a murder investigation. Again. I hoped the new detective would treat me better than the last one. Then it dawned on me. Jasper had installed cameras in the patisserie to keep an eye on his employees after Lacie started working for him, and he began losing customers.

"Check on the video feed from Jasper's cameras. It'll show who killed Lacie and you won't even have to get another detective involved." I mentally patted myself on my back for solving the crime already.

"Ms. Carmichael, I'm afraid that type of camera doesn't have a video backup feed." One of the new officers to Oak Creek spoke up. He appeared young, maybe in his mid-twenties, and he had dark circles beneath his eyes. He didn't know me well enough to feel comfortable calling me Carissa or even Cari. Yet. "It's the same system we use in our baby's room and playroom."

Darn. "Wait. I seem to remember there are security cameras in front of the patisserie that record. You used the security feed the last time..." I couldn't bring myself to say the last murder I had found myself involved in.

"Unfortunately, a week ago the camera in front of the patisserie was vandalized. Jasper had plans to replace it but he hasn't gotten around to it." My dad burst my hoped-for solution to solving the crime. "I've argued repeatedly with the city council about installing security cameras in the high traffic areas, but they don't feel like it's a priority since we're a low crime town."

He was right, despite this new murder. Even with the flocks of tourists that descended upon Oak Creek Valley every weekend, year-round, and every single day during the summer, there had been virtually no robberies or thefts over the years. With our close proximity to Los Angeles, a mere hour-and-a-half drive, depending on traffic, our small town of about eight thousand people was home to, or at least a weekend getaway, for celebrities and the wealthy.

It also hosted as the backdrop to many movies and television shows, and often, film crews and movie stars wandered around our arcade of shops and restaurants. Because of that, along with the talented artists and New Age retreats, busloads of people came to visit and enjoy all that our bountiful valley had to offer. I hoped this new murder wouldn't scare away the tourists that we heavily relied upon for our livelihood.

My dad gestured to his second in command. "Go with Bryon and give your official statement. I want you to stay at my house tonight. There's no need for you to be out in the boonies after all this."

"Do you really think it's necessary? Lacie's death has nothing to do with me." My dad might be right, but I didn't want to admit it even though exhaustion made me want to lie down right then and there. The thought of driving the few miles to my farmhouse in pitch black darkness, through avocado and Pixie tangerine orchards, didn't sound appealing. Still, I needed to assert a modicum of independence.

After the last murder, I'd lived with my dad for almost a month before I'd felt secure enough to move back to the isolated farmhouse in the middle of an avocado orchard my grandmother had bequeathed to me. I'd seriously contemplated selling it and moving into town, but, in the end, I couldn't part with something that connected me to my much-loved and much-missed grandmother.

"Just for tonight. You're tired, and it's going to be a late night."

"Okay. You're probably right." I grabbed Bryon's arm and pulled him toward the door.

"Make sure you wait for Bryon to follow you to the station. Don't go driving off by yourself."

I waved my hand over my head without turning around to look back at my dad. My car was parked on the curb just a few shops away from the patisserie, so there wasn't any need to get a police escort. But I did as my dad said so I wouldn't have to face a lecture later on.

Once we were seated at his desk at the station, Bryon had me go over everything that had happened with Lacie that day. I had a lot to cover. And then he had me go over it again. After the third time, Bryon started questioning me about my tarot card reading and the Ten of Swords card. Had anyone else been in the vicinity and seen what cards I had drawn? I didn't think so. I had to give Bryon credit. If he felt skeptical about the coincidence of the Ten of Swords card and Lacie's stabbings, he didn't show it. My dad would have been a different story.

"I think you've answered enough questions tonight,

kiddo. I'll follow you to the chief's house and make sure it's secure."

"Honestly, you don't have to do that. I'm not connected to this, and I'm not a target this time."

He rubbed his face. Bryon looked as haggard as I felt. Despite heading toward his late thirties, Bryon usually had a baby-face freshness, which is why he kept his blond hair cut military short. Tonight, he looked his age, if not older. "If you're sure. I need to get this typed up and ready for the detective. He'll want this first thing in the morning."

I looked at my watch. It was already after midnight. I yawned. "Nope, I'm good. I'm not a target, and I'm not going to get involved, so you and my dad don't need to coddle me."

Bryon stood up. "Let me at least walk you to your car."

I held my hand up, palm toward the officer. "No. I parked at the corner. It's not that far from the entrance, so I'll be fine. Besides, who'd be crazy enough to ambush me here?"

I pushed through the glass doors after the elderly night clerk, Bernard, unlocked them for me. A cool breeze caressed my face and blew tendrils of my raven-black, curly locks away from my round cheeks. It felt heavenly after the stifling August heat our valley had been experiencing, and I hoped it indicated the heatwave would break soon.

I'd parked my Ford about fifty feet from the entrance, and I retrieved the keys from my purse as I walked toward it. I punched the remote unlock button, and the SUV's lights went on, illuminating something that had been placed beneath the windshield wipers. I hesitated, then fumbled in my purse for a packet of tissues. I pulled one out and gingerly picked up the rectangular card that had been left for me. A chill slithered up my spine when the light illuminated the scythe-wielding skeleton tarot card. It was Death.

I ran back to the police station and banged on the glass door. Bernard opened it up for me, not looking nearly as tired as when I'd left moments before. I yelled for Bryon and hoped he hadn't decided to get in a cat nap the second I left. He came running out of the break room. Coffee dripped from the front of his shirt, and he pulled at the fabric to move the hot liquid away from his skin.

"What's wrong? Are you hurt?" A look of terror passed across Bryon's face. He knew if anything happened to me on his watch, my dad would probably kill him. Figuratively, of course.

I gingerly handed him the card, keeping the tissue in place to protect any fingerprints. "I was wrong. Someone is targeting me."

After wiping his coffee-stained hands down his trousers, he took the Death card and placed it in an evidence envelope. "Do you think your life is in danger?"

I shook my head. "I think someone is trying to frame me for Lacie's murder but wants to shake me up and scare me away from asking questions before I even start."

A droll smile formed on Bryon's lips. "You do have a reputation."

I waved a dismissive hand. "It's a small town. Everyone knows everything about everyone."

"I can't argue with that. Let me get my keys, and I'll escort you to the chief's house."

CHAPTER SIX

The robustly bitter fragrance of coffee filled my nose, and a gentle nudge woke me. My dad placed a steaming mug of coffee with a generous splash of milk on the table in front of me. The golden glow of sunrise filled the room and made the walls look a cheery shade of yellow instead of the ivory shade I knew they were painted.

"Good morning. I hope you weren't trying to wait up for me." My dad sat in the cushy reading chair adjacent to the couch I had slept on.

"No. I assumed you'd probably work all night long." I sat up and took a sip of coffee. "Thanks for fixing this. I need all the caffeine I can get. Did you get any sleep at all last night?"

"No. I came home to take a quick shower and change into clean clothes." He rubbed his smooth cheek with his palm, then smoothed down his still-wet hair. Dark shadows lay beneath his bloodshot eyes. "I'm meeting Detective Martin at eight, and he'd like to talk to you at nine."

I clenched my eyes together and tried to block out the

memory of finding Lacie's body the night before. I couldn't banish the vision, though. "Did you find out who might have killed Lacie? Or at least some good clues?"

"You know I can't talk to you about the case."

"But you did last time."

"There were extenuating circumstances. This time will be different." He stood to leave. "I need to get to the station to read over your statement before Detective Martin shows up."

"Before you go, what can you tell me about him? Is he any good?"

"I've never met the man, but from what I can tell, he has a good reputation."

"That sounds promising." I picked up the warm mug and held it between my hands. Even though the day would be hot, goosebumps prickled my arms. Had I caught Jasper's illness? What a miserable potential girlfriend I'd been. He'd been carted away to the hospital by ambulance, and I hadn't given him any thought except to worry about how contagious he might have been. I needed to fix that. "Have you heard how Jasper is doing?"

"He has pneumonia, but some antibiotics will have him on the mend in a few days." My dad dipped his head down and scowled. "You haven't checked on him yet?"

"Um, no, but I plan on doing that this morning." Shame warmed my face, and I put the mug of coffee back on the table. "I didn't get home until after midnight, and then I had a lot to think about with Lacie and everything. Didn't Bryon tell you about the card left on my Ford at the station last night?"

My dad plopped himself back down in the chair. "No. He'd already left by the time I got back to the station, and I didn't want to disturb his sleep. What card?"

I explained my tarot card reading with Madame Bonsail and the three cards I'd drawn. I pulled up a Google image of the Ten of Swords card and handed my phone to him. His face scrunched up before he handed my phone back. Next, I found the Death card image, a skeleton standing below phases of the moon, wielding a scythe, and showed it to him.

"It's more than a coincidence that I drew the Ten of Swords card, and then Lacie had ten knives stuck in her back. Someone is trying to warn me or scare me by leaving the Death card." I hated to admit it, but it frightened me. "Did you notice how there wasn't any blood left by the knives? Did she die before they stabbed her?"

"You know I can't discuss this with you, Cari-girl." Dad rubbed his cheek with an open palm and sighed. "But to put your mind at ease, she was strangled, and the knives were fake. It appears the killer used some kind of agricultural wire since there were traces of dirt left behind. It'll be much harder to determine where it came from with all the orchards in the county. Anyone could've stopped off at the side of a road and snipped off a length to use."

I swallowed hard. Lacie didn't deserve death, especially a death that was painful like strangulation. "What do you mean, fake? I saw the knives sticking out of her back."

"They're fake, like what a magician would use with a retractable blade." Dad made sure he had my full attention. "This information can't go any further, do you understand me?"

I nodded my agreement.

"Whoever murdered Lacie planned ahead. The bottom of each knife hilt had been fitted with a magnet, and then, he or she placed a magnetic mat beneath Lacie's shirt. It's how they got the knives to stand up. It was quite a theatrical gesture, which now makes sense with your tarot card."

Relieved she wasn't stabbed ten times, Lacie's death still horrified me. But who would have had ten fake knives lying around to stage Lacie's death? It had been less than six hours from the time I'd drawn those horrid tarot cards to when I found her body.

"How difficult is it to buy those kinds of knives?"

"They're readily available on online retail stores and any Halloween shop." Dad cocked his head at me. "We're checking on that angle so you don't need to get involved. Talk to Detective Martin, and then you and I will have a long discussion over dinner this evening. I'll cook my famous beans and franks."

I inwardly groaned. I wasn't a fan of my dad's favorite meal. So far, since moving back to my farmhouse, I'd avoided his weekly Friday dinner of beans and franks. "But it's Tuesday, not Friday. I can cook some chicken or salmon for dinner."

"A situation like this calls for comfort food, and there's nothing more comforting than beans and franks." He patted my knee.

I could think of a lot of other things that were way more comforting, like Jasper's triple chocolate rolls. The thought made my mouth water, which reminded me that I'd been a horrible, self-centered friend. I needed to find a way to help Jasper, who was stuck in the hospital, and Lacie, who was no longer among the living.

"Okay. We'll talk during dinner."

"We should plan on going to your house afterwards and packing your necessities." He raised an eyebrow as if daring me to argue with him. "You'll stay here until you're no longer a target."

"I agree, but Pixie is going to have to stay here too."

While Ashley, and especially Hunter, would love to keep my pup, I needed to make sure she knew she belonged to me. She was a part of my family no matter how many other people loved her almost as much as I did.

"You know that's not a problem. I still have plenty of food and treats left in the pantry for her." He squeezed my hand and then left for work.

I took a quick shower, dressed in clothes I'd left behind in my old bedroom closet, and downed another cup of coffee along with a piece of toast slathered in local orange blossom honey. With my appointment with Detective Martin set for nine, I had plenty of time to stop by Misty's Blooms and pick flowers up for Jasper before visiting him in the hospital. How had he gotten so sick so fast without me noticing?

When I entered Misty's shop, I breathed in the scents of roses, stargazer lilies, and fresh greenery. Just like my aromatherapy, it brought a sense of calmness. I made a mental note to spend some quiet time with essential oils today and center myself.

"Carissa!" Misty rushed over and held me in a hug. "What a terrible thing to happen to you. And well, of course, to Lacie. I hate to speak ill of the dead, but she courted trouble. Still, she didn't deserve to be killed with ten knives."

I stepped back and gazed at Misty. Despite being middle-aged, she dressed and acted like a teen. Her aqua-tinted short spiked blonde hair complemented her tie-dyed T-shirt that brought the ocean to mind. She wore her usual low-slung skinny jeans that were strategically ripped. "How did you know that? The investigators haven't released any information yet."

"You've been here long enough to know one single whisper leads to the entire town knowing all the details. And to think you pulled the Ten of Swords yesterday. Who would have thought that could happen?" Misty walked to the refrigerated arrangement glass enclosure and pulled out a treebark-looking container that held a variety of succulents. A few brown seed pods were tucked between the waxy leaves. She handed the arrangement to me.

"Who told you about my tarot cards? Shouldn't a reading remain private? Kind of like confession or attorney-client privileges?"

"Oh, it's all over town. I think Delaney told me about it last night. And then I got another phone call from Bobbie right after I hung up with Delaney." She must've seen the confusion on my face. "You know Bobbie, don't you? The teller at OCV bank?"

I shook my head. I didn't know Bobbie, but apparently, she knew me.

"Then there was Xavier and Larry from the mini-mart who told me this morning before I opened the shop." She stopped when I held up my hand. "Never mind who all told me. It's just obvious everyone knows, and someone used your cards as a way to frame you for the murder."

I'd done my utmost to avoid thinking Lacie's murder could be connected to me in any way. But the townspeople had already drawn that conclusion no matter what I wished for. "At least people know I'm being framed this time instead of assuming I'm guilty."

Misty see-sawed her hand back and forth. "I'd say about fifty percent think you're being framed, and the other fifty percent are waiting to see how the investigation plays out."

I groaned and would have cradled my face in my hands

had I not been holding the arrangement. I hadn't ordered anything yet, so it couldn't be for me. "Where do you want me to put this?"

"I knew you'd be in to pick something up for Jasper, so I made it as soon as I got in this morning."

"How do you know about Jasper already?"

Misty's loud laughter rang in the shop. "You're too funny. Everyone knows Jasper's in the hospital with pneumonia. I told him last week he needed to see the doctor. Men. They think they can tough it out."

"I hate to admit it, but I didn't even know he was sick last week."

"He was downing cough syrup and ibuprofen to cover it up." She winked at me. "He's in room three-oh-five, in case you didn't know."

I paid for the arrangement and felt even worse for not noticing he'd been sick. Was I that self-absorbed? My face must've shown my remorse.

"Don't beat yourself up, Carissa. The only reason I know is that I caught him having a coughing fit behind his shop and saw him down half a bottle of cough syrup and pop a handful of ibuprofen pills. I gave him a piece of my mind for treating his body that way, but I couldn't force him to get to the doctor."

Come to think of it, Jasper had seemed strangely busy this past week, and I'd only seen him in passing. When I'd invited him over for dinner, he'd made a vague excuse and promised he'd have time for me soon. When I saw Jasper, he was going to get a piece of my mind, too. What had he been thinking by not taking care of himself?

By the time I reached the hospital, I was in a funk. I couldn't get the image of Lacie's body out of my mind. The murderer must've been looking for an opportunity to kill her, and my tarot card reading gave them the inspiration they needed thanks to loose-lipped Madame Bonsail. I'd talk to her later today, and she'd get a piece of my mind too. It looked like I was going to get involved in the murder investigation whether I wanted to or not.

CHAPTER SEVEN

I knocked on Jasper's half-opened hospital door before pushing it open and stepping into the room. He was propped up in bed and had an IV line going from the back of his right hand to a plastic bag that held clear liquid. Other wires snaked from beneath his hospital gown, and a steady beep from the monitor above his head indicated a strong heartbeat. A tube blew oxygen into his nose, and I could hear a faint hiss with each breath he took. His face was ghostly pale, and the dark shadows beneath his eyes looked ominous. My stomach dropped. He looked so vulnerable.

He opened his eyes as I approached his bed. I placed the arrangement on the nightstand so he could see them. "Hey. I didn't mean to wake you up."

"I'm awake. It's next to impossible to sleep in a joint like this." He smiled but it wasn't his usual carefree smile where his adorable dimple popped on his left cheek. It looked like it took effort to curve his lips upward.

"How are you feeling?" I moved to stand at the end of his bed since I wasn't sure how contagious he was.

"Better than last night." He dragged his hand down his stubbled cheek. "I'm sorry you had to see me so sick, but thanks for coming by and bringing the plant."

"You should have told me you were coming down with something when it first hit you. I have several essential oils that might have helped your immune system plus some reflexology could have alleviated some of your symptoms." I bit back my urge to chide him for downing cough syrup and ibuprofen to mask his illness.

"I knew you were busy getting ready for the event. I didn't want to be a bother."

"You're never a bother." My gaze locked with Jasper's green eyes for a moment and I felt my cheeks warm. "I wanted to come by last night, but it was way past visiting hours by the time I was done with Bryon's questioning."

"I'm sorry you had to find Lacie." Jasper grimaced. "I promise I won't get angry this time if you need to investigate me as a murder suspect. But I hope you know I'm innocent."

I smiled even though inwardly I cringed. My suspicions had almost ended our friendship the last time I found a body. "Of course, you're innocent and just so you know, I am too."

"Does this mean you're investigating again?" Jasper struggled to sit up. When he tried to reach for the water cup, I handed it to him and then returned to stand at the foot of the bed. He took a sip and then rested the plastic cup on the bed.

"I'm supposed to talk to the new detective at nine this morning." I looked at my watch. There were five more minutes to spend with Jasper and then I had to dash to the station. "Supposedly he's good at his job and, I hope, open-minded enough to look beyond circumstantial evidence."

Jasper shook his head. "You're evading my question which I guess is answer enough."

"Yeah, you're right. Someone's trying to frame me and scare me away from asking questions. That makes it personal, and I can't sit around and let it happen."

"That's my girl."

My insides glowed. I was his girl? Yay! Or was it the drugs speaking? I shook off my doubts and asked the one question I needed to know the answer to. "Do you have any idea who might have wanted to kill Lacie?"

"Besides you?" He shook his head. "She was the friendliest person I've ever known. I just don't understand why you two never got along."

Lacie had certainly done a snow job on Jasper and had never allowed him to see her true self. I wouldn't burst that bubble while he was so ill, but it was certain that Lacie had earned many enemies. The question was who had hated her enough to murder her?

I left Jasper and sent a text to Ashley as I walked to my car, asking her to open Aromatherapy Apothecary and hold down the fort until I could get there. My phone immediately rang.

"No." Ashley is normally bubbly and bright. I hadn't expected such an abrupt response from her.

"I'm sorry, Ashley. I'd open, but well I'm not sure how long I'll be tied up." Had I gotten our schedule mixed up? I'd been certain Ashley was supposed to work with me this morning. I hated to think my shop would remain closed until I was finished with the detective, but it looked like that's what would happen.

"I mean, no, you can't text me and expect me to wait on pins and needles until you show up to tell me about Lacie's murder." Ashley's voice went shrill when she said Lacie's name. She hadn't experienced all the drama I'd had with the woman, but she'd heard enough to know Lacie was toxic. "What in the heck is going on, especially with that horrid tarot reading? Why didn't you call me last night?"

"I'm sorry, but I didn't want to wake you so late. You have Hunter and my dog, and if I disrupted them, it wouldn't have been a good thing."

"I know but you could've called me first thing this morning. You know Hunter is up at the crack of dawn."

"I had to rush to take Jasper some flowers. He's in the hospital with pneumonia."

"So I've heard. How is he?"

I pulled the phone away from my ear and looked at it. Did everyone know what was going on except for me? "He's on antibiotics and might get released tomorrow. I've got to call his part-time employees and explain the situation to them. Although, they've probably already received the memo not to come to work until they hear from him."

Ashley's throaty chuckle sounded over the airwaves.

"What are you laughing for?"

"You always seem so surprised and put out that there are no secrets in Oak Creek."

"You know me too well. I'm late for my appointment with the detective, but I promise I'll give you all the juicy details as soon as I can." I disconnected and started my car. Ashley was wrong. There was one secret in Oak Creek, and the killer would do anything he or she could to keep it that way. That secret was the murderer's identity.

I sat across from Detective Frank Martin in the interrogation room, err, the interview room. He offered me coffee, but I declined the battery acid over-brewed concoction.

"Ms. Carmichael, I've read your report you gave to," he paused and checked his notes—written on a yellow legal pad instead of an iPad most detectives now carried— "Officer Zabor late last night. I'd like to go over it with you."

"All right, but I really don't think I can add any new information since I gave him the information less than ten hours ago." I tapped a toe, impatient to get to work.

He furrowed his snow-white bushy eyebrows, and his mouth remained in what I thought was probably a perma- nent frown. "That might be, but I need to hear it directly from you. Written reports don't always convey the meaning behind the words."

He probably hoped my body language would betray any lies I might have told to cover up my involvement. Detective Martin was destined to be disappointed. I purposefully turned my gaze to focus directly on his clear blue eyes. "I didn't kill Lacie nor do I know who did."

"I'm not accusing you of killing her, Ms. Carmichael." He smoothed down his black tie, then tugged at the sleeves of his white shirt. "But someone did, and I want to know who and why. Since you were the first person at the scene of the crime, it'll be helpful for you to give me, verbally, all the details leading up to finding her and what you witnessed upon finding her."

And so, we did. Backward, forward, up and down. He tried to see if he could pry any details from me that I'd forgotten while trying to make sure I hadn't made any details up. I had my facts straight and I stuck to them.

Detective Martin sat back in his uncomfortable chair and rubbed his neck. He stretched and stood, so I did, too.

He motioned me to sit back down. "If you'll wait here a moment, I need to collect something from evidence."

"Sure." I wasn't going anywhere, although I was getting antsy. I needed to get to work.

Once the detective had closed the door as he left the room, I looked at the two-way mirror, did a princess parade wave, and gave a cheesy fake smile. I was certain either my dad or Bryon sat behind the glass, observing and taking notes. It wouldn't hurt to lighten the atmosphere a bit even though I was here on a serious matter. I tried to resist the temptation to turn on my phone. Detective Martin had me turn it off before the interrogation, err interview, but that was two hours ago. I was sure I had all sorts of messages and emails piling up. Before I had a chance to press the on button, the door opened. Detective Martin walked in with another man I'd never met before.

"Ms. Carmichael, this is Detective Raaf. He'll be assisting in this investigation."

The new detective was much younger than Detective Martin. His skin was sallow beneath the fluorescent light, and while he wasn't classically handsome, his thick wavy hair added a certain flair to his demeanor. He had a thin nose and full, rosy lips that he kept pressed together. His light brown eyes were cold and with his black eyebrows drawn together, it looked like he was scowling at me. Too late, I realized it wasn't my dad I had been doing the princess parade wave to. It was Detective Raaf, and he wasn't amused.

I gestured toward the two-way mirror. "Um, sorry about that. I thought my dad was there. I didn't mean to..."

Detective Raaf's scowl deepened. "I hope you realize this investigation is no laughing matter. A young woman has been murdered."

"Yes, sir. I realize this is serious. I didn't mean to jest..." I let my words trail off when a plastic evidence bag was tossed in front of me. The Death card.

"Is this the card you handed to Officer Zabor last night?" Detective Martin practically growled at me.

"Yes. At least it looks like it's the same card."

"And you used a tissue to keep from touching the card when you pulled it from your vehicle and took it to Zabor?" Detective Martin looked down at his notepad to check my answer from our earlier conversation.

"Yes."

"Tell us where you first saw it." It was Detective Raaf's turn to growl. They both seemed very angry, but I didn't understand why my silly princess wave had caused them to get so agitated.

I started to tell them about walking to my SUV and seeing it stuck beneath my windshield wipers.

Detective Raaf interrupted. "No. Tell us about seeing this card at the event at the Oak Creek resort."

"You mean with Madame Bonsail?"

"Yes."

"I have no idea if it's the same card, but the picture is the same as far as I remember." Why were they asking about the tarot card reading? Surely, this was a card from another deck, purchased by a demented killer.

"Please continue with what you saw and touched during the reading at the event." Raaf didn't ask, he commanded so I complied.

"Madame Bonsail had a deck of tarot cards. She shuffled them, then divided them into three piles, face down. Then, I turned over the top card of each pile and put it on the table. The last card I drew was one just like it." I pointed at the Death card.

"What happened to the cards after that?" Detective Raaf crossed his arms in front of his chest.

"I don't specifically know. I left the cards on the table and went to my booth." I crossed my own arms in front of my midriff and leaned back in my chair. "I assume Madame Bonsail continued to use the same deck with the rest of her clients."

"Who entered her booth after you left?" Detective Martin finally sat in the chair across the table from me.

"I have no idea. Shouldn't you be asking Madame Bonsail these questions?"

"Why did you enter the Jean Luc Patisserie after hours?" Raaf loomed over me. "Did you feel the need to continue the altercation with Ms. Simmons? Did it get out of hand?"

"What? No!" I bit my lower lip to keep myself from spewing out a sarcastic reply. "Jasper and I are good friends, and I thought he was in the patisserie prepping for the next morning. I thought I'd help him out. As far as I knew, Lacie had gone home after the event ended."

"Could there be a lovers' triangle that made you lash out at Lacie?" Raaf sneered, and I got the feeling he couldn't see how anyone would be interested in me.

"No! Jasper and Lacie are co-workers. That's it."

"Tell me about Officer Zabor. Did he coach you on what to say for the report?" Detective Martin leaned in toward me. "He's been your father's friend for many years. Did he do anything to help you cover up the truth?"

"Absolutely not! Officer Zabor is an exemplary peace officer. There was nothing untoward that occurred when he took my statement."

The two men exchanged a look I couldn't decipher. Detective Martin relaxed his posture and rested back in the chair. "How well do you know Madame Bonsail? Have you used her services before yesterday?"

"Yesterday was the first time I've had my cards read and will certainly be the last." I heaved out a long breath. Would any of this happened had I not tempted fate and had my cards read? "I know her as a passing acquaintance and fellow business owner. That's it."

Out of the blue, Detective Raaf extracted a paper from the leather folder he had set on the table. He held it out to me, and I took it. My name was typed on the top of the page, and ten fingerprints were lined up: five from my right hand on the top row and five from my left hand beneath. Below the two rows of fingerprints were three additional prints, the photos enlarged to about double the size of my official prints.

"What's this?" I handed the page back to him.

"These," he paused to point to the three enlarged prints, "are your thumb, index, and middle fingerprints that were found on the card you handed to Officer Zabor last night. The top and middle rows are prints you already had on record so you can see the evidence backs up our discovery. We think you placed the card there to divert attention away from your actions that resulted in the death of Ms. Lacie Simmons."

CHAPTER EIGHT

I gulped, and my face turned hot. This couldn't be happening again. Were they trying to trick me? Still, I'd had enough experience being on the wrong side of the law to know not to say anything except for six simple words.

"I'd like to call my attorney."

"There's no need to do that." Detective Martin's voice turned to honey. He knew if I called my lawyer, they wouldn't get any more information out of me. "We're only having a nice conversation here, throwing out ideas and seeing where they go. I'm sure you can explain how the card got on your vehicle."

I shook my head. "I'd like to call my attorney."

"Have it your way." Detective Raaf stood and practically stomped from the room.

I followed him out the door and walked to my dad's office to use his phone. He wasn't there. The two detectives had probably sent him on a useless errand or fact-checking mission so they could have a go at me. Detective Martin stood in the doorway as I placed the call. If I hadn't been so angry at the two detectives, I might have worried about why I'd memorized my attorney's phone number.

When the receptionist answered the phone, I identified myself and asked to speak to Alfred Sanchez. I blew out a long breath when she told me he'd been expecting my call and she'd connect me right away. I turned and saw the detective still standing there, staring at me.

"Carissa, I was hoping I was wrong, and you wouldn't need my services."

"Thanks for taking my call. I have a quick question for you. Am I supposed to be given absolute privacy to place this call to you?" I looked over at the door, and Detective Martin was gone. "Never mind. I was feeling a bit harassed, but they got the message."

"Have they arrested you yet?"

I got up and closed the door, probably a little more forcibly than I should have. The bang echoed down the tiled corridor, and I'm sure everyone in the station heard it.

"No. I hope it doesn't come to that. I'm just afraid that's where they're heading, so I thought I'd better call you before it went any further."

"I can be there in about ten minutes."

"Thanks, Alfred. I appreciate it." I didn't bother asking how he knew I'd need his assistance. The entire town had probably told him before I even knew I'd be a viable suspect myself.

I exited my dad's office and went to the front of the station to wait for my attorney.

Detective Martin sidled up beside me. "You're free to go but don't leave town. We'll have more questions for you as we collect evidence."

"I'll be around. Please be sure you look at the evidence

you collect through unfiltered conjectures. You might be surprised that other suspects are out there."

He looked taken aback. "Ms. Carmichael, rest assured I'm not going into this investigation assuming you're guilty. Quite the opposite. I heard how you were treated in the last investigation you were involved in, and I promise you, that won't happen under my watch."

Gazing out the window, I impatiently waited for Alfred to arrive. I didn't believe Detective Martin's words for a second. He was probably trying to lull me into a sense of complacency, and then wham, I'd be in the slammer. I fiddled with my phone and checked for messages while ignoring the man standing too close to me.

I had several texts, but I wasn't about to open them and read them while the detective practically breathed down my neck. When I was about ready to tell him to back off, my attorney pulled up in the front of the station in a brand new, shiny black Mercedes S-Class car. I turned my back on the detective, waved my fingers at the receptionist, and hurried to the car before Alfred had a chance to turn off the engine.

"Thanks for coming to my rescue so quickly." I buckled the seat belt. "It's amazing that a little threat from my attorney made the detectives see reason and let me go."

"I guess my stellar reputation precedes me." Alfred chuckled. "Let's go to my office, and you can fill me in. I need to sort through what's gossip and what the facts are."

Once we were settled in Alfred's conference room, his assistant, Gabriella, provided us with fresh coffee and crois-sants, and I told my story for the umpteenth time. I didn't have to stop to remember the sequence of events after repeatedly telling it to Bryon the previous night and then to the detectives. Alfred took careful notes and asked a ques-tion or two, but for the most part, he let me talk. I concluded with the bombshell that my fingerprints were on the Death card left on my SUV.

Alfred steepled his fingers together, and the furrow between his thick, bushy brows became more pronounced. "I don't like that I've already heard almost all the facts about the events that have taken place from the gossip going around town. Someone, either the killer or one of the persons attached to the official investigation, is sharing every single detail. This is going to make the investigation harder."

"Why would someone do that?" I took a bite of the croissant. It wasn't as good as Jasper's, but it would fill my growling stomach.

"That, my dear, is a very good question." He wiped a crumb from his lips with one of the linen napkins Gabriella had placed on the table. "Is it to point the investigators toward you, or is it to confuse them and allow the perpetrator to slip away unnoticed?"

I shrugged. My mind was spinning, and I couldn't make heads or tails out of what was going on. It was like someone had pulled me into a game, except they forgot to tell me what the game was or how to play it. I decided to change the subject a little and collect my own information. "Do you know Detectives Martin and Raaf?"

"I've come across Martin a few times, but I believe Raaf is new to the area. He transferred from the Bay area. Martin's a fair guy. Tough and expects people to toe the line, but at least he's fair."

"Uh-oh. Do you think that's why Raaf came down so hard on me? He saw all the news reports about my, uh, arrest last year?"

"That's certainly something to take into consideration should he arrest you for Ms. Simmons's death. If it goes to trial, we can claim pre-prejudice or something similar in your defense."

"I don't want to get to that point."

"We can hire a private detective. Let them dig around the victim's background and see what comes up."

"There's no need to waste money. I know about Lacie's background, and so does everyone else in this town."

"Didn't she move away for quite a while with her husband and then move back to Oak Creek after what's-his-name divorced her?"

"Brett Palen. Yes, but I don't know where she went." I wondered if Brett could have had something to do with Lacie's murder.

"See? You don't know everything about her."

"Maybe I don't, but trust me, most of the gossipers in Oak Creek can supply me with the juicy details. All it will cost me are some cookies." It was time to ingratiate myself and let the gossipers provide the information.

"Remember what happened the last time you started asking questions?" He slid his index finger across his throat. "You had a close call, and as your attorney and your father's friend, I have to caution you not to get involved. You need to keep a low profile and not draw any attention to yourself."

"It'll be fine. I'm not going to talk to the killer. What harm could come from chatting with the little old ladies who sit around gossiping over their three-martini lunch while complaining about what the town's mischievous kids are getting into?"

"The problem with that reasoning, Carissa, is you have no idea who the killer is."

CHAPTER NINE

On the walk back to Aromatherapy Apothecary, everything is within walking distance in downtown Oak Creek Valley, I stopped by a local farm-to-fork café. Their Mac & Cheese lunch special tempted me, but instead, I ordered two organic salads with grilled chicken to go. They included thick slices of garlic bread with the order, and my mouth watered the entire way to my shop.

It was almost one, and I worried about leaving Ashley on her own to deal with customers. The least I could do was bring her lunch. With the town's gossip mill apparently in overdrive, Ashley would be giving me more details about the case than I would be able to give her. I hoped we'd have a few quiet moments to chat and enjoy the lunch without constant interruption. But it wasn't meant to be.

The second I opened the door, my senses were assaulted. A room full of shrill voices, all clamoring to be heard, filled the shop. Brightly-colored attired bodies pressed together in groups around the room, and the largest group held Ashley captive in their midst. My nose told me that someone had spilled a vial of my celebration blend along with a vial of peppermint essential oils. The contrasting fragrances blended with the overpowering scent of someone's Chanel Number 5 and, if my nose wasn't mistaken, someone else's La Vie Est Belle. It made my head hurt, and I fought the urge to turn my back and run away.

"Thank God you're here." Dillon's strong hand grasped my arm and pulled me in. I couldn't escape now. He was my dad's girlfriend's son. Nearly twenty years old, Dillon was mature for his age, and better yet, had an affinity for pairing the right essential oils with our customers' ailments. The elderly women who frequented my shop adored the tall young man who always had a ready smile and patience for listening to them.

"What is going on?" I'd never seen my shop so overrun with people. I hoped they were customers wanting to buy products, but I had my doubts.

"A bunch of senior tour buses have hit town, and for some reason they want a photo with you." Dillon's hazel-colored eyes swept around the room, and then he pointed toward the back wall, which I'd had painted with my shop's logo a bare month ago. Someone had removed the table displaying some of the aromatherapy accessories I sold, and a group of elderly people milled about the open area.

"Why me?" I groaned. "I don't think that's a good idea. How about I scramble to get someone to help you out, and I'll disappear?"

But it was too late. A blue-haired little old lady saw me and started a stampede in my direction.

"There she is! I saw her first!" Even though the elderly woman looked to be in her eighties and appeared frail, she whacked the crowd with her oversized purse and used her elbows to make a path straight for me. "I get first dibs on having my picture taken with you."

She pulled me, with bony fingers firmly attached to my arm, toward the back wall. I tried to dig my heels in, but the woman seemed to have superhuman strength as she dragged me forward. I was sure this wasn't what my attorney had in mind when he told me to keep a low profile. How was I going to explain this fiasco to Alfred and my dad?

The blue-haired woman positioned me next to the logo while someone yanked the sack of salads from my hand. Another elderly woman removed my ponytail elastic band and fluffed my hair. Someone said I needed to apply some lipstick. I ignored that comment. Blue-hair handed her iPhone, the latest model that released the previous week, to a friend.

She poked me in the ribs. "Say cheese, deary."

I felt like a deer caught in the headlights, but I did. The sooner I got through this, the sooner I could creep away and hibernate for the next ten years. Several times, I attempted to leave the wall in order to help Ashley at the register. But each time I moved, chaos followed in my footsteps, making it nearly impossible for Ashley to take care of the paying customers. I gave up and stood where it seemed safest for everyone concerned. Despite asking several of the seniors why they'd descended on my shop, I never received a coherent answer. Instead, they tried to pry murder investigation answers out of me, so I stopped all conversations and moved them along as quickly as I could.

After what seemed like a lifetime of standing and smiling until my cheeks ached, the line to have photos with me dwindled to a handful of latecomers. I looked around the shop to see how Ashley and Dillon fared and found Detective Raaf standing just inside the door, scribbling in a notebook. His jaw was clenched and his black brows were drawn together so tight, it appeared he had a unibrow.

He caught me staring at him. With a roll of his eyes and a shake of his head, he pushed through the glass door and disappeared. A feeling of dread hit me as I looked around my chaotic shop. How could I make Detective Raaf understand that I hadn't instigated this mayhem?

I'd just as soon chase these people out so I could lock the door and wallow in sorrow. As much as Lacie and I had a contentious relationship, she was still a member of our community and would never experience love, friendship, or motherhood now. Instead, thanks to the powerful influence of social media, I had to smile and act like nothing tragic had happened.

An ancient man, who looked close to a hundred years old, came to stand beside me. He was half a head shorter than me, and sported a liver-spotted bald head and bad dentures. He pinched my bottom.

"Hey, you don't need to do that." I slapped his hand away when he rested it on my back, way below my waistline. "Move it or lose it."

He gazed at me with cloudy eyes and then fiddled with his hearing aid. "Eh? Whad'ya say?"

"Nothing. Just smile at the camera, okay?" I wondered if he'd heard more than he let on because he clasped his hands in front of his body and inched away from me.

He nodded at his companion, who held a top-of-the-line Canon DSLR, and immediately, the camera clicked and clicked and clicked. Apparently, it had been set on sports mode.

After what seemed like at least a hundred photos had been taken, I gritted my teeth and said, "Time for the next guest."

Instead of walking away, he turned and slipped a piece

of paper into my hand. "Here's my number, doll. Call me, and let's have dinner sometime."

I tried to smile politely, and instead of meeting his gaze, I motioned for his companion, who hurried to take the elderly man's arm. "Enjoy the rest of your visit to Oak Creek Valley."

The next woman in line had bright orange hair, which did nothing for her wrinkled complexion. Her hair clashed dreadfully with her hot pink lipstick and lime green muumuu, and the colorful combination standing next to me wouldn't be doing me any favors either. She must've seen the exchange between myself and the fresh elderly man because, instead of posing for the camera, she stepped in front of me to have a word.

"Don't worry about Melvin. He's harmless." She patted my arm. "He's on our bus, and we'll be heading out of town for Solvang in thirty minutes. I'll make sure he doesn't miss his ride."

"It was just a surprise to get pinched. I wasn't sure what to say."

"You handled him quite well, and it appeared he got the message. There's no excuse for any man to think they can put a hand on a woman."

I appreciated the woman's concern and felt bad about rushing our photo, but there were still people waiting impatiently in line. And to be honest, I was practically dead on my feet. "Thanks for letting me know. Are you ready to flash your charming smile for the camera?"

The woman chortled, and not only smiled to show off the dimples in her cheeks, she flashed the peace sign with both hands for the photo.

By four-thirty, I was ready to collapse, and from the fatigue that showed on Ashley and Dillon's faces, they felt like I did. Even though it was earlier than usual, I turned the closed sign on and locked the door the second our last paying customer left. I turned around in a circle to survey my decimated shop. It looked like an elephant had stampeded through, despite my worries that the guests were all lookie-loos, we had sold a huge amount of stock that day.

"I owe you guys big time." I sat on the floor next to Ashley, who had collapsed into the small cushioned chair, and rested my head on her slender jean-clad leg. "You're both my heroes, and I don't know how I would have gotten through the day without you."

Ashley stroked my tangled curly hair. After my ponytail had been released, I'd mistakenly allowed one of the women—who had to have been ninety if a day—to comb my hair and spritz it with hairspray. After my morning with the detectives, I knew my locks were a bedraggled mess, and if my picture was going to end up all over the place, I didn't want to look horrible.

After that, several other women had taken it upon themselves to comb, tease, hairspray, and bling out my locks with glitter and accessories to their liking. It had been a shock and awe moment as they scoured their capacious handbags for products and accessories to style me with. No matter how much I expressed my dismay, the elderly women ignored my feeble protests and did as they pleased. I could have been more forceful in putting an end to it, but I worried about getting a bad review on social media if one of them felt like I'd been rude in putting a stop to their fun. And if their giggles were anything to go by, they were having a blast. It's not easy saying 'no' to little old ladies having the time of their lives. I hoped never to experience another day like today, but I could ill afford to lose business in the long term if negative reviews were posted.

"I've never seen anything like that." Dillon folded his long legs, crisscross style, as he sat down on the other side of Ashley. "Who knew murder could be such a great marketing tool?"

Ashley sighed. "I can't figure out how all these people heard about Lacie's murder already and decided you're involved somehow. I know her death is tragic, but just think about all the publicity those hundreds of photos are going to provide on social media."

"If you're too tired to move, I can order pizza for some sustenance." I ignored their murder remarks and pulled my cell from my back pocket after I'd brushed glitter from Ashley's legs. "Or feel free to escape now while there's some peace and quiet. The cleanup can wait until tomorrow."

Ashley yawned, then pulled her wavy blonde hair up into a messy bun that looked elegant with her long, slender neck. "I'd better go home and relieve my mom. I thought once Hunter turned three, he'd be out of the terrible twos, but it hasn't happened yet."

Dillon glanced at his watch. "I'll pass this time, boss. I'm supposed to meet up with some friends for a gaming marathon, and I don't want to be late."

Ashley bumped her shoulder into Dillon's arm. "Thanks for coming in when I called. I wouldn't have survived without you."

"No prob." Dillon stood. "I'm glad I was around to help out."

I thanked my lucky stars that both of my employees were stellar. "I can't thank you both enough for putting up with the madhouse today. Once I tally up sales for today, I'll issue bonuses."

"And that's why you're the best boss ever." Dillon reached over and fist-bumped me. "Do you think it's going to be as crazy tomorrow as today? I'm supposed to leave for a waterskiing trip in the morning. I can cancel if you need me."

"Don't worry about it. I don't see being interrogated again so Ashley and I should be able to hold the fort down." I wished Mari wasn't on vacation. She'd be willing to help out the second I asked her. Even though she was in her seventies, Mari was my mentor and had been a lifeline during my scandal in San Francisco. She'd also been instrumental in helping me establish Aromatherapy Apothecary. Mari liked to say she was retired and living the quiet life, but she had too much energy to sit still for long and often spent time with me, offering free mini reflexology sessions for my customers.

"I'll be back home Thursday night, and you can count on me being here Friday through Sunday, however many hours you need." Dillon stood and patted my shoulder. "Don't forget my classes start in two weeks. You're interviewing for another part-timer, right?"

I groaned. The festival preparations and the onslaught of summer tourists had kept me busier than I had planned and I hadn't even advertised for help yet. "It's the very next thing on my list to do. I'll work on it before the crowds show up this weekend."

The Playwright's Conference and Festival would culminate with the participants showcasing their creations by putting on plays Friday through Sunday. Hordes of people would descend on our town to enjoy the entertainment and, with luck, be able to say they saw the start of a famous career if a participant hit it big. If today were any indication, all the shops in town would be swamped. It was good for our profit margin, but it was also exhausting. Besides another part-time employee, I needed to consider getting temporary help during the big festivals that came to Oak Creek Valley every month.

"How early are you coming in?" Ashley stretched her arms over her head. Her mint-green polo shirt pulled up, revealing her tiny waist and a glint of a belly button piercing.

"Maybe around eight. That should give me enough time to clean and restock the shelves before we open." I eyed the painted logo and wondered if I should cover it with something. I didn't want future customers to use it as a shock and awe photobooth opportunity because I never wanted to go through another day like today.

"I'll meet you here and help."

"Why don't you wait until nine? That'll give you some time with Hunter before work."

"He's been getting up at five every morning. By the time I get here, I feel like I've already put in a full day." She nudged my shoulder. "At least we've had Pixie to keep Hunter occupied and playing quietly without demanding my attention."

"Ouch. That's early." Dillon visibly shuddered.

"Tell me about it. He's just like his father was. Up at the crack of dawn with more energy than should be legally allowed." Ashley's rosebud mouth turned down at the corners at the mention of her deceased partner. A Marine, he'd been killed in the line of duty overseas before she'd even had a chance to marry him or tell him she was expecting their first child. She hadn't had an easy time of it since his death.

I hugged Ashley and then pulled her to her feet. "Do you want to bring Pixie in the morning? Or I can pick her up as soon as I finish closing the shop."

"I promise we won't steal your dog, but if we could keep

her another night, that would be great." Ashley crossed her fingers. "Pixie has helped Hunter cut down on his tantrums, which makes it so much easier on all of us."

"If you're sure. I hate to take advantage of your dog-sitting services."

Ashley giggled. "We're the ones who should be paying you to rent your dog for Hunter. It's a win-win for all of us."

I unlocked the front door. "Come on, you two. Get out of here and get some rest."

Once the pair were on their way home, I glanced around the shop and decided I could wait until the morning to straighten it up. After setting the security alarm, something my dad had insisted be installed after a murder took place inside my shop, I turned off the lights and headed to my SUV. I scanned the area around me, looking for anything or anyone that might pose a threat, but I didn't see anything except tourists strolling down the street on their way to dinner. It saddened me to see Jasper's patisserie closed and reminded me I needed to visit him after dinner.

On the drive home, I checked my rear-view mirror, hoping I wouldn't spot anyone, especially one of the detectives following me. Somehow, I didn't think they were through with me yet. When I reached my dad's house, I parked in the driveway at the home I'd grown up in. I didn't see his vehicle, so I assumed he was still at work.

Exiting my SUV, I made sure I locked it before limping toward the front door. My stomach grumbled. I'd never gotten around to eating my salad. On auto-pilot, my hand tugged open the screen door before my eyes could register the skeleton card taped to the oak front door. It was another Death card.

CHAPTER TEN

My hand jerked back like it had been about ready to touch a snake or a spider. Sweat broke out on my brow. Someone knew where I was staying and knew my dad wasn't around to protect me. I turned and ran toward my SUV, all the while fumbling with my key fob to unlock it. Instead, I set off the panic button, and a shrill siren split the air. While that wasn't my intent, I decided it wasn't a bad thing even if the shriek had almost given me a heart attack. If the person stalking me was hanging around watching, the siren would scare them off.

I had one hand on the key fob turning off the panic alarm and my other hand on my door handle to open the vehicle when a noise in the oleander bushes bordering my dad's property from his neighbor caught my attention. Just as my head swiveled to take a look, something solid hit my shoulder and knocked me to the ground.

I pushed up onto my hands and knees, ready to protect myself, and stared straight into the pulsing red eyes of a skull. A screech erupted from my lips. I leaped up and kicked the grotesque thing, which sent it wobbling down the sidewalk. Panting, I scanned the area to see if any more attacks were coming, but nothing else happened.

"Cool Halloween decoration." Ethan, a ten-year-old neighborhood boy my dad was always talking to, hopped off his bike and scooped up the skull that sat spinning on the sidewalk. "Do you have candy?"

It was too late when I realized the kid might have contaminated potential evidence. "Uh, no. Someone was playing a trick on me."

"Scared ya, huh?" He laughed and held the skull up to get a better look at the eye sockets that beamed out pulsing red light. "Can I keep it? I'm going to be a pirate for Halloween, and this'll go great with my costume."

"I need to let the police take a look at it first." I held my hands out, hoping he'd get the hint to give it back to me. Not that I wanted to touch the thing. I couldn't help but notice his scabbed knees sticking out beneath his camo cargo shorts and the scabs dotting his arms. He must've had a tumble off his bike recently, and I was happy to see that he wore a bike helmet over his red hair that curled beneath the edges of the safety gear. "As soon as they're done with it, I'll drop it off at your house."

Ethan reluctantly handed me the skull and seemed to examine my face. "You're the one that found the dead lady at the bakery."

I hesitated, then nodded. A ten-year-old shouldn't know about murder, but apparently, things were different than when I was his age.

"Was there a lot of blood? I heard she was stabbed with a lot of knives."

"Um, I need to get to the police station. I'd better go now before they close."

Ethan twisted his face and squinted his bright green eyes at me. "The police never close."

He had me there. "Well, the people I need to talk to don't work at night."

"They do if there's an emergency." He pointed at the skull. "Is this an emergency? Did someone threaten you?"

Oh-em-gee. When did kids get so smart? I realized I was better off being honest, and maybe he'd go home and leave me alone. "I think someone's trying to scare me, but that's all. I need to talk to the detectives who are investigating, and since they live in Thousand Oaks, I want to see them before they leave for the day."

"They're not leaving. They checked into the Blue Jay B & B this morning." Ethan blinked at me, and then he turned his attention to one of his friends riding past us on a bike. "I gotta go. Don't forget to give me the skull when forensics is done with it."

"Wait!" Were all ten-year-olds connected to the town's gossip hotline? Did they all watch CSI with their parents and know how crime scenes and clues were processed? "How did you know the detectives are staying in town?"

"That's easy. My aunt owns the B & B. They're lucky someone canceled their room at the last minute 'cause the festival means everything is booked already."

With that, he rode away and joined up with three more boys on bicycles. I'd rather have the detectives forty miles away instead of in my backyard twenty-four hours a day. I climbed into the Ford and tossed the skull into the passenger seat. At this point, there wasn't any use in trying to protect fingerprints. I was certain there wouldn't be any besides my own and Ethan's. I started the vehicle, but instead of driving to the police station, I called my dad.

"Hey, kiddo. I'm just leaving now." He turned the

volume of his radio down. Garth Brooks had been singing about friends in low places. I could relate. "Do you need me to pick anything up from the store on my way?"

"No, but you probably want to bring a forensics team home with you."

The phone went silent for several long seconds. "Say that again?"

"Someone left another Death card on your front door, and when I ran for my car, they threw a Halloween skull at me."

"Are you okay? Are you hurt?" The chief of police was back on the job.

"I'm fine, and they're long gone. I didn't touch the card, but Ethan from down the street picked the skull up before I had a chance to protect any evidence on it." I laughed. "He wants me to give him the skull once forensics is done processing it."

My dad chuckled. "He's addicted to CSI and can probably tell you about every single episode that's been aired."

"Should I stay here and wait for you or meet you at the station with the skull?"

"If you feel safe enough, stay there. I sent Bryon a text, and he should be there soon." His scanner spewed out some unintelligible words to me. "I'd hate for the perp to swoop in and take the card if no one's there to keep an eye on it."

"I hear the siren already. Are you going to alert the detectives, or do I need to do it?"

"I'll take care of them once I get home." My dad's siren came to life. "See you in a couple."

And then there was nothing but dead air on my cell.

Bryon showed up and placed the skull in an evidence bag. Even though it was dinner time, a gaggle of kids on bikes, boys and girls alike, clustered on the sidewalk in front of the house. Ethan was holding court and telling them what had happened to me and then went into great detail on how forensics would process the skull. I got the feeling he hoped he would have to go down to the station and provide them with his fingerprints.

Before Bryon could make his way to the front door, my dad pulled into the driveway and parked behind my SUV. I was glad he'd turned off the siren before entering the neighborhood. He gave me a quick nod, then strode to the front door and carefully examined the card without touching anything. He motioned for Bryon to put the card in the evidence bag, which he did with little ceremony. My dad put the bag in his vehicle, while Bryon dusted the screen door and the front door for fingerprints. I was certain he'd find nothing except my dad's and my prints. It was obvious whoever was stalking me knew what they were doing.

"Can you show me where the perp was standing when they threw the skull at you?" His radio squawked, and Dad turned the volume down.

I took him over to the oleander bushes and pointed to where the person had most likely been hiding. He looked at the ground and at the broken branches. "We'll need to process this and see if we can get a shoe print. Hopefully, they left some fibers and hair behind, too."

"Did you contact the detectives?"

He nodded. "They were in the middle of dinner but said they'd come by when they finished."

"Good thing it wasn't an emergency."

My dad gave me a look like he used to give me when I was a little girl. Without him saying a word, he'd warned me that I was getting too sassy and to watch my attitude. I might have huffed a little, annoyed that he knew me so well.

"Rumors are going around that you had quite a circus

going on at your shop this afternoon." Dad kept his focus on the bushes in front of us while he placed yellow crime scene tape around the area. "Do you think it's wise to make such a spectacle with everything going on?"

"You have to believe me when I say I was ambushed. I had no idea what to do, so I went along with it with the hope that those senior citizens would go on their way and leave me alone." I didn't want to have this conversation. I wanted to eat an entire pizza by myself, have a couple glasses of red wine, shampoo the stuff out of my hair, and then crawl into bed for the next seventy-two hours. "Those senior bus tour people are ruthless. Look what they did to my hair."

Whenever I moved my head, a shower of glitter floated around me like Tinkerbell. It would take an hour or more under the showerhead to wash it out of my thick, curly hair. "Every time I objected, they'd shush me or pretend I hadn't said a word. It was like I was a mannequin. They would have given Gram a run for her money."

"There has never been nor could there ever be anyone as strong-willed as your grandmother." My dad's mother was a force of nature, and even he, as chief of police, wasn't able to stand up to her.

"Yeah, I know. Now, just imagine one hundred Grams banding together and ganging up on you. That's what I faced today, and I was clearly the loser."

"You're exaggerating."

"Uh, no. I promise, I'm not exaggerating." I pointed my finger at him. "Go ahead and ask Dillon and Ashley about it. They're just as shell-shocked as I am. Maybe more so because they didn't know Gram."

He held up both hands, palms facing toward me. "Okay, I give. Why don't you let yourself into the house using the back door and get something to eat while we wait for Detectives Martin and Raaf to show up? You'll feel better once you get your blood sugar stabilized."

"Why are two detectives assigned to Lacie's murder? It seems a bit much."

"The Playwright Festival draws a lot of famous people, and the mayor doesn't want the negative publicity over the murder not getting solved right away. He thinks two detectives are better than one."

"Ah, so that explains why Raaf, at least, would rather pin his hopes on finding me guilty. A nice, easy solution with little effort."

"I still think Martin will be level-headed and fair. Raaf has something else going on besides the need to please the mayor." Dad lifted his eyebrows. "Does his name ring any bells from your San Francisco days?"

"I wondered if there was a connection the second I'd heard he'd recently transferred to Southern California." I shook my head. "But, unfortunately, no. It's an unusual enough name that I would have remembered."

"Keep your ears and eyes open, Cari-girl. This isn't going to be as easygoing as I'd hoped."

"Does that mean you'll give me information about the case so I can help solve it?"

Dad rolled his eyes. "No. It means if you hear or see anything, no matter how trivial, you tell me right away."

"Sure." Except I wouldn't be sitting by and waiting to become the next victim. It was time to get busy and delve into the occult, starting with how my tarot card reading had spread all over town. Madame Bonsail had better have some good answers for me.

CHAPTER ELEVEN

With a bowl of canned chicken noodle soup warmed up in the microwave, I sat at the kitchen table and ate it along with a stack of saltine crackers. Madame Bonsail had responded to my text and agreed to meet me at her home at nine that night. She indicated she had unfinished business with my reading and wanted to resolve it. I wasn't thrilled with the idea, so I made a few notes on my phone about the questions I should ask her. Hopefully, it would divert her from delving too far into the meaning of the cards I'd drawn.

The voices of loud males coming through the front door interrupted my solitude, and I hastily downed the soup left at the bottom of my bowl. While a glass of wine would have been nice, I didn't need my judgment clouded for the questions that would be thrown at me by Detectives Martin and Raaf.

"Ms. Carmichael, may we have a word with you?" Detective Martin stepped into the kitchen. "Might I sit down?"

I shrugged. "If you must."

Detective Raaf stood in the doorway with his arms crossed tight in front of his chest. He must have dressed rapidly for my interview, because his tie and his shirt looked rumpled, and his lips were pressed tightly together in a downturned glower. My incident had interrupted his evening off.

Detective Martin pulled out a small notebook and his cell phone. After scrolling through the various apps, he found one and opened it before placing the phone on the table between us. "Do you mind if I record our interview?"

Like I had a choice. "That's fine."

"Let's talk about your complete disregard for the integrity of this investigation and your scheme for personal publicity and financial gain from cashing in on the brutal murder of Ms. Simmons."

Stunned, my mouth fell open, and my mind raced. Weren't the detectives here to investigate the attack on me? Detective Raaf's glower had turned to a smirk, and I realized he had it in for me. "There is no scheme. Someone is going out of their way to besmirch my reputation and make me feel like I could be the next victim."

"That's not what it looked like down at your shop this afternoon." Raaf had uncrossed his arms and had placed his hands on his hips.

"That circus started while I was being interviewed by you, and then by my attorney. I have no idea why all those senior citizens descended on my shop, and I certainly had nothing to do with it. It was an ambush, plain and simple."

Detective Martin picked his phone back up, and opened a new app. Whatever it was, he scrolled and scrolled, frowned and scratched his head, then scrolled some more. Finally, he handed the phone to me. It was Aromatherapy Apothecary's Instagram account.

A graphic using my shop's logo and my photo invited people to visit my shop today for a chance to have their picture taken with a murder suspect. There would also be a grand prize drawing for a one-thousand-dollar Visa gift card. To enter, the participant only had to post their photo that was taken with me, and include #murdersuspect, #aromatherapyapothecary, #carissacarmichael, and #justiceforlacie on social media. They could gain extra entries by posting the photos and hashtags on all social media sites. No purchase was necessary.

The phone clattered from my hands, and my stomach plummeted like I was on a runaway elevator heading for the center of the earth. "Who? Why? Why would someone do this to me? Who did this? You have to stop them."

"That's a ridiculous question, Ms. Carmichael. This graphic is on your business Facebook page and X as well. It went viral." Raaf approached me. "Tell me, how much profit did you make today off of Lacie's murder?"

"Let me be very clear. I did not, nor did any member of my staff, create this graphic and post it to social media. You need to find out who hacked into my accounts and did this." I grabbed my cell phone from my pocket and opened Instagram. Except, instead of seeing the feed, I was met with the login page. I entered my password, but it wouldn't accept it. I hit the 'Forgot password' link and tried sending a reset password link to my email and my phone. Neither my email nor my phone received the link. I didn't bother checking Facebook and Twitter,...err, X. Someone had been messing around with my account and had frozen me out. I showed both detectives.

"There's no proof you didn't have one of your staff members change it for you in case you were questioned." Raaf hovered above me, and I had to tip my head way back to see him. It was uncomfortable but I wouldn't give him the satisfaction of knowing it bothered me.

"And you have no proof that I didn't get hacked." I hoped it was the case of innocent until proven guilty scenario.

"You need to freeze all your social media activity while tech takes a look. Until it can be ascertained if you're involved, I'd better not catch you posting anything, especially about the murder. I'll keep a close watch." Raaf had hijacked the interrogation and wouldn't let Martin get a word in edgewise. "Furthermore, we've gotten a judge to issue a gag order. You are not to talk about or even mention the murder from here on out. If you do, you'll be subject to prosecution. Do you understand?"

I nodded.

"I need to hear you give a verbal agreement." Raaf bent at the waist and placed his large hands palms down on the table in front of me. "I'll be watching you very, very closely because I know you can't help but meddle in things that don't concern you."

"I understand, Detective Raaf." I practically spit his name out. I fumed. "Now, would you care to tell me what you're going to do about the lunatic who keeps leaving me Death cards and attacks me in broad daylight? It seems to me that someone is going out of their way to make sure I don't talk."

"Nice try. There aren't any witnesses to anyone leaving the cards or throwing Halloween decorations at you." Raaf's smirk was back. "You're a pathetic attention seeker, and it's obvious you're manufacturing these incidents for your own gain."

"That's enough, Raaf." Martin inserted himself. "We're here to find the truth, not harass our witness. If what Ms.

Carmichael says is true about someone hacking into her accounts and stalking her, we have more than a murder to solve."

Raaf snorted. "By all means, have it your way. We'll go by the book but mark my words, this woman is nothing but poison."

Once the two men left the house, I poured myself a glass of wine with shaky hands. In hindsight, I should have called my attorney but I had erroneously thought they were coming to investigate the Death card and the skull. And what did the gag order mean? They hadn't left me any legal documents, so did that mean they were bluffing?

"Hey sweetheart, how're you holding up?" Dad wrapped his arms around my shoulders and gave me a hug.

"I've had worse days, but this has been pretty bad." I gulped some wine down. "Are they looking for footprints or fibers in the oleanders?"

He winced. "No. Raaf said he's pretty sure you fabricated the story, and they wouldn't waste their time or resources."

So that's how it was going to play out. The perp would get away, and I would be left trying to put my world back together. "I need to talk to Alfred but I'll call him tomorrow morning during business hours. There's nothing he can do right now. He probably should have been here, but I really thought they came to talk about the card and the skull."

"I thought about calling Alfred myself, but like you, I assumed they would take your statement regarding the Death card and investigate the threat." He sat down at the table beside me. "I'm sorry I didn't come in, but I was warned not to get involved. It could've made matters worse had I stuck my nose in. It probably should have tipped me off that they were here to investigate you and not the card."

"That's what I thought. Raaf is playing hardball, and we need to find out why." I pulled a beer out of the refrigerator and handed it to my dad. "So, any physical evidence hiding in the oleanders will just be destroyed by the elements?"

"Bryon is doing a thorough job of combing through it and cataloging every strand of hair and every fiber he comes across. He'll look for evidence even if Raaf won't." Dad took a sip of beer. "Are you ready for some beans and franks?"

"I had some soup but I'm still hungry." I pulled a pan out and placed it on a burner. "While it's heating, I'll make a salad. Do you want to ask Bryon to join us?"

"Naw. He has a hot date with some blonde tonight. I believe it involves pizza and a movie featuring baby lions and a monkey or two on the television."

I was happy for Ashley and Hunter. Bryon was a good sport and seemed to care about both mother and son. I busied myself with preparing dinner while my dad scrolled through his emails or something on his cell.

There must not have been much to catch up on because he cleared his throat to get my attention. "Why aren't I seeing any photos from your Instagram account?"

Wait. What? "You have an Instagram account? When did that happen?"

"I'm not the old fogie you might think. I'm on X too."

"No way!"

"Yes, way." Dad showed me the screen on his phone and pointed to the icons. "I'm not ready for Facebook. Too much angst goes on there."

I had to agree with his assessment. "What made you get on social media?"

He looked sheepish. "Dillon convinced me, then showed me how it works."

"Good for him." Although, to be honest, I was a bit

irked because my dad had never listened to me about getting an account.

"So, what am I doing wrong? I can't find your pictures."

"I'm not sure what's going on. My social media sites were hacked, and while I can't access my accounts yet, you should still be able to see photos in your newsfeed." Had the hacker closed my account, or were they preparing to do something worse? I worried how much damage that would do to my business and my reputation.

"How did that happen?"

Before I could explain the horrible graphic to my dad, my phone chimed with a text from Ashley, wondering why she couldn't access Instagram to upload some photos from today.

"Do you mind if I call Ashley and put her on the speaker? I'll explain to both of you what happened." I tapped on the phone icon and found Ashley's contact number. While I might have my attorney's phone number memorized, I hadn't done the same with my friends.

"That's a good idea. Maybe you should conference Dillon in, too, and keep him in the loop." Dad wouldn't meet my gaze.

I pushed away my curiosity about why Dad was so chummy with Dillon. Sure, he'd been dating Dillon's mom, Sandy, for a while, but I hadn't thought it was anything serious. Now, I had to wonder. That mystery could wait. Right now, I needed to protect my business and my reputation. "Sure. I'll send him a text and see if he's free."

Dillon immediately responded with a thumbs-up emoji, and I responded that I'd conference him in with Ashley and my dad.

I called Ashley and explained that I wanted the four of us on the call together. After asking her mom to watch

Hunter and my pup, she was fine with it. I hoped Pixie wasn't making a nuisance of herself.

When we were all on the line, I jumped straight to the issue. "Someone hacked into the shop's social media accounts and locked us out. To make matters worse, they posted a graphic using my logo and photo, luring people to the store for a chance to have their picture taken with a murder suspect. They also promised there would be a grand prize drawing for a one-thousand-dollar Visa gift card for anyone who posted their photo with me on their social media sites. It explains why today was such a zoo." Just talking about it made me sick to my stomach.

Ashley sputtered. "But how? I mean, why? Why would someone do that?"

"Duuuddde..." Dillon drew the word out. "Do you think you're going to need to have the accounts closed and start over?"

"I truly hope it doesn't come to that." I rubbed my eyes and tried not to think of all the time and work Ashley had invested in making our social media sites inviting and posting daily photos. "Somebody seems to want to ruin my reputation. I assured the detectives that none of my staff nor myself had anything to do with this."

"Of course we didn't." Ashley huffed out air. "I can't believe they'd even consider for a second that you'd sabotage your business and reputation by pulling a stunt like that."

"You have to admit it did bring in a ton of new business, though," Dillon said. "But I didn't mean to imply that using the murder for marketing is acceptable in any way, despite my insensitive comment earlier. And I hope you know I didn't have anything to do with this."

"I never for a second thought either of you did this. In

the meantime, I can't reset the passwords to our social media sites so I'll have to figure out how to get it done." I dreaded having to deal with it.

My dad looked like he was in shock, his eyes wide open, and his mouth hung down. I squeezed his hand.

"Law enforcement has said in no uncertain terms that we're not supposed to post anything to the sites, assuming I can even figure out how to access them. In the meantime, use extreme caution on who you talk to about the murder. Someone is using the town's gossip mill to make it look like I'm sabotaging the investigation. Apparently, the detectives even convinced a judge to issue a gag order against me."

My dad stood up abruptly. His chair tipped back and fell over, creating a deafening cacophony as it hit the tiled kitchen floor. "That's it. I'm going to have a word with Raaf. This is all his doing."

I grabbed his hand. "Do not do that. He's fishing for reasons to escalate the tension. Let's talk to Alfred in the morning and see what he suggests."

His shoulders drooped, and he set the chair upright and sat back down. "You're right. But karma is going to catch up with that man. Mark my words."

CHAPTER TWELVE

Dad cleaned up the dinner dishes while I took the speediest shower of my life and dressed in a pair of comfy, colorful board shorts and tank top. I saw I wouldn't make it to the hospital before visiting hours ended at eight-thirty. I decided to take the chance that they'd let me see Jasper anyway, if only for a moment, instead of kicking me out the second I arrived.

Sending a text to Madame Bonsail, I explained I'd be later than nine and asked if she'd rather reschedule. When she didn't immediately reply, I headed to the hospital where the head nurse took pity on me, and allowed me to see Jasper. He didn't appear as pale and weak as he was that morning, and I was relieved to see the oxygen tube had been removed.

"How are you feeling?" I started toward his bed, but he held up his hand in a stop position, so I stayed where I was.

"Better, but the doctor told me I might be contagious for another day while the antibiotics kick in. You probably should keep your distance. I didn't know that this morning when you came by. Sorry." He gestured toward the arrangement I'd dropped off that morning. "I don't think I thanked you for the succulents."

"You did, but you were kind of out of it this morning."

"I do appreciate them, so thank you."

"You're welcome. When are you going to get to go home?"

"Most likely by tomorrow afternoon. I've responded well to the antibiotics, and I'm not running a fever anymore."

"You're not planning on opening the patisserie as soon as you're released, are you?" I looked around his room and noticed numerous get-well cards were arranged on a side table, along with other bouquets of flowers. "You need to give yourself time to recover."

"Is that your expert medical experience talking?" Jasper grinned, then chortled to let me know he was kidding. "John and Luke flew in this afternoon from Seattle and will open it tomorrow for me. They said they'd stay at least a week or so until I get back on my feet."

"You mean John and Luke, the founders of Jean-Luc Patisserie?"

Jasper nodded. "They heard what happened at the patisserie and called me. When they found out I was in the hospital, they offered to help."

"That's wonderful. Is there anything I can do to help them out?" Not that I had any extra time, but if needed, I'd do what I could.

"Can you stop by tomorrow morning and thank them for me?" He paused as a coughing spell took hold. I was relieved that he used a handful of tissues to cover his mouth and nose. After a sip of water, the coughing subsided. "I'll drop by as soon as I'm released here."

I gave him a long look and shook my head. "I suppose

there's no trying to reason with you to go straight home and get into bed when you're released."

"I'll be fine."

I rolled my eyes, exasperated. "Yeah, and look where ignoring your symptoms got you. Why didn't you see a doctor when you got sick?"

"You don't need to lecture me. I've been hearing it all day long." He rubbed his palm over the reddish-gold stubble that covered his jaw.

"I'm just worried about you and hate to see you so sick." I wanted to reach over and clasp his hand, but instead, I stayed close to the door. "The whole town probably feels the same way I do."

"So...you're worried about me?" Jasper's green eyes glinted, and a dimple appeared on his left cheek. "Does that mean you'll nurse me back to health once I go home?"

"Will you settle for essential oils and reflexology? I can mix up a blend of eucalyptus, thyme, ginger, and clove essential oils and bring it by tomorrow evening." My stomach fluttered. I'd never visited the apartment Jasper lived in over the patisserie. "I can bring some soup for dinner too."

"I'd like that." His dimple deepened as his gaze met mine. "You can leave dessert up to me."

I could barely contain the smile that wanted to take over my face. "Sounds good. I'll try to be there around six-thirty after I close up the shop."

He lowered his voice. "I can't wait."

By now, my stomach was doing flip-flops. I jumped when the on-duty nurse stuck her head in the room.

"It's time to go, Carissa. Visiting hours are long over."

"Okay. I'll be out in a moment."

She left to return to her duties, and her shoes squeaked as she walked back to the nurse's station.

I glanced at my watch. "I need to meet Madame Bonsail at nine anyway, so I'd better make the nurse happy and leave."

Jasper raised his eyebrows.

"It's a long story. I'll tell you about it tomorrow night." I waggled my fingers at him. "If you need anything in the meantime, call me."

"Thanks, Carissa. It means a lot to me that you came by."

Once I left the safety of the brightly lit hospital, I kept a close watch on the surroundings and kept my finger next to the emergency call button on my phone until I made it to the SUV. With the doors locked, I drove to Madame Bonsail's home, a mere three blocks from the hospital. I would have walked had I not been so nervous about a killer targeting me.

She must have kept an eye out for me because as soon as I locked my vehicle, she stood at the opened door of her Craftsman bungalow. Golden light spilled from the doorway and illuminated the flagstone walkway leading to the house. Small Malibu lights were strategically placed in the California drought-resistant landscaping.

"Come in, my dear. I have herbal tea and lavender cookies for our session." She winked at me. "I bought the cookies from your beau a while back and keep them stashed in my freezer for when I need them."

"You mean Jasper?" What did she mean by beau? We hadn't been on many dates, and Lacie managed to disrupt our time together more often than not.

"Of course. It's obvious you two are meant for each other."

"I don't know about that. We're only getting to know each other, so it remains to be seen."

I followed Madame Bonsail down a hallway with thick, dark-red carpet that muffled our footsteps. Ornate, antique-gold-colored sconces, reminiscent of the Gilded Age, provided dim lighting. She motioned for me to sit when we entered a cozy sitting room. Two overstuffed armchairs, upholstered in wine-red velvet, faced an ornately carved white marble fireplace hearth. I chose the chair closest to the door, relieved she hadn't built a fire. It was warm in the room as it was, and the vintage burgundy-colored cabbage rose wallpaper made it feel closed in. A round, marble table situated between the two chairs held a white china teapot, two delicate white cups, and saucers. A dainty, gold plate displayed a half dozen cookies that held flecks of lavender in the pale rounds, and she thoughtfully added several rose-colored napkins on the side.

Madame Bonsail sat down in the remaining chair and poured tea into the two cups. The brew had a red-blush color, and the fragrance of rose and hibiscus greeted my nose. After handing me one of the filled cups balanced on a saucer, she picked up her teacup and took a sip. I did the same and was pleased that she had tempered the tartness of the hibiscus with honey. With a sigh, she placed the cup and saucer back on the table and steepled her fingers together.

"Now, young lady, we must address your reading." She took my cup and saucer and placed it back on the table. "May I examine your left hand?"

I held it out to her while I tried to avoid knocking the cups over. She turned my palm to face the ceiling, and smoothed my hand with her soft fingers. I couldn't help but notice that her nail polish was almost the same color as the tea and the same color as the flowing caftan she wore.

She guided my hand back to my lap and sighed.

"What did you see?" Not that the cards or my palm had anything to do with Lacie's death. Instead, a killer had heard about the cards I drew and had used the opportunity to kill Lacie and frame me. The rest was all coincidence.

"Between your card reading and your palm reading, I think fate is trying to tell you that you're being targeted by evil forces." She closed her eyes and leaned back in her chair.

With my palm positioned in front of my face, I tried to see what she was talking about. I didn't have a clue, except that anyone who had listened to even half the gossip circulating town could have said the same thing. "What does that mean?"

"I merely pass on the reading. You'll have to find the answers within yourself." Madame Bonsail shrugged. "Or perhaps you did something in a former life, and you're paying the price for it now."

"How can I get myself untargeted?" I wasn't sure I believed what she'd said, but I'd been a victim a few times too many. Perhaps she could help me change my fate.

She motioned for me to place my hand into hers, and once again, she turned my palm facing up and ran her fingertips along the lines creasing my palm. She released my hand, and I placed it back on my lap.

"You have a strong intellect and a quizzical mind. That, paired with your compassionate nature, make you want to right wrongs." She turned to gaze into my eyes. Her light blue eyes looked almost black in the lighting. Her voice lowered to a hoarse whisper that sounded like nothing I'd ever heard come out of her mouth before. "But, beware of Death. It will be your downfall."

CHAPTER THIRTEEN

I reared back in my seat. The scenes of finding Lacie sprawled in the walk-in refrigerator with ten knives sticking from her back flashed through my head, while a skeleton card mocking me from my dad's front door made my heart rate escalate. Who was targeting me and why? Despite Madame Bonsail's pronouncement, I didn't believe unseen evil forces would be my downfall. Instead, it was an evil human intent on making me pay for their crime.

"What do you mean? Who or what is Death?"

Madame Bonsail shivered, then twisted her head away from me. Her voice turned squeaky. "What?"

"What death are you talking about?"

Her face scrunched together as if trying to puzzle over my question but she didn't say anything. I realized I hadn't told her about the Death cards left for me, so I filled her in on what had happened.

Instead of responding, Madame Bonsail picked up her teacup and sipped. Her teacup rattled against the saucer as her hands shook.

"What's wrong? Can't you tell me what's going on?" I

wanted a sip of tea, but my hands quivered. Madame Bonsail's distress was contagious. I tucked them beneath my legs and took a deep breath to calm myself.

She placed her teacup and saucer down, and finally gazed back at me. "This is worse than I thought. Dark forces are gathering against you. If you press forward with your quest, all will be lost."

Ugh. Something creepy was going on, but it wasn't some supernatural death-type thing. "Madame Bonsail, would it be possible for you to put aside your, ah, profession, and think back to the event on Thursday? Was anyone around that could have heard or seen the cards I drew? Or did you tell anyone about my cards?"

"Oh dear..." Her eyebrows furrowed together, and she pursed her lips. "I didn't think..."

From long practice while waiting for my dad to collect his thoughts, I allowed silence to fill the air and barely allowed myself to breathe, worried I'd distract her. My patience paid off.

"I owe you an apology. This is all my fault." She picked up a paper napkin and twisted it so harshly it shredded onto her lap. She stared at the bits and pieces that blended into her caftan. "My dear, I told everyone who came to my booth that day. I've never seen or even heard of anyone drawing those three cards together. I never would've thought someone would use that information to commit murder."

This was even worse than I could have possibly imagined. Those people probably told everyone they knew, who, in turn, passed on the gossip. By now, there were probably about ten thousand people who knew about the cards and could have killed Lacie. "What happened to the deck of cards you used with me?"

She rolled her eyes up toward the ceiling while she

thought. "I put them aside since I didn't want your aura interfering with other attendees' readings. Funny thing is, I couldn't find the deck when I packed up to come home."

"Would it have been easy for someone to have taken them after their reading without you realizing it?"

She shrugged. "I left the deck on the side table and didn't give them another thought until I went to pack up. You know how busy it got. I didn't have even a minute to breathe between each session."

I nodded. "It was exhausting. I'm going to have to rethink my participation in these types of events or rotate the mini sessions with another reflexologist so we each have breaks."

"Ashley would be a good candidate."

"She would be my first choice, and her practice is paying off. Unfortunately, I'm short on staff as it is and I can't afford to close the shop for events."

"Hmmm. Let me make some inquiries. I think I know someone who would be a good fit with your staff. Are you looking for a full-time employee or part-time?" She poured some more tea into our cups and took a sip. Her hands no longer shook.

"Part-time for now once Dillon starts college, but the hours would increase during festivals and events if they were available." I picked up a cookie and took a nibble. The sandy, melt-in-your-mouth buttery texture almost made me swoon, while the delicate flavor of the lavender filled my mouth with happiness. I'd have to put an order in with Jasper for our private after-hours, "Make Your Own Healing Salve" special workshop Ashley and I had scheduled for Thursday. If it went well, we planned on making it a monthly event, and the fragrant cookies would tie in beautifully with the lavender essential oils used in the salve.

"I'll make some calls tomorrow."

"Thanks, I appreciate it." I took another cookie and warned myself not to eat the remaining four left on the plate. "Back to the missing cards. Do you have any inkling who visited your booth and had issues with Lacie? It has to be someone who knew her."

"My dear, you probably know better than anyone that Lacie created chaos in all her relationships, whether casual or close."

"Hmph. Everyone except Jasper, but I suppose once she got her talons into him, he'd have eventually seen the real Lacie." I gave myself a mental slap. It wasn't nice to speak ill of the dead.

"Jasper is a Pisces and thoroughly exhibits the empathetic and compassionate nature of his sign." Madame Bonsail took a sip of tea. "But back to your question, Ms. Walton was particularly angered by Lacie. I had a difficult time reading her cards since her negative aura encroached on the session."

"I don't see a famous person like Rachel Walton following Lacie and then killing her. Besides, with all the events going on, she's sure to have an alibi."

"Ms. Walton is a Capricorn, so don't rule her out."

I tried not to roll my eyes. This wasn't getting me any answers. All I had wanted was a list of people who had visited Madame Bonsail and not their birth signs, which, in my mind, didn't influence whether they could murder someone. Plus, if she was a real psychic, wouldn't she already know who the killer was?

She must have sensed my impatience because she briefly touched my arm. "My gift doesn't work that way."

Surprise must've shown on my face. How had she

known what I was thinking? I hadn't said it out loud, had I? My face heated.

"Your face is an open book, Carissa. Plus, I've had enough experience with people having preconceived ideas about what I do. I can take a good guess at what their thought process is, given the emotions displayed on their faces."

"I'm sorry. I didn't mean to belittle your..." I waved my hand around the room, "err, expertise."

Her laugh tinkled like a tiny bell. "Your questions don't belittle me, and I realize the zodiac signs of my clients don't mean anything to you. I suppose any number of people, pushed hard enough, could seek murder as a solution. Let's see, there was Delaney Allman, and she had a lot to say about being forced to work with Lacie at the event."

That surprised me since Delaney seemed sympathetic to Lacie when we'd chatted after the event. "Really? I wonder why she stayed in Jasper's booth most of the time then? Wasn't she supposed to only help out until Lacie came back?"

"Apparently, Lionel thought Lacie wasn't capable of manning it on her own, and he always puts the reputation of the resort first. He didn't want to risk attendees experiencing a negative run-in with Lacie."

Could Lionel have been so angry at Lacie for potentially ruining the inn's reputation? Especially after her derogatory remark to the famous Rachel Walton. I seriously doubted it. From what I could see, the event had been a huge success despite that snafu. "What about Lacie's ex, Brett? I saw him briefly before the doors opened."

Madame Bonsail shrugged. "They had a contentious relationship, and the divorce made it even more so. Even though I didn't read his cards, I could see that there's a dark red aura with black edges surrounding him. My advice to you is to steer clear of him... he could be dangerous."

CHAPTER FOURTEEN

A cold nose and a warm tongue licking my cheek nudged me awake. My puppy, Pixie, gazed at me with soulful toffee-colored eyes. Her apricot-colored furry tail did a helicopter twirl, which made her entire body shake. I reached over, stroked Pixie's silky ears, and glanced at the doorway. My best friend, Ashley, gave me a huge smile and a finger wave.

"Sorry to wake you, sleepyhead, but it's already eight thirty. Didn't you want to meet at the shop at eight?"

Groaning, I squinted at my childhood clock sitting on the bedside table. Ashley wasn't lying. It really was that late. How had I overslept for so long? Why hadn't my dad woken me? I rolled out of bed, and Pixie danced around my feet.

"Let me throw some clothes on, and I'll be ready in a couple of minutes." I ran my fingers through the tangles of my unruly hair. It would have to be a messy bun day. "Thanks for waking me. I'm surprised my dad let me sleep in this late."

Ashley cleared her throat. "I don't think he slept here last night."

My hand fell from the shirt that I'd been ready to yank from the clothes hanger, and I turned to gape at her. "What do you mean? How'd you get in the house if he's not here?"

"When you didn't show up at the shop by eight, I went to the patisserie and ran into him there. He gave me his house key and suggested I check on you." Ashley's shoulders lifted, and she wiggled her eyebrows. "He and Sandy looked very cozy and lovey-dovey eating their pain au chocolat and sipping cappuccinos."

"Oh no! I promised Jasper I'd stop by early this morning and see if John and Luke needed anything. Did you see them?" Not waiting for an answer, I threw my oversized sleep T-shirt off and donned a camisole and a clean sage-colored polo shirt that sported my shop's logo. Once I'd stretched black leggings over my generous thighs, I slid ballerina flats onto my feet. I put off thinking about my dad not coming home last night and his progressing relationship with Sandy.

"I don't think you need to worry. They have everything under control. It's almost like they never left." Ashley handed me a hairbrush. "Come on. There's a latte and cinnamon roll waiting for you at the shop. They didn't have your favorite chocolate ones this morning."

"You're the best friend ever!" I leaned over and bussed her cheek, then scooped Pixie up and held her close. "I suppose we can open the shop a little later than usual since we have so much cleanup and restocking to do."

"Mari and Dillon are already there, so we'll be fine."

"Wait. What?" My head still felt sleep-addled, so I wasn't sure I understood. "Wasn't Dillon leaving for a waterski trip today? And Mari isn't supposed to be back from Hawaii until Saturday."

"Mari heard about Lacie's murder and came back early.

She said you needed her." Ashley patted my shoulder. "And Dillon's friend broke his leg yesterday so the trip was canceled."

It didn't take long for me to finish getting ready. I jumped into my SUV and followed Ashley's vehicle on the few blocks drive to my shop. Gnarled oak trees and California pepper trees lined the streets, providing shade for pedestrians who were out for their morning walks. Ashley and I circled the block until we both found parking close together.

The second I walked into the apothecary, my mentor, Mari, gave me a tight hug. I breathed in her fragrance, a blend of citrusy orange, woodsy sandalwood, and spicy sweet nutmeg essential oils, and felt myself relax. Mariska, or Mari as she preferred to be called, Kemp had come to my rescue once again.

She'd found me drifting in a temporary job when I'd quit college after losing my mother to cancer. Hiring me on the spot, she taught me reflexology and aromatherapy skills and made me a vital part of her shop. When I struck out on my own, she supported my fledgling business in San Francisco. And when I'd been led away in handcuffs, thanks to the scandal my no-good boyfriend had involved me in without my knowledge, Mari had been there to help me pick up the pieces. After I'd slinked back home to Oak Creek Valley to wallow in my shame, Mari had retired and offered to help me set up my Aromatherapy Apothecary shop. I owed her my life.

Mari released her tight hug and placed her nut-brown, wrinkled hands on my moon-shaped cheeks. Her golden-brown eyes gazed up into mine. "You should have called me the second you received your reading from Madame Bonsail."

"I didn't want to interrupt your vacation with Ira." I gripped her hands after she released my cheeks. "You deserve to enjoy your romantic getaway without me needing rescuing."

"Bah! We're just a couple of old people who enjoy companionship. Don't make it out to be anything other than that." She released my hands, bent over to ruffle Pixie's fur, then scooped my pup up and held her close.

I didn't believe her for a minute that there wasn't a spark between the two, but Mari kept whatever was going on a closely guarded secret. "Fine. But you still didn't need to rush back home and ruin your trip."

She waved off my concern. "I'm here now, so let's get to the bottom of this tragedy and get your shop open."

"You're right. Let's get to work." I'd been friends with Mari long enough to know not to keep gushing my thanks. I looked around the shop to see what needed to be done before opening. Dillon mopped, trying to scrub up the last of the glitter that had scattered all over the floors. Ashley had grabbed a swiffer cloth and dusted the bare shelves. They made a great team and made me proud. "Put Pixie in my office so we don't trip over her, and then I'll start restocking the single oils if you want to stock the blends."

Many of our customers liked to make their own blends of aromatherapy essential oils at home, so they purchased single oils. Others, especially those starting out, liked the convenience of purchasing a vial or tube application of essential oils that I'd blended for specific needs. One of my most popular blends was intended for headache relief. It included essential oils of peppermint, eucalyptus, rosemary, and lavender, mixed with a combination of organic grapeseed oil and locally grown organic olive oil. I sold the blend in vials along with roll-on tubes, which made applying to the user's neck and temples a breeze.

With a long sigh and a wish that I'd had a chance to chug the latte Ashley had bought for me, I unlocked the front door and welcomed a busload of senior citizen tourists. Thanks to Mari standing by my side, we wouldn't be overwhelmed if a mob showed up again.

CHAPTER FIFTEEN

A steady stream of tourists and locals alike, wanting gossip about Lacie's murder, kept us on our toes all morning. It wasn't until almost lunchtime when Dillon sidled up to me and nudged my shoulder. I tore my attention away from an aromatherapy resource tome I consulted after a customer had called in and asked me to create a safe, organic blend to use in her garden to repel plant-eating insects.

"Can we break for lunch?" Dillon's hazel-colored eyes were wide.

"Sure. You didn't need to stay this long since you weren't supposed to work today." When concern flitted across his face, I hastened to reassure him and patted his shoulder. "I'm grateful you showed up, though. We couldn't have opened on time without you."

"I mean, can you and I break for lunch together?" Dillon ran his long, thin fingers through his light brown hair until it stood on end. "We need to talk about my mom and your dad."

I gulped. This could prove to be the conversation I'd

been dreading ever since I'd hired Dillon in the spring and found out my dad was dating his mother. "Sure. Let me check with Mari and see if she can stay while we're gone."

Mari shooed away my concerns about her working longer than she'd intended. She gave me a knowing grin after glancing at Dillon, who waited patiently by the front door. "Carissa, be happy for your father. Sandy's a good woman."

"I know, but I feel like they're moving the relationship along too fast." They'd been dating for about six months, and maybe, for people their age, it wasn't too fast. But I was having a hard time accepting someone taking my mother's place.

"They're adults. Give them some credit for knowing what's right for them." She shook her head. "Go on. Get out of here before another group of customers come in. Ashley and I can handle it."

I gave Mari a quick hug, then retrieved Pixie from my office. After clipping her blinged-out leash to her collar, she scampered to Dillon and danced on her hind legs as if begging to be picked up. He acquiesced and snuggled Pixie to his chest. I couldn't help but smile at the way everyone loved my pup.

"I almost don't need a leash since everyone spoils you so much and carries you around like a little princess." I ruffled Pixie's ears before opening the glass door to step out onto the expansive sidewalk.

We waved hello to our neighboring shop owner, Fiona, and I drooled a little over the enticing aromas of the fragrant teas she sold at Tea Breeze. Right before my grand opening a few months before, Mari had consulted with Fiona's sister at their Santa Barbara location, and created a tea that embodied my celebration essential oil blend. We sold packets of the tea blend in my shop, and it had proven to be a big seller. My customers generally hopped over to Fiona's shop once they found out the connection.

I picked out the spicy scent of cinnamon and aromatic vanilla wafting from Tea Breeze, and decided I'd pick up iced tea for Ashley and Mari after lunch. Fiona had opened the shop in Oak Creek only a couple months before, and I was greatly relieved we got along so well. Unlike the previous shopkeeper's son, who had made it his mission to make my life miserable. Even after his tragic death, I shuddered when I thought about the ugly scenes he had caused.

"Where do you want to eat?" I pulled my gaze and nose from the tea shop, and turned toward Dillon.

"We could hit Paco's tamale truck at the farmers' market." His brows furrowed together. "If that's okay with you? Otherwise, if we go to a restaurant we'll probably have a long wait for a table and we won't have a lot of privacy to talk."

"You should know by now that you never have to ask me twice to eat tamales." My *abuela* had taught my mama, as a young child in Mexico, to make tamales and they, in turn, had taught me to make them. Given the time-consuming steps to prepare the traditional dish, it was much easier to order from Paco's. They were just about as good as I remembered my *abuela* making for our Christmas and birthday dinners.

We meandered past the patisserie—I was happy to see, for Jasper's sake, that it was crowded—then down through the historic arcade with its graceful arches and Spanish-tiled sidewalks that reflected the town's heritage. Across the street, the farmers' market was in full swing with tourists stocking up on produce and local arts and crafts to take home. The mouth-watering aromas of grilled meat, spicy chilies, and buttery-sweet caramel corn filled the air the closer we got. Typically, the farmers market was open only on Sundays. But when bus-loads of tourists descended on the town for festivals, the market expanded its operating days to make the most of the tourist dollars our town heavily relied upon.

We joined the long line for Paco's famous tamales, and we chatted amiably about Dillon's upcoming college classes, new aromatherapy oil blends for the shop, and my failed class at Pixie's dog training session.

"I don't understand why the trainer told me to try back in a month and to practice saying no and following through every day." I stroked Pixie's silky ears. "She said my dog wasn't the problem, it was me."

Dillon's laughter rang out, causing several people in line in front of us to turn around and stare. I gave them a finger wave.

With his free hand he swiped the back of his hand over his eyes. "You're too funny. I could have predicted you'd fail doggie training class."

I stuck my bottom lip out in a pout. "What? I love Pixie, and I don't see why that would make me flop."

"It's not a question of love but of making sure Pixie understands and respects your expectations." He leaned over and shoulder bumped me. It made me realize that Dillon was already like a younger brother to me. "For example, how many times have you tried to take her for a walk on her leash?"

"Almost every day! You can't say I don't try."

"And what happens when she sits down and refuses to go more than twenty feet from the door?"

I snorted. Dillon knew me so well. "I hate when you're a mister smarty pants."

He guffawed again as we inched closer to the order window. He raised his voice to falsetto. "Awww, poor puppy is tired already. Let me carry you and hand-feed you dog treats."

Punching his shoulder, I couldn't help but giggle. "Okay, okay. I get it. But she's so cute when she looks up at me with those big teddy bear eyes, and I can't resist."

"Case closed." Dillon handed Pixie to me, reached into his pocket, and extracted his wallet. "What do you want on your tamale?"

"You're not buying for me. It's my treat." I tried pushing Pixie back into his arms.

"I'm the one who asked you out to lunch, so I'm buying." Dillon turned his back on me, so I had no choice but to hold on to my dog.

The order window employee, a fresh-faced teen girl, waved us up. "Hey, Dillon, what can I get you?"

"Hey, Karri. Two pork tamales with salsa *verde* with sour cream and a coke for me." He turned and nudged my arm. "What do you want?"

"I'll take a pork tamale with salsa *rojo* and cilantro, and an iced tea." Karri didn't appear to be happy when Dillon paid for both of our orders. She looked me up and down like she was trying to figure out why he would be with an older, chubbier woman like me. Maybe she had a crush on him, and I didn't want to mess up any chances just in case he reciprocated. "Thanks, Dillon, although as your employer, I should be the one buying lunch."

The teen's shoulders visibly relaxed when she handed Dillon his change. From my vantage point though, apart from being friendly, Dillon hadn't given the girl a second glance. Maybe he wasn't aware of her crush. I wondered if I should mention something to him and then decided to keep my nose out of it.

Once the steaming tamales and drinks were in our hands and Pixie was on the ground, forced to walk, we ambled as we looked for an empty table to sit at. Not a single chair was free, so we headed for the base of an oak tree with an expanse of scraggly grass surrounding it.

"Is picnic-style okay?" Dillon gestured at the ground. "I probably should've brought a blanket or beach towel."

I plopped down and secured Pixie's leash around my ankle. "Works for me."

We ate in silence as we consumed the velvety corn masa imbued with an earthy, spicy sauce that the succulent pork had braised in until it became melt-in-your-mouth tender. Once my paper plate was practically licked clean, I leaned back and sighed with contentment. "I could eat these every single day."

"I agree." Dillon popped the last bit of tamale into his mouth and finished off his coke. He picked up our trash, placed it in a nearby receptacle, and then sat back beside me on the grass. He gazed up at the oak branches spreading above us, then looked around to see if anyone was within hearing distance. "This is awkward... Has your dad talked to you about his, ah, relationship with my mom?"

I scratched my nose, unsure I wanted to have this conversation. "Uh, not really. He's private that way. Has your mom said anything to you?"

Dillon closed his eyes and lowered his voice to barely above a whisper. "I was supposed to be on the waterski trip and didn't tell my mom it was canceled. I kinda got a surprise when I walked in on them last night."

I held my hand up in the 'stop right there' position.

Awkward was right. I truly did not want to think of my dad and Sandy being caught in the act so to speak. "I really don't need or want to know any of this. I don't even want to think that's happening between them."

"Ugh. Oh god, no! It wasn't that at all." Dillon's face turned a bright shade of neon-red. "I'll be scarred for life just thinking what I could have walked in on."

I cocked my head and tried to think of what else Dillon could have found awkward by coming home unexpectedly. I bit my tongue and waited.

He let out a long exhale and fanned his face with a napkin left over from our lunch. "Robert was down on one knee with a small jewelry box in his hand."

"What?!" I lowered my voice and glanced around to make sure I hadn't attracted any attention. "My dad proposed to your mom?"

Dillon nodded. "You didn't know he was going to?"

"No! Definitely not." Madame Bonsail's words came crashing down on me. She'd had a premonition that my dad would soon experience a major life change. It didn't get any more major than this. My neck prickled, and goosebumps popped out on my arms.

"Whew. I was going to be mad at you if you knew and didn't warn me." He puffed out another exhale. "This is unexpected to say the least. I mean, I like your dad and everything, but doesn't this seem a little fast?"

"It does seem fast. I like your mom, too, but I think they should get to know each other better before taking this step. They've been dating for all of six months or so?" I rubbed the goosebumps from my arms.

"About that, at least that's when my mom mentioned she was seeing your dad. Maybe they were seeing each other before that or were at least friends?"

"So, what did they say when you walked in?"

"Nothing. I don't think they even knew I'd come in, so I snuck out and stayed at a friend's house last night." He pursed his lips together. "But I did hear my mom say yes before I got out the door."

While I knew it was ridiculous to feel a twinge of regret that my dad was moving on with someone other than my mother, I realized this had to be much harder for Dillon. I, at least, had my own home and was an adult. Dillon was a teen and still lived at home. This could be a major change in his life. I reached over, gave his arm a quick squeeze, then put Pixie in his lap. Dogs were great givers of comfort. "You doing okay with this?"

He shrugged. "I guess. Maybe I should look into moving into a dorm when school starts. I don't want to intrude on them."

"No!" Pixie startled at my exclamation. I patted her head to calm her as I tried to figure out how to make Dillon feel wanted. By all of us. "I don't think you need to do that at all. I know my dad isn't going to want to disrupt your life or make you feel unwanted. In fact, he probably sees you as the son he never had and the little brother I never knew I needed."

Dillon's face turned red. Again. "That's a nice thing to say, but I'm old enough to be on my own. I really don't want to be in their way."

"But if you move into a dorm, you won't be able to save as much money when you transfer to a university." I wanted to give him a reassuring hug but worried it was too much, too soon. We still needed to navigate the step-family dynamics before I showered affection on him. "And you won't be around to work for me. I can't be losing my best male employee."

"I'll think about it." Dillon pulled his knees to his chest and dropped his head to rest his chin on his kneecaps. The corners of his mouth were turned downward.

"Besides, they just got engaged. Maybe they'll wait to get married until you leave for university in two years." We could hope anyway.

CHAPTER SIXTEEN

The motion of a bright purple caftan billowing in the light breeze caught my attention. Partially hidden in the trees, close to the walking trail that meandered through groves of oak trees, I could make out the features of Madame Bonsail. Had I conjured her while thinking about her premonition? I shook my head at my imagination.

I leaned forward to get a better look. She stood facing a man, and it appeared they were having a heated discussion. I squinted to get a better look. The man resembled Brett. Lacie's ex-husband. I nudged Dillon, then pointed at the pair. "Do you think you can sneak behind the trees and get close enough to hear what they're arguing about? I think that's Brett arguing with Madame Bonsail."

My request had the results I'd hoped for. Dillon perked up, and a sparkle appeared in his eyes. "So, we're investigating, huh?"

"When an opportunity presents itself, it's hard to ignore." I patted his shoulder before he stood and handed Pixie to me. "Besides, you're thin enough to hide behind trees. They'd see me coming a mile off."

Dillon offered me a fist bump—which I returned—then cautiously darted to a tree twenty feet away from where we'd sat. I kept my eye on Madame Bonsail and Brett while Dillon edged closer, holding my breath each time he broke cover as he moved from one tree to the next. Within a couple of minutes, Dillon reached a tree about fifteen feet from the pair, shot me a thumbs up, then leaned into the oak tree, hidden from their view.

My heart beat faster when it appeared the argument had escalated. From where I sat, I could hear the anger in his voice, although I couldn't discern the words. I jumped when Madame Bonsail waved a rude finger gesture at Brett and stomped off, thankfully heading away from where Dillon hid. Brett watched the woman until she disappeared around the bend in the trail, then turned and made his way back to the farmers' market. Dillon edged his body behind the large oak tree trunk, so when Brett passed within ten feet of the tree, he didn't notice the teen.

Before Brett had a chance to notice me, I scrambled to my feet and clutched Pixie tightly to my chest. Darting to the other side of the tree that had sheltered us during our tamale picnic, I tried to hide my body as much as possible. Stroking Pixie's ears and gently holding her muzzle, I hoped Pixie wouldn't think we were playing a game and start barking. After a couple minutes, I peeked around the tree to make sure Brett was out of sight. I didn't see him. Dillon made his way back to me, still darting from tree to tree, as a precaution, I presumed.

When he reached my hiding spot, he grinned. "That was fun."

I grinned back, happy that the melancholy over the engagement seemed to have disappeared. "Could you hear what they were saying? Did you find out anything?"

"They were shouting a lot of insults at each other, but I think Madame Bonsail wants money back that Lacie stole from her. Brett said he doesn't have it and, get this, he accused Madame Bonsail of being a thief!"

This put a new light on Lacie's murder. She'd been vindictive and rude, but I hadn't known she'd been a thief. If she had stolen from Madame Bonsail, perhaps there were other victims too. "Did you find out anything else?"

"Not much. By the time I got close enough to hear, they were at the tail end of the argument. But right before it ended, Brett threatened Madame Bonsail."

"What?" That didn't sound like the Brett I'd known. "What did he say?"

"Something to the effect that if she didn't give him the money, she'd be sorry." He raised his palms upward. "That's all I got."

"You were awesome. I never would have been able to sneak close enough to overhear." I pulled a shriveled oak leaf from my tangled hair. I'd have to track Brett down and have a chat with him. "Come on, I'll buy us dessert, and then we'd better get back so Mari and Ashley can get a lunch break."

My mouth watered as the fragrance of warm cinnamon and sugar lingered in the air while we waited in line for hot churros. The deep-fried pastry was a favorite Southwestern dessert, with its crispy, sugar and cinnamon-laden exterior, and the soft interior. It was similar to a donut, except denser and chewier. Once we had several in hand, we quickly made our way back to Aromatherapy Apothecary. I had planned to buy iced teas for Mari and Ashley from Tea Breeze but decided the churros were a better reward for holding down the shop.

I exhaled a breath I hadn't known I'd been holding

when we entered my shop and saw it wasn't a zoo like the day before. Several customers, representing a variety of ages, browsed while one woman, who appeared to be in her sixties, held an animated conversation with Mari. I held up the bags of churros, and pointed at Mari and then toward the break room. Mari nodded at me, then returned her attention to the client. Ashley had just finished ringing up a customer. She wrapped the product in sage-green tissue paper and placed it in a white gift bag printed with my logo. As soon as the customer headed for the door, I motioned for Ashley to take a lunch break. She nodded and walked toward our small employee lounge, which was smaller than some walk-in closets I'd seen.

I dropped Pixie off in my office, which was even smaller than the break room, and smiled when she trotted to her cozy bed. She stretched out and closed her eyes as if she were exhausted, like she'd walked far more than she'd been carried. After closing the lower portion of the Dutch door, I joined Ashley. She pulled a brightly colored reusable lunch sack from the refrigerator and set it on the tiny bistro table.

"Were there any problems while I was out?"

"Nope. No crazy seniors showed up wanting their photos taken with a suspected murderer."

I collapsed onto one of the bistro chairs and handed her one of the bags containing two churros. I placed the remaining sack on top of the microwave. Mari could eat them as soon as she was done with her consultation. "Thank goodness. I'm not sure I could have handled another day like that."

Ashley returned her sandwich to her bag and slipped a churro out. She inhaled the cinnamon-y aroma and closed her eyes. "Dessert for lunch. Thanks."

She opened her eyes, took a huge bite, and then pointed

the churro at me. "What did Dillon want? He's not quitting, is he?"

"No." I twisted my mouth to the side. Did Dillon tell me about the engagement in confidence? Was I supposed to keep it a secret? Did my dad and Sandy want word to get out before they made an announcement? "Dillon's fine, but I'm not sure how much I can tell you. It's about my dad and...."

"Oh-em-gee! They're engaged, aren't they?" Before I could finish my sentence, Ashley jumped up and started doing a happy dance. "How'd he ask her? What does the ring look like? When's the wedding?"

"Whoa! Settle down girl!" I grabbed Ashley's hand and directed her back to the chair. "They haven't told us yet. Dillon walked in when it happened, although they didn't see him, and he got out of there before they even knew he'd been home."

"Oh. Right. He was supposed to be on his trip."

"Yeah. So, we're not supposed to know anything." I fiddled with the basket of napkins sitting on the small table. "Don't you think it's kind of fast?"

She pursed her rosebud lips. "Rumors about your dad dating a redhead started about a year ago. I think that's about the time Sandy and Dillon moved to town. So, presumably, they've been together under the radar, so to speak, for at least that long."

"You could be right. I guess since I just met Sandy a few months ago, it feels like they've only been dating for a short time."

"I know it can't be easy for you to see your dad move on, but Sandy seems to make him happy." Ashley took another bite of her churro.

"That's true. I am happy for him, but I have some

emotional adjusting to do." I circled my hand in front of myself. "It'll be fine."

Ashley leaned in toward me and lowered her voice. "Have you made any progress in the investigation?"

"Not yet. There are quite a few people I need to track down to find out their alibis, but I haven't found the time yet."

"Have you talked to Brett? They say the husband or ex is often the perpetrator."

"He's on my list of people. The weird thing is, Madame Bonsail warned me that Brett is a dangerous man because of his aura." I rolled my eyes. "And then Dillon and I saw them arguing in the park while we were finishing up lunch."

"Do you think he could be dangerous?" Ashley's eyes went wide. "Maybe you shouldn't talk to him on your own."

"I don't know…" I twisted my mouth to the side while I thought about my high school ex-boyfriend. "The Brett I knew back then didn't have a temper and certainly wasn't violent. Even when Lacie told lies that I'd cheated on him while we were together, he was hurt but didn't get angry."

"So that's why you broke up." Ashley huffed. "You wouldn't talk about what happened, so I thought it was Brett who'd cheated on you with Lacie."

"It was easier to let people think that instead of wondering if there was some truth that I'd been the cheater." Despite Brett's denial, most of our friends had assumed he'd dumped me for Lacie, thanks to her reputation for stealing boyfriends. "But I guess people do change, and Lacie has, or had, a way of bringing out the worst in people, including me."

"Just be careful when you talk to him."

Mari stuck her head into the doorway. "There's a detective here to see you. I'll stay until Ashley's done with lunch, but then I have an appointment I need to get to."

Startled, I jumped up, and bumped the table. Ashley's bottled water teetered then fell over, spilling water onto the remaining churro. I grabbed a handful of napkins and tried mopping up the water as it streamed over the table's edge and onto the floor. "I'm so sorry! Go buy more churros and I'll reimburse you."

"Naw, I'm fine. I really didn't need the extra calories anyway." Ashley pulled the soggy napkins from my hands. "Go see what the detective wants."

"I'll share mine with her." Mari gestured toward the sack sitting atop the microwave, where two churros peeked out from the top.

"Ms. Carmichael." Detective Raaf's voice sounded impatient. He nudged Mari from the doorway and crooked his index finger at me. "I'm running an investigation and don't have all day waiting for you to finish your gossip, or whatever it is you're doing."

"I had a little accident with the water and...." I stopped speaking when his glare deepened, and his face turned red. "Shall we speak in my office?"

"No. You need to come down to the station." Detective Raaf crossed his bulky arms over his chest. "This is a formal questioning."

"Then you'll have to give me a moment and let me call my attorney." I stood up straight, trying to muster an appearance of height despite only being less than five-and-a-half feet tall. "I won't answer any questions without him there."

"If you want to play this the hard way, then I'll just arrest you right now, and you can call your attorney from jail." His eyes narrowed into slits, and his rosy lips disappeared into a flat line. "It's your choice whether you want your customers to see you walked out in handcuffs or not."

Ashley must have seen my hands trembling because she reached out and gave my hand a tight squeeze. I barely heard her whisper behind my back. "Go. I'll call Alfred."

Nodding to the detective, I tried to paste a smile on my lips. It probably looked more like a grimace. "Fine. Have it your way."

"I know Mari needs to leave for her appointment, but you don't need to worry. I'll eat my sandwich, and then she can go." Ashley stood and touched my arm. "I've got the shop and Pixie covered as long as you need me."

Squeezing her hand briefly, I turned and picked up my purse from the floor. It seemed only minutes ago I had dropped it before collapsing in the chair to talk with Ashley.

I followed the detective out to the sidewalk and watched as he yanked the back door of his department-issued SUV open. He motioned for me to get in. I shivered as the cage partition caught my attention. It made the back seat appear tiny, and I was certain there wasn't enough room for a grown adult to fit.

"Uh-uh. No way." I crossed my arms in front of me and scowled. I never ever wanted to sit in the back of a police vehicle again. Not after my perp walk in San Francisco. "Either I sit in the front, or I'll drive myself."

He slammed the door shut and glowered at me. "Don't be so high and mighty. It's only a matter of time before I get to snap the bracelets on you and haul you in for good."

His venomous tone made me shudder. I needed to find out why Detective Raaf had it in for me. Sooner than later. "I think I'll drive myself. My car is just around the corner, so I'll meet you there."

CHAPTER SEVENTEEN

Without giving him a chance to disagree, I spun on my heels and practically ran toward my car. Just before I turned the corner, I glanced back at where the detective had been standing. There was no one there, and an ancient VW Bug of a faded, indeterminate color was pulling into the now-empty parking space.

Once the door was unlocked and I'd crashed into the driver's seat, I tried to calm my breathing while blotting my forehead with tissues retrieved from the console. My hands shook, and my heart pounded in my chest. I wanted to call my dad, but knew I'd only make the situation more incendiary. Instead, I called my attorney's office as I pulled away from the curb.

When Alfred's assistant, Gabriella, answered the phone, I skipped the pleasantries and got straight to the point.

"Can Alfred meet me at the police station? Detective Raaf insisted I go there for questioning, and he threatened to arrest me." My voice quivered despite the deep breathing I'd tried to do.

"Oh dear. He's on his way back from a client meeting in Woodland Hills. Hopefully, he'll be back in town within forty-five minutes, but then he has another meeting after that." The clickety-clack of her keyboard sounded loud and clear. "Let me reschedule his meeting, and I'll let him know to meet you at the station instead."

"Thanks. If something changes or if Alfred gets delayed, can you send me a text?"

"Will do." Gabriella rushed through our goodbyes as her phone began ringing.

While I drove the short few blocks to the police station, I scoured my memories of the aromatherapy reflexology sessions I'd done for the city's planning commissioner along with other officials and developers, before being led away in handcuffs. While innocent of the bribery and corruption crimes my then boyfriend, Vincent, had been convicted of, I'd still been an unknowing partner. None of the names that had been associated with Vincent were Raaf. That, I was certain of. I wondered if my attorney in San Francisco could give me any information. I had to find out why Raaf seemed so intent on harassing me instead of focusing on finding other viable suspects.

As I parallel parked at the side of the station and exited my vehicle, I received a text from Ashley.

Just spoke with Gabriella. Alfred on his way within 45 min. Sit tight!

Thanks!

After hitting the send button, I squared my shoulders and pushed my way through the doors. Detective Raaf stood waiting for me, arms crossed in front of his barrel chest, scowling.

"My attorney won't be here for another forty-five minutes, so perhaps we should reschedule."

"That doesn't work for me, and I'd prefer you answer my questions now instead of wasting my valuable time."

"I'm not talking without my attorney here, so I suppose we'll just have to wait for him." I clasped my hands in front of my midriff.

"It's your choice to do this the hard way, Ms. Carmichael." He jerked his head toward the back of the station. "You can wait in the interview room."

I followed him toward the back of the station down a long, narrow corridor. It was eerily quiet, and I wondered where everyone was, especially my dad. The detective opened a door and motioned at the nondescript, beige interrogation room. "Stay here. I have things to do while we wait for your attorney to show up."

I entered the room and settled into the hard plastic chair. I refused to look at or acknowledge Detective Raaf. A few moments later, the door forcefully shut, and his heavy footsteps echoed down the hallway as he made his way toward the front of the station. I pulled my cell phone out. The cell service was sketchy but I called Alfred's office anyway. It took a few attempts as I walked around the room and held my phone at different angles, hunting for a better connection, but I finally reached Gabriella.

"I wanted to let you know that Detective Raaf has insisted I wait here until Alfred shows up for questioning. I'm in the back interview room instead of waiting in the front." My arm was tired as I awkwardly angled the phone to keep the connection.

"I'll let him know. And it must be your lucky day since there's not much traffic. He'll probably reach you in thirty-five minutes." Once again, Gabriella disconnected without much fanfare as her phone rang.

Woodland Hills was at least an hour's drive from Oak

Creek Valley with no traffic. Gabriella was right. I was lucky since Southern California freeways were rarely without bumper-to-bumper cars.

While waiting, I decided to do my own online search for Detective Raaf. Nothing popped up on the first page when I googled him, so I delved deeper as I clicked through the pages. Again, there wasn't anything.

I wondered how someone could remain private in the world today when everyone else seemed to splash their lives all over the internet. I switched to my Facebook app and tried searching that way. Unfortunately, I didn't recall ever hearing his first name so that was a complete bust. I tried LinkedIn, but again, not knowing his first name was a disadvantage. I considered texting my dad, but decided he'd start asking questions I'd rather not answer.

Next, I accessed the San Francisco police department's website, hoping they'd mention detectives. Another bust, but it didn't surprise me since it would be a safety concern to tout the names and photos of those who served the community. Without getting my dad involved, I had one last attempt. I searched my contacts for my San Francisco attorney, Jorge Alvarez. He was one of the best in his field of work, and he'd gotten the charges against me dropped, but his brusque manner made me hesitate to contact him. I recalled that his administrative assistant, Suzie Benson, had proven to be a good source of information and comfort while in the middle of my scandal. Maybe she could find out if there was a connection to Detective Raaf.

Standing on my tippy-toes, angling the phone up toward the ceiling as I leaned against the station's exterior wall, my call to Suzie connected.

"Jorge Alvarez's office, this is Suzie, how can I assist you?" Her rich, contralto voice purred over the phone.

"Hi Suzie, it's Carissa Carmichael. I don't know if you remember me, but..." I stopped talking when her voice boomed over the cell.

"Carissa! How the heck are you? Don't tell me you're in trouble again. I told you to stay away from those bad boys." Suzie sucked in a breath, then continued. "Are you back in San Francisco? Let's meet for drinks or dinner soon."

That was Suzie through and through. Take charge while making you feel like you're her best friend. I glanced over at the two-way mirror and wondered if Detective Raaf was listening in. He didn't need to know I was researching him. Hopefully, he'd think I was talking about the death of Lacie.

"I live in Southern California, but had a question about my case. Um, I'd rather not talk about it on the phone in case someone overhears me. Can I send you a text or an email?"

"Sure. Do you have my company email address?"

"No. All I have is your boss's address."

She rattled off her email, and I asked her to wait while I found a pen and an old receipt floating around my purse to use as scratch paper. I wrote it down, then repeated it back to Suzie to make sure I'd copied it correctly. She acknowledged I'd gotten it right.

"When are you coming back to The City?"

"I'm not sure. I recently opened an aromatherapy shop, and it keeps me busy almost twenty-four hours a day."

"Sweet. Guess I'll have to head down your way on my next vacation and check it out." She mumbled something I couldn't make out. "Hey, Jorge just got back, and I've got to get him ready for his next appointment. I'll be on the lookout for your email."

Before I could say goodbye, the phone went dead. I

spent the next fifteen minutes crafting an email to Suzie and once sent, I spent a while scrolling through Pinterest to see if there were any new aromatherapy trends. After that I watched several silly cat videos while glancing at my watch every few minutes. Cute puppies and mischievous goat videos replaced the cat videos as I sat, getting more impatient by the moment. I glanced at my watch. I'd been here almost one hour. Where was Alfred?

I stood and angled the phone to get cell reception, but this time, the bars never materialized. I sent Gabriella a text instead.

Will Alfred be here soon?

Impatiently, I watched for the three dots to appear on my screen. Finally her answer appeared.

Bad accident on Hwy 33. Should be there in 10 min. Sorry! Meant to let you know sooner.

I quickly answered her, trying to sound nice, even though I was a bit miffed she hadn't notified me earlier.

No worries and thanks.

It didn't seem right that Detective Raaf would make me sit here while we waited for my attorney. The iced tea I'd consumed at lunch had me squirming, so I decided to avail myself of the facilities while I waited. When I turned the knob and pulled to open the door, it didn't move. I tried again and realized that I'd been locked in.

My heart began to race, and the palms of my hands turned slick with perspiration. He'd locked me in like a criminal and left me here with no regard for my well-being. I turned and glared at the two-way mirror. If he were sitting there, gloating over my rising panic, he'd find out he had made a huge mistake. I pounded my fists on the door, hoping someone would hear me.

CHAPTER EIGHTEEN

Within a few moments, footsteps came down the hallway, the rubber soles of their shoes squeaking on the tile. With a click of the lock, the door pushed open, and I stepped backward.

"Carissa! What are you doing here?" Officer Bryon Zabor drew his eyebrows together as he gazed down at me. He looked back at the door and then back at me. "How did the door get locked?"

"Detective Raaf locked me in. I didn't know until I needed to use the restroom and couldn't get out." I rubbed my wet palms down the sides of my leggings.

"But why?" Bryon looked up and down the long hallway. "Where is he, and why are you here?"

"He came to my shop and said he needed to "officially" question me." I raised my hand and bent my index and middle fingers up and down as I emphasized the word officially. "I said I wouldn't talk to him until Alfred arrived. My attorney was tied up in another meeting, and I'm not sure when he'll get here."

Bryon's scowl deepened. "So Raaf just locked you in the room and left?"

"I didn't know it was locked, or I'd have been banging on the door a whole lot sooner." I peered over to the two-way mirror. "He's not back there watching me, is he?"

"Not that I'm aware of." He held the door wide open. "Come on, let's see if the front desk knows where he is."

After slinging my purse over my shoulder, I followed Bryon toward the front of the station, but then made a quick detour to the ladies' room. Nature called, and I'd had enough squirming for the day.

Finally comfortable, I made my way to the front and found Bryon resting his elbows on the front desk, his palms cradling his cheeks. He straightened and stood upright when he saw me. "Officer Davidson says Raaf left over an hour ago, but didn't indicate where he was going."

I glanced at my watch. "That must have been right after he locked me in. Why would he do that?"

Officer Davidson cleared his throat. "I'm sorry, Miss, but I didn't know you were back there. Detective Raaf didn't say anything to me before he left."

The station had been eerily quiet when Raaf brought me in. I'd found it odd, but in hindsight, I should have questioned it. I stuck out my hand. "I'm sorry, I don't think we've met before. I'm Carissa Carmichael. Chief Carmichael's daughter."

Officer Davidson, who had to be pushing retirement age or maybe gone beyond it, paled. His liver-spotted hands trembled when he reached out to shake my extended hand. His voice quivered when he spoke. "I am so sorry. I don't know how this happened."

"When Detective Raaf brought me in, I didn't see you, or anyone else for that matter."

"He, uh, sent me out to get some coffee and pastries. There was a long line at the patisserie, and it took a lot longer than I anticipated." The elderly man rapidly blinked his pale blue eyes several times. "He promised he'd stay and cover for me, and when I came back, he was still sitting right where I'm at now. He left just as soon as I returned."

My anger approached a boiling point. Raaf had purposely locked me in when no one was around and then abandoned me. What did he hope to accomplish besides making me want to commit murder? His murder.

Bryon rested his hand on my shoulder. "Come on. I'll take you back to work."

"I drove here. At least I wasn't stupid enough to get in the back seat of his car when he came to drag me here." I shook my head. "Do you happen to know Detective Raaf's first name?"

"Your dad and I will get to the bottom of this." He removed his hand and opened the front glass doors, ignoring my question. "Let Alfred know what happened so there's documentation, and let us figure out why he did this. You don't need to get involved."

"I know you'll do everything you can to clear my name, but what is Raaf's first name? I think there's a connection going back to my, err, time in San Francisco."

Bryon sighed and wouldn't meet my gaze. Fortunately, Officer Davidson hadn't discerned why Bryon was being so evasive. "Ms. Carmichael, I have his business card here."

I waited, a bit impatiently, while he rummaged through a drawer stuffed with receipts, scraps of notes, a mishmash of pens, pencils, and other office detritus. He finally found a bent business card and handed it to me. "I knew it was in there somewhere."

I glanced down and saw Raaf's full name. Detective

Erik Raaf. Special Investigator with the Ventura County Sheriff's office located in Thousand Oaks. Included on the card was his badge number and a phone number. I snapped a photo of the card with my cell phone, then handed the business card back to Officer Davidson. "Thanks. That helps."

Bryon shook his head while he looked heavenward, then pulled my arm and led me to the open doorway. He lowered his voice so that the other officer couldn't overhear. "Don't add any more stress to the Chief. He doesn't need to be worrying about you."

"I'm glad you brought it up. Where is my dad? I haven't seen him in a couple of days and hoped to see him here."

He led me toward my car, all the while keeping his voice low. "It was strongly suggested he focus on taking care of the playwright event."

"Seriously?" This was even worse than I'd thought. "Where's he spending his time? I haven't seen him around."

"He's been hopping around the various festival sites, but I think right now he's at the bowl. Last I heard, there was a big hoopla over a huge name band offering to show up this evening for an impromptu gig at the location. Security has been in an uproar since they decided it would be first come, first served for the seats."

I couldn't imagine the crush of people lining up with the hopes to snag a seat at the outside stage venue. "Have you heard who the band is?"

"Yeah, but I have no idea who they are. Some flower or something." He ran his hand through his short-cropped blond hair. "Word of mouth is spreading, and people are already lined up."

Taking my leave of the mission adobe-styled police station with its red Spanish tiled roof, I walked beneath the shade of Silver Dollar Eucalyptus trees that dotted the sparse, brown lawn surrounding the station. The ongoing drought that seemed to plague Southern California meant lush, green lawns were a thing of the past. The gentle drone of buzzing bees filled the rustling leaves and invited a sense of calmness despite my encounter with Raaf.

When I reached my car, I called my attorney's office and left Gabriella a voicemail that Alfred should call me instead of meeting me at the station. I headed back to work. As I approached Aromatherapy Apothecary, I couldn't help but notice the near-empty arcade walkway. The Tea Breeze shop was dark, and the closed sign hung in the window. When I entered my shop, I found Ashley dancing along to music she played in her tiny earbuds while dusting shelves with a feather duster. There weren't any customers in sight.

"Ashley."

She was startled when she saw me watching her, and her peaches and cream skin turned rosy-pink. She removed her earbuds. "Sorry! It's been dead in here for the last hour, and I've heard a lot of shops have closed for the day."

"Do you know why?" I walked toward my office to let Pixie out, and Ashley followed. Pixie yawned and stretched when I opened the door, then scampered to my feet, begging to be picked up. I obliged.

"How have you not heard that the Platinum Magnolias are making a surprise visit at the Bowl?" She reached over and tousled Pixie's ears. "Dillon sent me a text. He's in line and thinks he might be able to get a seat. I'm so jealous!"

"That's nice." It was great for the festival to bring this kind of entertainment to our town, but bad for business since it took tourists away while they waited in line for hours to see if they could get a seat. "Why don't you head home? I'll close up early since I'm having dinner with

Jasper, and I promised to bring food. I think I'll run out to the farmhouse and shower since I overslept this morning."

Ashley sniggered. "You'd better wear a cute sundress and sandals, too. It might help the patient recover more quickly."

"Oh, stop. We're just friends." My face heated because we were more than 'just friends', but I wasn't sure where our attraction was headed. "I'll see you in the morning."

"You know I'll be bugging you for all the details, so come prepared." Ashley threw me an air kiss as she walked through the doorway.

CHAPTER NINETEEN

It didn't take long to close out the register and set the shop up for opening the next morning. Ashley had worked hard, and most of the work was done. I mixed up a blend of eucalyptus, thyme, ginger, and clove essential oils, then diluted it with sweet almond oil for Jasper. I transferred the mixture to a vial, topped with a glass dropper, wrapped it in colorful tissue paper, and then placed it in my purse.

I strapped Pixie into her safety harness and headed home. I could hear my dad saying it wasn't safe since there was a murderer on the loose. But since I hadn't received any more Death cards nor had anything happened that day to make me think I was still being targeted, it should be safe enough. Whatever Detective Raaf had going on with his vendetta against me was a whole different story.

The dusty green oblong leaves of the avocado trees greeted me as I drove down the quarter-mile gravel road through the orchards, to my farmhouse. I remembered, when I was little, the excitement my grandmother displayed when she bought the house and orchard right after my grandpa died. I turned the last corner and drove into the large clearing that held the white adobe ranch-style farm-house. It was all mine, thanks to the generosity of my grand-mother's bequeath.

As soon as I'd placed Pixie on the ground, she scampered to the sparse lawn and rolled on her back. I'd have to brush the dried grass from her fur, but she looked like she was having too much fun to tell her to stop. While I fumbled to find my house key, Pixie sniffed around the hydrangea bushes that framed the front window and watered a few. When she heard the front door open, she dashed up the steps, scurried into the house, and started barking. I quickly turned off the alarm, picked her up to shush her, and froze. A ransacked mess littered my house.

Backing out of the house, Pixie clutched close to my chest, I turned and ran toward my car. Not bothering to buckle in Pixie or myself, I started the car, performed a U-turn that barely missed mowing down an evergreen shrub, and headed back to town. I pulled into the parking lot of the convenience store at the edge of town and called 9-1-1.

"What's your emergency?" The crisp, efficient voice of Peg Godwin matched her straightforward self. She'd worked with my dad for at least fifteen years and knew me well.

"Hi Peg, it's Carissa."

"Don't tell me you've found another body?" Unfortunately, Peg had been the dispatcher who'd taken my call after I'd found a body a few months before and had, I was sure, listened to the recording of my emergency call after finding Lacie.

"No! Absolutely not! But someone broke into my house and ransacked it." My heart still pounded in my chest, and I tried to steady my breathing.

"Are you safe? Is the intruder still there?" Her no-nonsense voice steadied my nerves.

"I didn't see or hear anyone. Pixie and I are at the mini-mart, so we're safe." I gripped the phone tighter when my clammy hand started to lose its grip. The clack of keyboard keys being pressed sounded in my ear as Peg summoned help. "I didn't stick around long enough to determine if anyone was still in the house."

"Good. You did the right thing." She murmured something in the background. "Units are on the way to your house. But your dad says to stay where you're at with your doors locked. He should be there in five."

"Thanks, Peg."

"Do you want me to stay on the phone with you until he arrives?"

"There's no need. I'm fine." Physically I was fine, but inside, my anger boiled. Someone still targeted me, despite my wish that it was otherwise.

The wailing screams of sirens split the air a few seconds before two black and white patrol cars sped past the mini-mart, presumably heading toward my farmhouse. A couple of minutes later, my dad parked his pickup truck next to me. He leaped from the vehicle, slammed the door shut, and strode to my driver's side window, which I'd rolled down.

"What do you think you were doing, going alone to your house?" His hands clenched into fists. His voice went up another octave. "After all the ways you've been targeted, you chose to put yourself unnecessarily in danger?"

"It was only going to be for a couple of minutes. I needed some clean clothes." It was probably best I not share that I planned on showering and putting on makeup while I was there. "The front door was locked, and when I went in, the alarm was still on. It appeared safe enough."

He rubbed the palms of his hands over his face, then placed them on his hips. "You should have asked me, or at least Bryon, to go with you."

"You've been busy. Besides, Bryon is not my personal bodyguard. He works for the city, remember?" Now, I was sounding like a petulant teenager. Why did my dad always bring this out in me?

He opened my car door. "C'mon. You can ride with me to the crime scene and see if anything is missing."

Checking my watch, I was dismayed to see I'd never make it to Jasper's by six-thirty. I'd have to call him and cancel, but I'd wait until my dad wasn't hovering over me. After rolling up the window and retrieving Pixie and my purse, I locked the car and climbed into my dad's truck. It looked freshly washed and waxed, and smelled of oranges. Had the break-in pulled him from a planned date? I decided not to ask.

Silence filled the vehicle for a couple of minutes as he drove. I stared out the window, watching the rustic stone walls that surrounded orchards of olive trees, tangerines, and avocados as we sped past them. My dad finally cleared his throat. "I'm sorry. I guess I overreacted."

"It's okay, Dad. I know you're worried about me." I stroked Pixie's silky ears. "I can't be kept in a bubble. Besides, you've taught me to be hyper-aware of my surroundings, and not for a second did I think or feel there was any danger in going out to my house to pick up clothes."

He reached over and gave my hand a quick squeeze. "I can't bear the thought of anything happening to you."

My throat constricted, and my eyes stung, so I just nodded and squeezed his hand back. Pixie gave both our hands a lick, then nudged my hand to start rubbing her ears again, so I complied.

"You're spoiling her." He took his eyes from the road for a brief moment and looked down at Pixie. "What happened to doggie training?"

"Nothing. Just taking a break until Lacie's murder is solved." No way could I admit I'd flunked us out the first time around. Although, he probably already knew, given his deep chuckle.

Once he'd parked the truck alongside the two patrol cars, Dad paused with his hand on the door handle. "I know Jasper is expecting you for dinner, so I'll try to get you out of here as quickly as possible. I'll wait for you inside while you call him."

His chortle once again filled the cabin of the truck before he strode purposefully toward my home. Despite the circumstances of crime bringing us here and his initial outburst, my dad chuckled and teased me instead of lecturing me during the entire drive. I had to consider that his engagement to Sandy had something to do with it. Maybe it wasn't such a bad thing after all.

Jasper answered my call on the first ring. "Hey, Carissa, will you be here for dinner soon?"

"Well..." I cleared my throat. "There's been a bit of trouble at my farmhouse..."

"Are you okay? What happened?" Jasper's warm concern made my eyes water.

"I'm fine, but someone broke in and ransacked my house."

"I'll be there in twenty minutes. Is there anything I can bring to help you clean up?" A barking cough exploded across the airwaves. It was loud enough that I had to yank the phone away from my ear.

"Absolutely not. You need to stay home to rest and take care of yourself."

"I'm not as bad off as the cough makes me sound. Just let me know how I can help."

"You'll be doing all of us a favor if you stay home." I felt bad about squelching his offer to help. "My dad and Bryon are here, so they'll give me any assistance I need."

"If you insist." Jasper coughed again, but at least it didn't sound like a barking seal this time. "Come over whenever you get done there. It doesn't matter what time it is."

"All right. I'll bring soup with me, so don't go to any trouble for either dinner or dessert."

Disconnecting the call, I picked Pixie up to snuggle in my arms and made my way to the farmhouse. When I stepped through the doorway, Bryon walked toward me, holding a clear plastic evidence bag in front of him, a scythe-wielding skeleton plainly visible. It was another Death card.

CHAPTER TWENTY

"How? Why?" My knees felt like they were going to give out.

My dad gripped my elbow, led me to a kitchen chair, then filled a glass with water and placed it in front of me. Pixie stretched her neck out and licked the droplets of water that dripped down the side of the glass.

Bryon crouched beside me and held the card out. "Do you recognize this?"

"It looks like all the other cards." I wondered if someone could buy a pack of tarot cards that contained nothing but Death cards. "It's the same design. Where did you find it?"

Bryon glanced up at my dad. "It was taped to your bedroom mirror."

Shivers cascaded down my spine. My dad growled. "How did they get in? The door was locked, and the alarm was on when Carissa got here."

"It looks like the perp broke the lock on the outside electrical panel and then turned off the electricity." Bryon fingered the plastic-encased tarot card. "At least he was thoughtful and turned it back on before he left."

My dad growled again. He'd had multiple arguments, first with my grandmother and then with me after I'd moved in, trying to convince us to spend the necessary money to update and move the ancient electrical panel to the inside of the house.

"But I have a backup battery system for the alarm. It should have kept it on even if the power went out." I glanced at my dad. He'd insisted I install an alarm system in the spring after some taggers left a message trying to scare me. "The battery should last more than a few months. Right?"

Bryon nodded. "It should. Can you check your alarm app and see what activity it shows?"

I pulled my cell phone from my purse and scrolled through the activity log on the app. It showed the alarm was disarmed at two that afternoon, and then armed one hour later. I scrunched my face up as I showed Bryon. "How is this possible? I was stuck at the station…"

Too late, I realized I hadn't told my dad about Detective Raaf locking me in. Fortunately, Bryon must've seen the panicked look on my face because he handed the phone to my dad and asked, "Is there any possibility the perp could know your passcode?"

My face prickled with embarrassment. I didn't want to admit to these two men that while I'd meant to pull out the alarm owner's manual and figure out how to change the default code, I'd never actually gotten around to it. Even after a killer taunted me about keeping the same simple code to unlock my cell phone a few months ago. "Uh, he might have guessed. It was still the default code."

As expected, both men gazed at the ceiling and shook their heads. My dad was the first to scold me. "Carissa! How many times did I remind you to change the code?"

"You mean you never changed it from one-two-three-four?" Bryon practically sputtered out the numbers. "Every burglar knows that default code. You're lucky no one's broken in before."

"Can you change the code for me before you leave, Dad?"

He ignored me and, instead, turned toward Bryon. "Did the team dust the alarm touchscreen yet?"

Bryon shook his head. "They're still working on Carissa's bedroom. They dusted this card, though, and as expected, it's clean."

"Can you have them dust the alarm panel next? In the meantime, I'll have my daughter check to see if anything is missing."

"Hey guys, I'm standing right here. You don't have to talk about me like I'm not listening." They were in cop mode, and they were both irritated that I'd been so irresponsible with the alarm code. It hadn't escaped my attention that I risked my home and my valuables by not changing the code.

Dad tucked a lock of my unruly hair behind my ear and then ruffled Pixie's head. I took that to mean I was forgiven, at least I hoped that's what it meant. Again, I considered what a good mood my dad was in. I'd have to mention it to Dillon.

Bryon took the tarot card out to his patrol car and came back in with his crime scene kit. He stopped in front of the alarm touchscreen. I paused to watch him work, but my dad nudged me, then led us toward my office, a converted spare bedroom.

We stood at the doorway and looked at the papers strewn around the room and the file cabinets gaping open. "Let's see if you can determine if anything is missing. Try not to move too much around since I'll have Bryon check for fingerprints on the desk and the file handles."

My desktop computer sat where it always had. My iPad perched on the edge of a small wine barrel table. A cozy chaise, upholstered in vintage rose chintz fabric, was situated next to the table. I liked to curl up most evenings with a glass of red wine and read to unwind after a long day at work. The two electronic items would have been long gone if the break-in was a burglary. But they were still here, which made me wonder what the person had been looking for. I opened the desk's bottom drawer and found my personal and business blank checks, a few twenty-dollar bills, and two credit cards.

"Perhaps you need to get a home safe." Dad's voice sounded overly loud next to my ear.

"Guess you know what to get me for Christmas if you think I need one."

He grunted and pulled open another drawer on the desk. I could have told him there was nothing else of value there, just the usual pens, sticky note pads, and real estate scratch pads left on my front porch every month. I didn't want him to get any more ideas about me selling and moving to town so I pushed his hand away and closed the drawer.

"Everything of value in the room is accounted for. I doubt whoever broke in did so to steal my stapler and tape dispenser." I gestured to the remaining drawer. "They seemed to be after my files, but honestly, there's nothing of importance in them. It's all to do with my shop and aromatherapy ideas."

"What about your legal documents? Especially the San Francisco case?"

My answer would definitely generate a gift of a fire-proof safe for Christmas. "Um, they're in plastic totes. I keep them stored under the guestroom bed."

He raised his eyebrows but didn't scold me. Yep, I was getting a safe for Christmas.

"Okay. Let's go check that room out."

A few quick steps down the hallway from my office had us standing in the doorway of the guestroom. It appeared it hadn't been touched. Even the bed's dust ruffle, which hid the paper-filled plastic totes, had undisturbed pleats. Across the hallway was the guest bathroom. I peaked in and was relieved it looked untouched as well. With trepidation, I turned and plodded toward the primary suite.

CHAPTER TWENTY-ONE

Pausing in the doorway, I tried to keep tears from spilling down my cheeks as I viewed the destruction. All the contents from the dresser drawers, including my unmentionables, had been dumped and strewn about on the floor. Clothes from the walk-in closet had been pulled from their hangers and thrown about the room. Books had been tossed from the bookcase, and some of the covers appeared ripped. The lid of my grandmother's jewelry box gaped open, and the sentimental costume jewelry pieces that once belonged to her were scattered on the floor. The mattress of my bed had been pulled halfway off the box springs, the bedding crumpled on the floor beside it.

"Why would someone do this to me?" I swiped my eyes with the back of my hand, my other arm clutched Pixie close to my chest. When I hugged her even closer for comfort, she lifted her toffee-brown eyes and licked the salty tear that trailed down my round cheek. "What are they looking for?"

Dad stood beside me, his arms crossed in front of me, his feet planted in a wide stance. His voice was low and gravelly. "You could have walked in on this perp. Now, do you understand why I don't want you coming out here all by yourself?"

I nodded and tried to calm my quivering lips while I caught my breath. When another tear rolled down my cheek, Dad put his arm around my shoulder and pulled me in for a hug. "Did you have anything of value in here? Like jewelry or electronics?"

Shaking my head, I pulled away from the hug and pointed to my earlobe. "The only expensive jewelry I have are mom's diamond studs. I wear these all the time."

"What about paperwork or files? Did you store anything in here?"

Again, I shook my head. "Nothing. I think everything you see on the floor is what I keep in here."

Pixie squirmed in my arms and whined. It was obvious she was tired of being held and wanted to get down to scamper about. "Do you need me to stay and go through everything tonight?"

"No. Let the guys dust for prints, and I'll bring you back later, when it's convenient, and help you with the cleanup." He tugged on my elbow and began leading me down the hallway. "Let's go change your alarm code, and you can head over to Jasper's. I'll stick around and arm it after everyone leaves."

"I can stick around. You probably had plans with Sandy tonight." I watched him from the corner of my eye and saw color flood his face. "You've done enough for me today."

"Nope. I'm not going to leave you out here."

"I promise I'll leave as soon as your crew finishes their dusting."

He gave me his best 'dad is going to win,' look with one

eyebrow cocked high, but he didn't say anything. I raised my own eyebrows. I hated being treated like a child.

"Carissa, I'm done with the alarm panel. You can change the code now." Bryon's voice interrupted the stare-down I had going on with my dad.

Dad chuckled. "I win. Go see Jasper. He needs you more than you need to be here."

I forcibly blew my breath out through my mouth which made my lips vibrate together. I sounded like a snorting horse and it made Pixie bark. "Fine. Have it your way."

I marched over to the alarm panel and handed Pixie to Bryon. I didn't want to put her on the floor without a leash, which I'd left in my car in haste to get to my dad's truck. "Okay. What do I do to change the code?"

Dad hovered behind me and rested his chin on my shoulder. He pointed at the tool symbol on the touchscreen. Before I pressed it, I whipped out my cell phone and took a photo. I'd add it to my notes in case I ever had to go through this again. Perhaps I should hunt down the owner's manual.

Once I had pressed the symbol another screen popped up. My dad walked me through the steps, which I was ashamed to say weren't complicated, until it was time to enter a new code. I punched in the four-digit number and felt him poke my shoulder.

"That's my house alarm code. You should pick something different."

"Nope. This way, I'll remember it."

Bryon laughed and handed Pixie back to me. "She has a point. It'll be one less number for you to remember, when you need to come out here."

Bryon had been my dad's right-hand man for over fifteen years and knew my dad's alarm code, too. I didn't mind that he now had my code and, in fact, it made me feel a little more secure.

"Go on. Bryon can drop you off at your car and follow you to Jasper's."

I wanted to argue that I didn't need the officer to follow me, but I saved my breath. It was useless. It was two of them to one of me. I kissed my dad's cheek. "Fine. Let me grab some leftover soup from the freezer, and I'll be ready to go."

"Text me when you leave Jasper's so I'll know when to expect you at my house. Or better yet, I'll meet you there and follow you home." He tried giving me the stern dad look but I couldn't miss the twinkle in his eyes.

"I'll text you when I leave but nope, I won't wait for you to show up. I can drive two blocks without an escort."

I pulled two containers of vegetable tortellini soup from the freezer and hoped that Jasper had some bread or baguettes I could toast to go alongside. I'd planned on stopping by the deli and purchasing a picnic-worthy spread, but that wouldn't happen. At least I always had a stash of extra food in the freezer for last-minute emergencies. Once outside, I set Pixie down for a quick potty and exploration break, then slid into the front seat of Bryon's black and white sedan. He was on his phone, sending a text message.

As soon as the swoosh of the text being sent ended, Bryon secured his phone into the console. "Where's your car?"

"At the mini-mart." I wondered if they'd have any type of artisanal bread, then decided it would be better to show up empty-handed than admit where I'd purchased it. Besides, nothing could ever compare to the patisserie's delectable baked goods. "Are you going to tell Detectives Raaf and Martin about the break-in?"

"I've already sent them an email alerting them to that and the Death card."

"What did they say?" I turned to look at Bryon. He kept his eyes fixed on the road.

"I haven't heard back yet."

"Isn't that odd?" Before Bryon could answer, it dawned on me that not once had Detective Martin been mentioned earlier when Raaf, picked me up. "Where's Detective Martin been today? Why wasn't he involved in Raaf trying to question me?"

"This isn't their only case. It could be that they had other matters to attend to."

We rode the remaining few minutes in silence. When he parked alongside my car, I thanked him and opened the door. He placed his hand on my arm with a light touch. "I'm going to have to tell your dad about Raaf bringing you in today."

I closed my eyes for a brief moment, then turned to gaze into his gray eyes. "Can you at least wait until tomorrow?"

"Yep, I think that's a good plan."

My hand tightly gripped the door handle, but I didn't open the door. I wasn't sure if I should voice the suspicion that had been swirling in my head, ever since I found my house ransacked. "Can I ask you something? I mean, I know this is going to sound crazy, and I know it might be a coincidence..."

Bryon didn't break the silence while I searched for a way to explain. I hoped that meant he'd consider my suspicions. "Do you think it's possible Detective Raaf is the one who broke into my house?"

"That's a pretty serious accusation." Bryon stroked his chin's light five o'clock shadow. "What proof do you have?"

"It's odd that he locked me in the interview room when

no one else was around, then disappeared. What purpose did he have for doing that to me?" I wavered about telling him that I'd contacted my San Francisco attorney's assistant and asked her to research Raaf. In the end, I decided to keep that tidbit from him and avoid the lecture about letting the police handle the investigation. "And then nothing was taken at my house. It looked like someone was trying to scare me, especially by leaving the Death card."

"I don't see him doing it. It's pure coincidence, although I have no answer for why he'd lock you in." Bryon wagged his head back and forth. "What I think happened is that you've been asking questions, and Lacie's killer thinks you're a danger to them."

He was gearing up for a full lecture so I opened the door and stepped out. "I'd better check on Jasper. I'm not sure anyone has brought him food today."

"Carissa..." Bryon gave me a look that perfectly mimicked my dad.

"I promise I'll be careful." I shut the patrol car's door before he could finish his sentence.

CHAPTER TWENTY-TWO

True to my dad's request, Bryon followed me as I drove to Jasper's apartment. He lived above the patisserie with a stairway access from the courtyard side of the building. Apparently, most of the town's population and tourists were trying to snag seats for the concert tonight, so finding parking was a breeze. Bryon pulled in behind me, but didn't roll down his window to scold me. Instead, he waited until Pixie and I had climbed the stairs before driving off. I hoped he would have the chance to spend some time with Ashley. He needed to be soothed after he'd been riled up from my lack of attention to the lecture he thought I needed to hear.

Butterflies danced in my stomach as I lifted my hand to knock on the door, my other hand clutching the leash attached to Pixie, my purse, and the tote containing the frozen soup. After he found out I'd suspected him of being a murderer a few months ago, our budding relationship had chilled. It seemed we were beyond that and were moving in a new direction with this invitation. My hand stilled in mid-air, when the sounds of laughter came from inside the apartment. It sounded like Jasper already had company and I wondered if I should turn around and head to my dad's house.

Before I had a chance to decide, the door flung open, and Pixie took the opportunity to lunge forward. She pulled the leash from my hand, which caused me to stumble. My shoulder caught the edge of the doorframe, and I tumbled into the apartment, landing on my knees. The room turned completely silent, even Pixie stopped barking. Heat flooded my face as I attempted to shove the scattered contents of my purse back into place and stand up.

"You must be Carissa." A deep, gravelly voice sounded above my head. "You certainly know how to make an entrance."

I gazed up and saw a giant of a man with blazing red hair and a full, bushy beard of the same color. His eyes were small, almost lost between his equally bushy eyebrows and his round cheeks. He bent down and helped me to my feet, then retrieved the aromatherapy vial that had rolled away. His large hand nearly engulfed mine as he handed the vial over.

"Thank you." I glanced around the room and saw Jasper reclined on the couch, pillows propped up behind his back, and his legs covered with a colorful quilt. A blue mask covered the lower half of his face. I gave him a little finger wave, and he winked at me. Pixie took the opportunity to trot over to him and jumped into his lap.

Belatedly, I realized I looked downright dowdy. I still wore the same leggings, stretched out and baggy in the knees, which I'd thrown on in haste this morning. My polo shirt had wrinkled and showed a few blotches of essential oils that had splashed when I'd mixed Jasper's blend. I'd also neglected to freshen my makeup or brush my hair after the trauma of the break-in. Visiting Jasper had been a big mistake. "Uh, hi. Thanks for helping me."

"I don't think we've ever met, although I know your father, and knew your grandmother quite well." The giant towered over me as he held out his hand to shake. "I'm John, formerly of the Jean-Luc Patisserie."

"It's so nice to finally meet you, John. I've heard so many wonderful things about you." I shook his hand which, again, swallowed up mine.

"Can I get you a glass of wine? There's a charcuterie board in the kitchen, and Luke ran downstairs to get the desserts."

"Thanks, but I'm okay right now." I glanced around the room but couldn't decide where to park myself. Perhaps I should place the soup in the refrigerator and leave. I could come back tomorrow when Jasper was alone.

Jasper must've noticed my hesitation, or as my dad always said, I wore my thoughts on my face because he swung his legs around so his feet rested on the floor. He patted the couch cushion next to him. "Have a seat. I shouldn't be contagious with all the antibiotics they've shot me up with, but just in case, I'll keep the mask on."

I was happy he sounded more like himself, even if his skin was still pale. I held up the tote containing the soup. "I brought soup. Would you like for me to heat it up?"

"No, thank you. I've been well-fed by John, but if you're hungry, help yourself to anything in the kitchen."

"I'll leave the soup in the fridge, and you can eat it later." I turned to head to the kitchen, but John intercepted me.

"Sit and relax with Jasper. I'll bring you a glass of wine and something to eat." He plucked the tote from my hand.

"I understand you've had a harrowing evening and we want to hear all about it."

I sat after Jasper patted the couch again, leaving several inches between us. Pixie hopped off his lap and burrowed into the space between us. I held the back of my hand to his forehead. He didn't seem to be running a fever. "You're not coughing. Are you feeling better?"

"Much better. Thanks." Jasper reached over and grasped my hand for a quick squeeze.

"Don't let him fool you. He's still on ibuprofen, and I caught him sneaking some cough syrup." John poked his head from the entry to the kitchen and pointed his finger at Jasper. "You're still sick and need time to heal."

"I'm fine. I'll even work for a few hours tomorrow."

"Oh, no, you won't." The voice boomed from the doorway as a man, Luke I presumed, strode in with a platter of cupcakes and cookies. He was a good foot shorter than John, closer to my height of five-five, and thin where John was on the portly side. While it was hard to determine John's age with his blazing red beard covering half his face, Luke appeared to be in his fifties with thick gray hair expertly coiffed. He was handsome, in a classical way, with a strong face and mesmerizing blue eyes. "You'll listen to your doctor, and you'll listen to us."

"Luke, meet Carissa. She's Robert's daughter." John came back to the living room and handed me a glass of wine before taking the platter of desserts from his partner's hands.

Luke wiped his palms down the sides of his sharply pressed black slacks then moved toward me with an outstretched hand. "It's so nice to finally meet you. We've heard so much about you from your dad and your grandmother."

John snorted. "Yeah, especially from your grandmother. Boy, did she have stories to tell about you."

"Please share." Jasper's green eyes twinkled as he playfully poked my shoulder. "She hasn't been very open with me about her past."

"Oh, stop. There's nothing to tell." I tried to keep my tone light and teasing, but truth be told, I worried about what my grandmother might have shared. Granted, I'd told Jasper about some of my turbulent past. Like the time in high school when Lacie had pressured me to drink at her party, and someone drugged the wine cooler she'd shoved into my hands. She'd allowed me to get behind the wheel of my car, and I'd crashed. No one was injured, for which I was forever grateful, but I was arrested. And then there was my arrest in San Francisco, which I'd rather not ever talk about, but somehow, no one would ever let me forget.

I needed to get them off the subject of yours truly.

I opened my purse, retrieved the vial of essential oils, and handed it to Jasper. "I brought a blend of essential oils to help your recovery. Would you mind if I gave you some reflexology and use the aromatherapy on you?"

"Are you sure you're not too tired? You've had a long day already."

I shook my head. "I'm fine."

"If you're sure, then I'd like that. Thank you."

I took a quick sip of wine, then placed it on the coaster that protected the coffee table. Making my way to the bathroom, I conscripted the hand towel and saturated it with hot water. After wringing it out so it wouldn't drip all over the hardwood flooring, I brought it back to the living room along with a large bath towel. "Can you remove your socks, and I'll warm your feet with the towel?"

Jasper complied while I added a couple drops of the oil

blend onto the wet towel, then swiped it down the soles of both feet.

He inhaled deeply. "What oils are you using? I can pick out eucalyptus and cloves, but there's something else I can't quite figure out."

"There's thyme and ginger oils, too." I wrapped his feet in the warm, wet cloth, then settled myself on the floor, crisscross applesauce style, facing him. I unwrapped his right foot and balanced it on my legs. "Eucalyptus tends to overpower a lot of the other fragrances."

With gentle strokes, I applied the oil to the sole of his foot. Supporting the top of his foot with one hand, I began applying deep pressure with the thumb of my other hand three-quarters of an inch below his big toe on the sole. I walked my thumb toward his little toe, applying a great deal of pressure.

Jasper winced. "Is it supposed to hurt?"

"As long as it's not unbearable. The pain is in response to the inflammation in your lungs. By applying deep pressure, it helps increase the energy flow to the area to aid in breaking up congestion."

Jasper nodded for me to continue. "It's pretty tender but not terrible."

I applied more oil to my hands, then repeated the process with his left foot.

Luke scooted his chair closer and watched while I worked. "If Jasper would have started this as soon as he'd gotten sick, do you think he would have still come down with pneumonia?"

"That's hard to say. However, his body's immune system should have responded more vigorously between the essential oils and reflexology." I couldn't help but smile at Pixie as she snuggled deeper into Jasper's arms. "These methods aren't a substitute for modern medicine, and Jasper certainly isn't going to recover from pneumonia without taking the full course of antibiotics."

"You do realize I'm sitting right here while you're talking about me." Jasper angled his head toward John and Luke. "Tell me some of the stories Carissa's grandmother shared with you."

I flicked my index finger at his foot, not hard enough to hurt but enough to get his attention. "You're supposed to relax and meditate while receiving reflexology."

"I'll be meditating, don't you worry." His green eyes darkened as they gazed down at me. "Meditating on finding out all about you."

John and Luke chuckled in unison, and they nudged each other. My cheeks felt hot, so I lowered my head. "Let me have your hand."

Once he held it out for me, I added several drops of the oil blend. "Rub this into the back of your neck if you're not going to relax while I work."

I focused back on his feet while Jasper did as I'd asked.

"Actually, we're interested in what happened with the break-in at your house and Lacie's murder," Luke said. "Do you think they're connected?"

"I'm pretty sure that's a yes, given another tarot Death card was left at my house." Jasper's body tensed, and I looked up at him. "But it doesn't appear that anything is missing."

"Are you okay? You're not staying out there by yourself, are you?" Jasper's fingers lightly brushed my cheek. "I'm worried about you."

"I'm fine." I tried to relax my shoulders, which had bunched up around my ears. "I'm staying with my dad until this is resolved."

"I'm glad. He'll keep you safe." Jasper leaned back against the couch and began stroking Pixie's head. "Does he have any suspects? I feel out of the loop not being at the patisserie to hear all the gossip."

An unhappy groan practically exploded from my mouth. "It was strongly suggested he put his focus entirely on the playwright's events while the detectives from Thousand Oaks investigate their prime suspect. Which, in case you haven't heard, is me."

"Surely they have other suspects by now." Jasper's eyebrows drew together.

I shrugged. There was no telling what the detectives, especially Raaf, were doing aside from harassing me.

"Did you know Lacie's ex, Brett Palen, is in town? He came to the patisserie today. Poor guy hasn't aged well." John handed Jasper a cupcake. "He didn't have one nice thing to say about the deceased to whoever he was talking to on his cell. I wonder if he had anything to do with the murder."

"I saw him at the kickoff event for the playwright attendees. He got into a huge argument with Lacie. It sounded like it had something to do with him cutting off her alimony." I wondered how much I should share with John and Luke. For all I knew, they would broadcast it to whomever walked through the doors of the patisserie tomorrow. It was probably time to redirect the conversation again.

CHAPTER TWENTY-THREE

I placed Jasper's socks back onto his feet, then handed him the vial of essential oils. "Put a couple drops on the soles of your feet every night and morning for the next week. And for heaven's sake, stop taking the cough syrup. Your lungs need to naturally expel what's in there."

"Thanks, Carissa. I feel much better." He'd taken off his mask and had eaten half the cupcake in one bite. "Or maybe it's the dark chocolate."

Eying his fudgy cupcake, I decided there wasn't anything wrong with having dessert for dinner. Chocolate and sugar would be good for my nerves. Jasper must've seen me drooling because he pointed down the hallway. "Go wash your hands and bring the platter of dessert in here. I think I need to sample a few more things and convince Luke to share his recipes with me."

I settled myself back on the couch, ready to eat a chocolate cupcake and a chocolate pecan cookie, when my phone pinged. It was a reminder that I was in charge of the dessert and drinks for Ashley's skin healing salve workshop the following evening. The lavender shortbread cookies that

Madame Bonsail had served me were exactly what I needed. With Jasper under the weather and unable to bake, I wondered if he would share the recipe so I could bake a batch for the event.

"Is everything all right?" Jasper placed his mask back on and peered at my phone.

"Yes. It was just a reminder about an event Ashley and I are hosting tomorrow evening." I took a deep breath, then slowly exhaled. The worst that could happen was he'd tell me no. "I'm in charge of dessert, and I'd hoped to get some of your lavender shortbread cookies to serve for the event. Since you're sick, can you share your recipe with me, and I'll bake them tonight?"

Jasper drummed his fingers on the couch's upholstered armrest. Both John and Luke leaned forward in their chairs, appearing to wait with bated breath for his answer. The same as me.

"I'll do better than that. We can bake your cookies right now."

"You mean here?"

"I have plenty of supplies and one of these guys," he jerked his thumb toward John and Luke, "can go downstairs and get the dried lavender for us."

"I hate to be a bother and, besides, you should be resting, not baking."

"It's no trouble. I'll let you do most of the heavy lifting, and I'll sit and supervise."

John and Luke exchanged a smirk, which I tried to ignore.

"If you're sure, then thank you."

Luke stood and pulled a set of keys from his pocket. "I'll be right back with the lavender. Anything else I can bring back?"

Jasper shook his head. "I have everything else."

I cleaned up the dessert plates and wine glasses while Pixie snuggled into the warm pillows Jasper had vacated. He scrubbed his hands and then removed butter from the refrigerator. He chopped the cold butter into tiny pieces and scooped them into the mixing bowl. He saw me watching. "It's a trick for bringing the butter to room temperature quickly."

"Write down the measurements and ingredients, but don't let the guys see." He handed me a pad of paper and a pen. Next, he removed containers of flour, cornstarch, and salt from his pantry and carefully measured the ingredients into a medium-sized bowl, whispering the amounts each time. He gave me a small whisk. "Stir the dry ingredients together, and I'll start creaming the butter and sugar."

The whirl of the stand mixer made conversation difficult, but I couldn't help but watch and admire Jasper's broad shoulders and his narrow waist. He wore khaki-colored cargo shorts, and the muscles in his calves rippled, showcasing the bird tattoo that seemed to move in flight with each step he took. John leaned against the kitchen doorway frame, and when I glanced over at him, he waggled his eyebrows at me. Heat flooded my face, so I went back to whisking the dry ingredients, although I was certain I'd mixed them enough already.

Quiet filled the air when Jasper switched off the mixer just as Luke bounded into the kitchen. He held up the bag of dried lavender buds. "Mission accomplished."

Jasper deftly snatched the bag from Luke, then shooed the two men out of the kitchen. "No peeking at my ingredients. This recipe is proprietary."

"Don't get your knickers in a twist, chef. We're on our

way out." Luke waggled his index finger at us. "We'll leave you two love birds to your baking."

My gaze darted to Jasper and saw his face, at least what was visible above the mask, and his ears had flamed red, probably about the same shade as my face.

Before Jasper could respond, Luke grabbed John's hand and spun the large man around. "Ta-ta. We'll check on you tomorrow as long as you promise to save us a couple cookies to sample."

I avoided making eye contact and went back to whisking the dry ingredients. Jasper was silent until we heard the front door close.

"Sorry about that. They can be..." Jasper seemed to be at a loss for words when I gazed up at him. "I would have sent them on their way earlier. but with the playwright event this week, there's nowhere else for them to stay except with me."

"It's okay. They mean well, and I'm sure it's been a godsend having someone keep the patisserie open for you."

"I don't know what I would have done without them. First, I got pneumonia, then Lacie." He shuddered. "I don't know what I'm going to do now. She was a huge help to me and a good friend."

I bit my tongue. Now was not the time to disparage the dead, even if Lacie had completely fooled Jasper. Truth be told, she wasn't a nice person at all.

Jasper took the whisk from my hand and placed it in the sink. He turned back around to face me and casually rested his backside against the black granite countertop. "I know you've had a lot of issues with Lacie since your school days, but she really did change. She told me how awful she felt about what she did to you, especially stealing Brett, but she didn't know how to apologize."

A snort escaped from my nose. Jasper was way more gullible than I'd given him credit for. "She could have started by not making snide remarks about my weight or my business all the time."

"Look, I know she could be caustic at times, but if she tried to make you uncomfortable with who you are, then she was more disturbed than I thought. You're perfect just the way you are." He rubbed his earlobe and appeared to be contemplating something. "I think deep down she was an unhappy, injured person."

I had sensed that too, right before she'd been murdered. Was I somehow responsible for her emotional health or lack thereof? I shook off my misgivings. Lacie had been given plenty of time after high school to pull her life together. Instead, she had taken it upon herself, once I moved back to Oak Creek Valley, to make my life as miserable as she could.

Jasper moved to the island where I'd been working, pulled out a barstool, and sat down next to me. He rested his elbows on the countertop and grasped my hand. "I'm not saying you're responsible for her unhappiness. Ultimately, it was her choice to behave like she did. I just wanted you to understand that she went through a lot of things with Brett that stunted her emotional development."

"How do you know that?" If I remembered correctly, Lacie and Brett had moved away from Oak Creek before Jasper had come to town to work for John and Luke.

"Working together over the last few months gave us an opportunity to talk about things." He squeezed my hand when I stiffened. "I wasn't romantically interested in her, and she knew and accepted it. We were friends."

I nodded but didn't say anything.

He sighed. "I know you're asking questions and investigating the murder. You should take a closer look at Brett.

Lacie confided in me and said he had an uncontrollable temper. She suffered violence at his hands several times."

"Brett? You mean the same Brett I went to high school with?" I racked my memories and couldn't come up with any scenarios where Brett had exhibited any out-of-control anger when we'd been together. Still, people changed. Or perhaps substance abuse could have changed him. "What happened? Is that why they got a divorce?"

"I probably shouldn't say anything else." He released my hand. "She told me in confidence, and I don't want to influence you one way or another. Just be careful if you talk to him."

Thinking back to the event and the argument that had escalated between Brett and Lacie, it appeared she was giving just as much as she was getting, as far as verbal barbs went. "I'll be careful and I'll let my dad know."

"I didn't want to say anything while John and Luke were here, and you can't be spreading the gossip around. Promise?"

"I won't tell anyone who doesn't need to know." I flashed three fingers up. "Girl Scout promise. I won't even tell Ashley."

"Oh, god. Please don't tell Ashley, or it'll be all over town within a minute." He shook his head. "If that happens, no one will tell me anything when they come to the patisserie."

I gently nudged his ribs with my elbow. "I think you thrive on the gossip that goes around this town, more than anyone else."

"I can neither confirm nor deny."

Jasper returned to the sink and washed his hands again. "Let's get the cookies finished."

He pulled down a *molcajete*—a Mexican basalt stone

mortar and pestle—then had me add in a tablespoon of dried lavender, a tablespoon of sugar, and a teaspoon of vanilla extract.

"If you want to change the recipe up a bit, skip the vanilla and add a teaspoon of lemon zest." After instructing me to grind it into a coarse paste, Jasper put his hand over mine to show me the best way to use the pestle. Flutters filled my stomach, and even though Jasper's hand lingered on mine longer than necessary, I wished the lesson hadn't ended almost as soon as it'd begun.

He added the paste to the creamed sugar and butter, gave it a quick whirl, then added the flour mixture. After a few spins of the mixer's paddle, Jasper scooped the cookie dough onto a large sheet of plastic wrap, wrapped it tightly, then popped it into his stainless-steel refrigerator. "That needs to chill for thirty minutes, and then we can do some scalloped circle and square cutouts."

"I could have made the cookies at home so you didn't have to go to all this trouble." I gestured around his kitchen, which didn't look nearly as disastrous as mine would've been had I mixed the cookies on my own. Inevitably, I ended up with flour all over the counters and on my clothes, and sticky sugar granules on the floor.

"Truth be told, I'm not used to lying around all day. I'm feeling better, and it's good to have a quick project." Jasper gathered the containers of ingredients and returned them to the pantry. He handed me a bottle containing coarse white sparkling sugar. "Next time, let me know a few days in advance when you need these cookies, and I'll pipe royal icing lavender blooms on them. But for this batch, we'll sprinkle the sugar on top to give it a little jazz."

"Thanks, but really, you've done more than enough. Let me take the cookie dough home, and I'll bake the cookies there." I put the dirty bowls in the sink and started filling them with hot water. "You need to get some rest."

"I feel great. I think your aromatherapy massage helped." His eyes crinkled at the edges, so I knew he was smiling beneath the mask. He flashed me two thumbs up. "Besides, this cookie project barely took any time at all."

"Uh, hum." I raised my eyebrows, fisted my hands and, placed them on my hips. "Just how much cough syrup and ibuprofen did you take? It's masking your symptoms, not helping you heal."

Jasper wouldn't meet my gaze, so I assumed he knew he shouldn't have self-medicated like he did.

"Go sit down, and I'll bring you some herbal tea with honey." I turned back to the sink and added a squirt of dish-washing soap. "Then I'm going to do the dishes and take the cookie dough home. You've exerted yourself more than you should have today."

"You're no fun. But I'll do as you request as long as you promise to let me cook dinner for you as soon as I'm well." Jasper winked at me, then placed the cookie cutters and the sparkling sugar into my tote.

"You've got yourself a deal as long as you promise me no more cough syrup unless your doctor says otherwise." I opened his pantry and searched the shelves for honey and tea bags. He reached over my shoulder and pulled the tea down, while his other arm encircled my waist. He pulled me against him for a quick hug, then released me and handed me the tea. Jasper smelled of cinnamon and sugar, and the warmth of his arm sent the good kind of shivers down my back.

"If your cough gets worse after the medication wears off, drink more warm tea with honey. A squeeze of lemon juice would be good too."

It didn't take long to get Jasper settled and the dishes washed and dried. With the cookie dough added to my tote, I scooped Pixie up but refrained from blowing Jasper a kiss. He tried to get up to see me to my car, but, in the short time it had taken me to do the dishes, I could see his energy level had dropped and a low-grade fever had developed.

"I'm calling my dad right now to let him know I'm on my way. I'll keep him on the phone until I'm safely locked in the car, so stay right where you're at." I wagged my finger at him. "As soon as you finish the tea, I want you to go straight to bed."

"Yes, ma'am."

It worried me that Jasper didn't have any quips in response to my bossiness. "You can take a couple more ibuprofen before going to sleep, too. It should keep your fever under control, and you'll rest better."

"Yes, ma'am."

With a quick wave of my fingers, I let myself out and called my dad before I descended the stairs. I searched the courtyard, and I was glad it was brightly lit. I didn't see anything or anyone lying in wait for me.

"Are you on your way home?" Dad's voice sounded concerned. "You did have Jasper walk you to your car, right?"

"He's still sick, so it's best that he stays inside. That's why I called you before I walked to my car." I heard his sudden exhalation of breath that Dad did when he was irritated but didn't want to say anything.

Behind me, the door opened and spilled light onto the steps. Jasper came out onto the landing.

I turned around and furrowed my brows. "You're supposed to be resting and drinking your tea."

"Carissa, is everything all right? Who are you talking to?" Dad sounded worried.

"It's Jasper. I'll see you at home in a few." Without waiting to say goodbye, I disconnected the call. "Well?"

"Do you really think I'd let you walk to your car all by yourself? Especially after what's happened over the last few days?" He ran a hand over his strawberry-blond hair, which made his wavy curls pop up. "I'd never forgive myself if something happened to you that I could have prevented."

My heart did a little hop and skip. "You're a true gentleman. Thank you."

"My mama raised me right." Jasper's Texan twang made an appearance. It happened anytime he spoke of his mom or his boyhood home back in Texas. He stepped toward me, took the tote from my hand, and motioned down the stairs. "Ladies first."

I wanted to argue and tell him to stay put, and he could watch me walk to my car without exerting himself. He'd never agree, so I kept my mouth shut.

Once Jasper made sure there weren't any Death cards or tampering done to my car, I buckled Pixie in. He followed me to the driver's side and pulled me into a tight hug.

"Thanks for coming over tonight. As soon as I'm feeling better, I'd like to take you on a real date."

"I'd like that." I climbed into the car when he released me and started the vehicle. "Take care of yourself.

Before I pulled away from the curb, Jasper put his hand up to his ear, thumb and pinkie extended, and mouthed 'call me'. I gave him a thumbs up, then headed to my dad's house, where an interrogation awaited me.

CHAPTER TWENTY-FOUR

I dropped Pixie off at my office, with plenty of chew toys to keep her entertained, and locked the shop before I strolled several doors down to the patisserie. A line had already formed, even this early in the morning, and the small bistro tables and chairs that lined the pastel pink, white, and black-striped painted walls were full. I didn't look closely at the customers since, I assumed, they were tourists who had been drawn in by the aromas of cinnamon, sugar, and chocolate along with rich, dark coffee. My mouth watered, and my gaze fixated on the sweets ahead of me.

It felt strange not seeing Jasper's dimpled smile behind the long glass case that contained indulgent pastries and confectioneries. Instead, it was Luke behind the counter who gave me a wave as I joined the end of the line. A young man, perhaps in his late teens and the newest employee at the patisserie, assisted John by pouring brewed coffee or creating a barista coffee drink. Jasper mentioned the young man had joined one of the artist enclaves in Oak Creek Valley but needed to work part-time to supplement the funds his parents provided on a monthly basis. He was one of the many creative souls drawn to the energy of our valley and mountains. Oak Creek was known for its multitude of art galleries, and on occasion, one of our artists would obtain national acclaim, which would draw even more tourists to our town.

Standing in line, I strained my ears to listen to the conversations going on around me. There was chatter about the ongoing playwriting event and the impromptu concert the night before. Apparently, it had been a smashing success. But what caught my ear was the word murder. I swiveled my head around, attempting to locate the source of the conversation.

Tucked into the corner, as far away from the pastry counter as possible, I spied the back of a man's head with short, thinning blond hair. His shoulders leaned toward his companion as he jabbed his index finger in the air, directed at the woman. She appeared to be around my age, and she shrank back in her chair. Her cheese Danish sat untouched, and she gripped the porcelain coffee cup tightly between her two hands. The woman's short mousy-brown hair hung limp around her face while the black long-sleeved blouse she wore did nothing for her sallow skin. Her pale pink lipstick was half chewed off.

Even though I could only observe the back of the man, there was something familiar about him. When he raised his voice at the woman, I recognized it. Brett. Lacie's ex-husband. And he was angry.

"...nothing but drama." I couldn't make out the entire conversation over the din of the patisserie's patrons, and while Brett raised his voice on certain words, the rest of the time it sounded like he was hissing. "They'll blame me..."

What I could make out sounded like he was talking about Lacie's murder.

"...knives...her fault..."

The woman lifted her gaze from the coffee cup she cradled and caught me staring at her. I immediately turned back toward the pastry case but kept my ear tuned to Brett's voice.

He fell silent and I wanted to turn around to observe the couple again. But I forced myself to face forward. The scrape of the wrought-iron legs of the bistro chairs screeched as they pushed back from the table. I turned my head just enough to see the couple from the periphery of my vision. Brett and the woman were leaving. She gave me one last glance before she scurried behind Brett and out of the patisserie. I turned and gazed out the large plate-glass window, and watched as they strode away. Who was the woman? Could it be his wife or an assistant? Jasper was right, Brett did seem to have a temper, but I still needed to talk to him.

I gave a regretful glance at the pastry case and a quick wave to Luke, then hustled out of the patisserie. Heading in the direction Brett and the mystery woman had taken, I caught a glimpse of the pair as they turned the corner at the end of the long arcade walkway. There was a public parking lot at the far end of the block they had turned onto, so I picked up my pace. If they reached their car and left, I'd have to find another way to track down Brett. I briefly wondered if he was staying at the Oak Creek Inn and if perhaps that might be a better place to question him.

Upon turning the corner, I found Brett and his companion had reached his car. It was a bright red Mercedes convertible parked parallel alongside the curb. Breaking into a trot, I couldn't help but recall Lacie arguing with Brett over alimony because he claimed he was experiencing financial difficulties. If that were the case, how could he afford to keep such an expensive car? Brett was already seated in the Mercedes, and the engine rumbled to life as the woman fumbled with the door handle to open the vehicle.

"Brett!" I was still about fifty feet away, so I shouted to make myself heard over the growl of his car's engine. "Can I talk to you for a minute?"

When he registered who had hollered at him, Brett yelled something at the woman. She gave a quick glance my way, yanked the car door open, and hopped into the seat. Before she could even close the door, Brett pulled away from the curb, the tires of the Mercedes squealing.

I watched the red car speed down the road until it turned the corner, no longer in sight. Why had Brett avoided me? His action made me all the more determined to speak with him. I hurried back to my shop and popped a K-Cup pod into the coffee machine for my caffeine fix. While I wanted to go back to the patisserie for my pastry and a latte, I decided to make a phone call to see if I could track down where Brett was staying. I presumed he'd be in town for at least a few more days while Lacie's death was investigated. One of the things I wanted to find out was why he'd come to town in the first place. Was he connected to the playwright event, or had he used it as a cover for killing Lacie?

The time on my phone screen indicated it was already after eight, so I called the Oak Creek Inn. When the receptionist answered, I asked to be transferred to Brett Palen's room. It didn't take long for the ringer to sound in my ear. Knowing Brett wasn't in his room, I hung up. At least I'd found out where he was staying.

Next, I called Delaney Allman, the assistant to Oak Creek's event manager. I doubted the front desk would give me any information on whether Brett's companion was his wife and, if not, if they were sharing a room. I hoped Delaney might be able to find out for me.

"Delaney Allman speaking. How may I assist you?" Her voice was crisp.

"Hi, it's Carissa Carmichael." Before I could launch into my request, Delaney cut me off.

"Now isn't a good time. Can we meet for coffee around eleven?" The cacophony of ringing phones sounded in the background. "Meet me at the Oak Grill. It'll be my treat."

Before I could agree or suggest a different time, silence filled my ear. I looked at my phone to see if we'd been disconnected and, at the same time, a text popped up. It was from Madame Bonsail.

I found someone to work for you pt. What time should I bring her in this morning? She can start tomorrow.

Chewing my lip, I tried to come up with a tactful reply. It was one thing to interview a potential employee and decide they wouldn't work out, but it would be entirely uncomfortable meeting with someone who might have the idea they were already hired. Given the tarot cards Madame Bonsail had read for me, I didn't want to risk any further bad juju by rejecting this person.

Can u be here at 9 today? I'll need input from staff before I schedule any hours for her.

Hopefully, Madame Bonsail would get the hint that the mystery person's hire wasn't a done deal. Unfortunately, she didn't.

We'll be there at 9. She's flexible with any hours or days you want her to work. Willing to start today if you need her.

All I could do now was hope this woman was a good fit.

If not, I suppose I could limit her hours and days to when I was around to mitigate any problems.

Thanks. See you soon.

I downed my now-cool coffee and cleaned up the distillation room. The front door lock clicked, and the bells tinkled when the door pushed in. Pixie barked, then expressed whining chatters of excitement. My dog's nails skittered across the floor to greet the newcomer. It could only be Ashley who'd let herself in.

"Hi, Carissa." She made her way toward the back of the shop just as I came from the distillation room. She eyed the vials of lavender essential oils I'd filled. "You're here early."

"I couldn't sleep, so decided I might as well come in and get things done."

"Well?" She waggled her eyebrows.

I knew exactly what information she wanted to pry from me, but I decided to make her work for it. Besides, there wasn't anything to tell. Instead, I picked up the platter of cookies I'd left on the counter when I'd entered the shop earlier and handed her a cookie. "Jasper made us lavender shortbread cookies for our event tonight, and I made some lavender lemonade sweetened with honey."

Ashley held the cookie between her thumb and forefinger and waggled it in front of me. "Spill the details, girlfriend! A cookie baking date? It doesn't get much more romantic than that."

"It didn't seem like much of a date." A sigh escaped my lips. "John and Luke are staying with him while they help out at the patisserie, and even though they left for a while, Jasper's still under the weather."

"But is there at least hope for a future date?"

The corners of my mouth tugged upward. "Oh yeah. I

might have gotten a couple hugs from Jasper that made it seem like we might be more than just friends."

"I knew it!" Ashley's wide smile mirrored my own. She took a bite of the cookie. "Yum! I could eat the whole plate of these cookies. The extra sugar on top makes them even better."

"Jasper gave me the recipe so I can make them whenever we have an event."

"Or for my birthday, or Christmas, or Best Friends' Day?" She reached over and plucked another cookie from the platter.

"Of course." I picked up a cookie to nibble too. The batch had made more than we needed for the afterhours gathering that night. "What else do I need to do for the workshop?"

"Everything is ready at least until the shop closes. After that, I'll need your help setting up the table." She took another bite of the cookie. "It shouldn't take too long to get it organized."

I glanced at my watch and saw I had fifteen minutes before Madame Bonsail would arrive with my new employee. "Our solution for part-time help should be arriving at nine this morning."

"Tell me who it is and how you were able to hire them so quickly."

I gave Ashley an overview of what had transpired. "My only qualm is what to do if she's not a good fit. I'd hate to annoy Madame Bonsail if this doesn't work out."

She waved away my concern. "She's a businesswoman. I'd trust her to make the right recommendation."

I could only hope Ashley was right because right at the stroke of nine, the bells from the downtown tower pealed the hour, and a sharp rap sounded at the door. I scurried to answer with Pixie close on my heels.

CHAPTER TWENTY-FIVE

Madame Bonsail, dressed in a flowing turquoise, shell-patterned print caftan, had her fist raised to knock again. She lowered her hand when she saw me. I quickly unlocked the door and she glided into the shop, then turned and motioned her arm with a flourish. "Let me introduce you to my sister, Betty Kalakos."

The woman who stepped out from behind the turquoise fluttering fabric bore little resemblance to Madame Bonsail. Instead, she appeared to be much younger, perhaps in her early forties, with stick-straight candy-apple red hair that hung halfway down her back. Dramatic cat-eye black liner rimmed her eyes, and her dark burgundy lipstick color clashed with her pale ivory skin tone. Dressed in skinny acid-washed ripped jeans and an embroidered peasant blouse that slipped off her shoulder, the ensemble seemed better suited for a teen. The four-inch espadrille wedge sandals that encased her feet made her tall enough so that we saw eye-to-eye. Without the heels, she'd be a short woman.

I reached my hand out. "It's so nice to meet you, Betty."

She returned my handshake with a firm grasp, although her long, burgundy-colored painted nails almost raked my palm when she released my hand. In a breathy, almost Betty Boop voice, she answered, "Thanks for this opportunity. I've been at wit's end since I was forced to leave Venice Beach with hardly more than the clothes on my back."

"Oh no! What happened? Did your home catch on fire?" I tried to imagine what else could have caused her to lose her home with nothing more than the clothes on her back.

"Don't you pay Betty any mind. She's just exaggerating a bit." Madame Bonsail stepped closer to her sister and rested her hand on Betty's arm. "It's nothing as dramatic as that. Shall we discuss the duties you'd like her to do and talk about a schedule?"

Betty lowered her head to stare at the floor and shoved her hands into the pockets of her jeans. I gathered she wasn't pleased with her sister dismissing whatever situation had brought her to Oak Creek. Her response worried me, though. Why did Madame Bonsail try to gloss over Betty's trouble? Or did Betty exaggerate all the time, and she hadn't experienced anything so dramatic? "Uh, sure. We can sit at the counter and talk about what is needed. Can I offer you some tea or coffee?"

Without waiting for Betty to respond, Madame Bonsail answered for them both. "We're fine. Thank you."

She pulled her sister over to the narrow marble-topped counter island that ran six feet down the center of the shop. They sat down on the black leather padded barstools. While Madame Bonsail looked relaxed, Betty appeared stiff, and the furrows that had formed in her forehead earlier had yet to disappear. Before they'd arrived, I'd placed an employment application and pen on the counter. I pushed them toward Betty.

"I'll need you to fill out the application for my records and tax purposes." Before I could go further with my spiel, Madame Bonsail interrupted.

"Surely you can forgo this rigmarole?" She glanced over to where Ashley stood, dusting the front window shelves, and lowered her voice. "Just pay her cash, under the table so to speak. It'll save you both money in the long run."

I'd never experienced this side of Madame Bonsail before, and I didn't like it. "Even if I hired her as a consultant and paid cash, I'd still need her information to issue a 1099."

She lowered her voice even more. "That's not really necessary. We won't tell if you won't tell."

Betty sat quietly, her gaze bouncing between her sister and me. I was getting more uncomfortable by the moment, but I wasn't going to court attention from the IRS for anybody. I'd had enough attention from law enforcement to last me a lifetime. I also had to wonder what they were trying to hide. Inspiration struck, although it wasn't actually factual. But they didn't need to know that. "I'm sorry, but that's not possible. My dad, who you know is the chief of police, does a lot of the accounting for me and helps file the taxes. He'd notice in a second if there was unaccounted money going out."

"Bertha, it's okay." Betty reached out and laid her hand on her sister's arm. "It's not a big deal. I'll fill out the form."

Having never heard Madame Bonsail's first name, I was caught by surprise. The banality of it didn't seem to mesh with the larger-than-life image she exhibited. I supposed I should continue to call her Madame Bonsail until she indicated otherwise.

Madame Bonsail sighed. "We can try to figure something else out."

I tilted my head and blinked while I examined the two sisters. There was definitely more to the story than wanting to avoid paying taxes. What were they trying to hide? Trying my best to remain patient, I stayed silent, waiting to see what they decided to do.

Betty looked at her sister, shrugged, and then pointed her chin at Ashley. "You said Carissa could be trusted. How about the other one?"

Madame Bonsail nodded but didn't take her gaze away from mine. "We're putting Betty's life in your hands, Carissa, by filling out that form."

What were these two women trying to get me involved in? I was pretty sure I didn't want any part of it. I had my own problems. But then tears started dripping down Betty's cheeks, leaving trails of black streaks. I reached beneath the counter and extracted a box of tissues, which I handed to her. She wiped her cheeks and pressed trembling lips to the back of her hand. I waved at Ashley to come sit with us. "If you want to tell me what's going on and still desire to work here, Ashley needs to know what's going on. She's my right-hand woman, and I trust her one hundred percent.

Neither woman protested, so Ashley settled in next to me. Once Betty seemed to have gotten her emotions under control, she slid the red wig from her short, brunette hair and started talking. Except, the Betty Boop voice was gone, and instead, a polished contralto voice fell from her mouth. "I apologize for the deception, but I'm afraid my husband is going to kill me. The restraining order has done nothing but make him angrier, so I'm hiding."

"I'm sorry you're going through that." That would certainly explain the remark about having to leave with nothing but the clothes on her back. "Are you certain he'll track you down here? Venice Beach is a long way from Oak Creek."

"My husband used to live in this area, and he knows my sister is here." She glanced at Madame Bonsail, who blew out a noisy breath of air.

"What Betty is saying is he's already been snooping around. Someone recognized my sister last week and told him she's been staying with me." Madame Bonsail's face turned red, and she knit her eyebrows together. "Neither of us can afford to move, and Betty needs to start earning some money to retain an attorney. We thought the disguise would throw him off her trail but we didn't think the IRS requirements through."

"Look, I wish I could avoid employment tax requirements, but I can't." I pushed the form toward Betty. "How about you fill out the form, and I'll have my dad lock it in his file cabinet at the police station? No one will be able to access your personal information there."

The two women glanced at each other and then nodded at the same time. While Betty filled out the form, Ashley disappeared into our break room and I could hear the Keurig gurgling as it dispensed cups of coffee. It didn't take long for my friend to set down four cups of piping hot coffee along with a plate of lavender shortbread in front of us.

I decided to ask Madame Bonsail some questions with the hope we could provide a safe environment for her sister. "Who is the person who recognized Betty? I'd like to be able to give her some warning should they show up."

Madame Bonsail waved her hand dismissively. "It's no one you need to worry about. They're no longer in town and won't be bothering my sister."

Betty's hand holding the pen trembled. She put it down

and massaged her fingers. "Sorry. Every time I think about my husband finding me, I can't help but get shaky."

"It's okay. I understand." While I didn't understand how a spouse could be so intent on murder, I'd experienced how terrifying it was to have someone targeting you. "Can you give us a description of your husband? That way, if we see him lurking around, we'll give you a heads up."

Again, the sisters exchanged a look before Madame Bonsail answered. "He's fifty-eight, six-foot-two, about two hundred and twenty-five pounds. Salt and pepper buzz cut hair and hazel eyes. He has several tats on his forearm, the largest of which is a blue anchor on his right arm. Ex-navy, but he's a defense attorney now. He has some pretty rough clients who know better than to mess with him. He's a mean one."

How had Betty gotten involved with someone like that? She must've guessed my thoughts.

"I started out as Hank's paralegal seven years ago. He'd just gone through a bad divorce and was setting up his own firm. Back then, he was quite charming, and it seemed like the perfect match, being able to start the law firm together." She gulped. "Everything was a fairy tale until he put the ring on my finger. It went downhill from there, especially after he hired his daughter as our receptionist."

Betty bent her head down and picked up the pen. I waited, hoping she'd tell us more, but the shop remained quiet. Was her step-daughter still around, or worse, had the murderous rage extended to her as well? I turned toward Madame Bonsail. "What happened to his daughter? Is she safe?"

"She's the root cause of this." She gestured at her sister. "As far as I'm concerned, she deserves whatever karma comes her way."

"Now, Bertha, don't be so harsh." Betty looked up from the application. "From what I gather, my step-daughter had a tough childhood and then married a man every bit as mean as her father. I never quite understood why she decided to reconnect with Hank and work for him, after her divorce. Maybe she was hoping to get all of her daddy's money instead of sharing with me."

"I did her cards a few times. She's a greedy little witch, is all I can say." Madame Bonsail took a bite of a cookie. "You got Jasper to make you the lavender shortbread cookies. You should stock them in your shop in little gift boxes to sell."

"That's a great idea. I'll talk to Jasper once he's back on his feet." I swiped my phone on and made myself a note.

Betty signed her name with a flourish and handed me the application. "I've listed Bertha's phone number for now since I'm in the process of getting a new phone.

Tamping down my curiosity to examine her information immediately, I brought up the subject of scheduling. "Do you have any specific days you can't work?"

She shook her head. "I have nothing else going on. Just tell me when to show up."

I turned toward Ashley. "How many customers do we have signed up for the event tonight?"

"Ten. Eight ladies and two gents." Ashley pursed her lips for a moment. "Having an extra set of hands to help out would be great. It'll give Betty a chance to hear our spiel and try out some of our products alongside the others."

"Can you work from six thirty to around nine thirty tonight, Betty?"

She nodded enthusiastically. "Thank you for this chance. I truly appreciate it."

Once the two women were on their way, Ashley and I

hustled to clean up. I took a moment to peek at Betty's application. As I suspected, there was a different name listed, and her real name was Yvonne Lakeland. I'd just forget I'd ever heard that name in case anyone ever came looking for her. I shoved the application in my purse so I'd remember to ask my dad to safeguard it for me. At exactly ten, I unlocked the door and turned the sign hanging in the window to 'open'. Within a mere moment, the bells dangling on the door jingled to alert us we had our first customer. It was none other than Rachel Walton, the famous playwright. I'll admit I was a bit starstruck now that I'd found out who she was.

"Hello, Rachel, welcome to Aromatherapy Apothecary." I extended my hand to her, which she ignored, and instead, pulled me into a hug. From her perch at the register, Ashley raised her eyebrows at me, and her eyes flew wide open.

"I wanted to say thank you in person for your advice in seeking a thyroid test. You were spot on." Rachel's smile widened. "The Inn recommended a doctor who was able to do a rush test and prescribed thyroid medication for me to start taking right away."

"That's wonderful! I'm glad you didn't have to wait until returning home to get the test done."

"I know it's too early to see any benefits, but having someone acknowledge I'm not imagining all these symptoms makes me feel better already." She swept her gaze around my shop. "This is a lovely space and I adore the fragrance."

"I've been distilling and bottling lavender this morning. Would you like to sample some of our moisturizing oils?"

"I'd love to, dear, but you also mentioned you could

concoct a blend to aid in my thyroid function and dry skin issues."

"Of course. Let me show you what I have." I led her over to the marble counter and got her settled onto the padded stool. I was relieved to see that Ashley had already cleared the coffee cups and wiped down the counter for stray cookie crumbs.

After unlocking the cabinet beneath the counter that contained the bottles of pure essential oils, I pulled several out and set them onto the marble top. Next, I poured 100 milliliters of almond oil into a beaker, then poured the same amount of the jojoba oil into a second beaker.

"I have two mixtures to make for you. The first is for you to massage a couple drops on your neck every morning." I opened the notes app on my phone to check the ratios of essential oils I'd researched. I added small measures of rose geranium, lemongrass, and myrrh oils to the almond oil, and explained what each essential oil was. Next, I stirred the oils with a disposable stick, commonly found in coffee shops for mixing sugar and cream into beverages, then carefully poured the mixture into an opaque blue bottle. I tightened a black plastic cap and showed Rachel a screw top bottle dropper. "When you get home, you can keep the bottle dropper in instead of the cap. But for now, I'd recommend the cap to prevent any oils from seeping out into your suitcase."

I used the stir stick to wipe residual oil onto the back of Rachel's hand and massaged it in. She held her hand up to her nose and sniffed. "I never would have thought a combination of floral and citrus would meld together so nicely. And there's a scent of sweetness too."

"That's the myrrh oil. It reminds me of figs, but Ashley says she smells plums." I pointed at Ashley, who was busy ringing up a customer. She gave a quick wave, then turned her attention back to wrapping the purchase.

I quickly entered the ingredients and usage on a small handheld label machine, then attached the printed label to the vial. It wasn't the most decorative, but after trial-and-error, Ashley and I had decided it was better to be accurate than pretty. We'd toyed with the idea of an expensive system that required the use of my laptop, but decided speed and ease of use were key to moving clients along.

Mixing the second blend, I described the two ingredients used. "This is a simple blend containing only cedarwood oil and jojoba oil. Both are known for their moisturizing properties. Cedarwood can also help you relax for better sleep. Rub a small amount into your feet every night before bed, and if you can stand it, wear socks after the oils have been absorbed."

Rachel insisted that I walk around the shop with her while she examined it, and much to my delight, she picked up aromatherapy gift items to purchase. We chatted about the events going on around town and which ones she was directly involved in. While Ashley rang up another customer, Rachel looked around and, seeing no one nearby to overhear, leaned in toward me and lowered her voice. "Did you know that the police consider me a suspect for murdering that horrid woman from the opening event?"

My eyes widened, and my lips formed an 'o'. It was given that they'd question Rachel after her argument with Lacie, but I never thought for a moment she'd be a serious suspect. "I'm sure it's a mere formality of questioning anyone who had interaction with her that day."

"Oh, it's much more than just questioning. I've been told not to leave town in no uncertain terms." Rachel fingered a gold medallion that dangled from a thick gold chain that encircled her neck. "The problem is I don't have an alibi."

"How is that possible? Wasn't there a cocktail party and dinner for the award-winning playwrights right after the opening event?" Had I gotten the schedule of events mixed up?

"You're correct, there was. I went to the cocktail party, but a dreadful man, mind you, I won't slander him and say his name, cornered me. He's been after me for several years to write something for his outrageous, and frankly, untalented son." She glanced as if to see if anyone was within hearing distance. Despite us being alone, aside from Ashley by the register, Rachel lowered her voice even more. "I was so annoyed I skipped out and hid in my room."

"But surely security cameras would verify that, right?" Nowadays, security cameras seem to be everywhere, although when you really needed them, they weren't available.

She waved her hand dismissively. "The detective is claiming I went out through my balcony door that overlooks the golf course. The cameras are located sporadically, and he claims I knew where they were and avoided those areas."

"Let me guess, it's Detective Raaf who's accusing you?"

"No, dear. It's the older handsome fellow. Detective Martin." She reached up and zigzagged the gold medallion across the chain, back and forth. It made a sawing noise that filled the quiet shop. It must've caught Pixie's attention because I could hear her whine from inside my office. "Oh, do you have a dog here?"

"Yes. She's my puppy, Pixie, and she gets to hang out in my office while I work." I didn't want the conversation to veer away from the investigation. "What else has Detective Martin said about the case?"

"He hasn't given me one iota of information. It's all about him collecting evidence and trying to find potential suspects who had issues with the victim." Rachel pursed her lips. "Your name came up multiple times."

"I swear I didn't have anything to do with her death." There was no way I would tell her I was probably the last person to see Lacie alive, aside from the killer. But, of course, I should have been prepared for not only towns-people to be dialed in to the gossip hotline but out-of-town guests as well.

"That's not what I heard. In fact, you were the one to find her with ten swords stuck in her back."

"Actually, they were ten fake knives. Not swords." I realized I needed to convince her I wasn't a killer, especially when I could spout personal knowledge about the crime. "Truly, Rachel, I'm innocent and had the misfortune of being at the wrong place at the wrong time."

"It doesn't really matter if I believe you or not. I just find it interesting and want to explore all angles of the human reaction to such a violent death." She smoothed her hair back and tucked a strand behind an ear. "It's good research for perhaps a future script."

Not sure if I liked that explanation or not, I decided to move Rachel on so I wouldn't be late meeting Delaney. Besides, I doubted this famous playwright had murdered Lacie, and I doubted she had any further information to add to my investigation. "I'm sure the detectives will get to the bottom of it and arrest the murderer."

She eyed me and cocked her head to the side, then shook it. "You're probably right, dear. I suppose I should complete my purchases and let you get back to work. Thank you for a most eye-opening conversation."

I led her over to the register, where Ashley rang up the sale. I wrapped each purchase in sage-colored tissue paper, then gently placed them into a gift-sized bag. Rachel chit-chatted amiably while she waited for us to complete the transaction.

Walking toward the door, she stopped and turned back to face us. "Do you have tickets for my play on Saturday night?"

Ashley and I both shook our heads. Her play, one of the highlights of the event, had sold out within minutes of the tickets being released.

"I'll send someone over with four tickets. Front row seats if you're interested."

"That would be fantastic. Thank you!" I could feel Ashley practically bouncing on her toes next to me. "What do we owe you for the tickets?"

Rachel waved away my question. "Absolutely nothing. You've done more for me than I could ever thank you for."

"Then, doubly thank you! We can't wait to see your production."

She turned and swept through the doorway and down the sidewalk. I could see a few people walking by, turn and watch her. They nudged each other and mouthed a few words, no doubt excited to have seen a famous personage out running errands.

"Oh my gosh, oh my gosh! I'm so excited." Ashley clapped her hands. "I've got to call Bryon and make sure he can go with me. I hope Mom can watch Hunter, or I'll have to get a sitter."

I smiled, happy to see Ashley excited about this opportunity. I checked the time. If I didn't leave immediately, I was going to be late for my coffee date. "Can you hold down the shop? I'm meeting Delaney Allman at the Oak Grill for a quick coffee."

"Uh-uh. And some investigating, too?" She nudged me. "I'm fine. It's been a quiet morning, and I'll even take Pixie out for a break."

"I don't know what I'd do without you, ya know?" I gave her a quick hug before I flew out the door.

CHAPTER TWENTY-SIX

I found Delaney seated at a table on the patio, shaded by the massive branches of ancient oak trees. The Oak Grill came by its name honestly. Two to-go cups of steaming coffee and a bakery bag of biscotti were placed in front of us by a server dressed in white shorts and a white polo shirt. As the day progressed, the August heat would become unpleasant, although guests returning from soaking in the cool waters of the crystalline pool often wanted to sit outdoors. At the moment, though, it was warm but not uncomfortable.

"Thanks for inviting me." I gestured at the coffee and biscotti. "Your pastry chef makes some delicious cookies."

Delaney's tinkling laugh caught the attention of a pair of golfers heading to the grill. Their heads swiveled to get a better look at her. She ignored their stare. "I'll agree she's good, but no one can compare to Jasper's pastries and cookies."

"True, but then again I'm a bit prejudiced in that regard." I smiled and my cheeks heated thinking about mixing the lavender shortbread dough with Jasper the evening before.

"I know you probably need to rush back to your shop." She stood. "But I thought it would be best if we could walk around while we talk and act like I'm giving you a tour for your potential event."

I cocked my head. "What event?"

She leaned in close to me. "I don't want employees or my boss to think I'm gossiping, so if we pretend you're thinking about holding an event here, it'll make sense that I'm showing you around."

"Good thinking."

I picked up my coffee and the biscotti as Delaney led us away from the patio restaurant and onto a wide path. A sign pointed in the direction of the pool and spa. "Speaking of gossip, I hear you're investigating Lacie's murder."

"I might be asking a few questions here and there." I looked behind us to make sure no one else was headed toward the pool. The pathway was empty. "Why? Do you know something?"

"I assumed that was the reason you called and asked to meet up." She glanced at her slim gold watch, the face rimmed with diamonds, which encircled her wrist. "I have about fifteen minutes before I have to oversee the set up for the lunch buffet and keynote speaker, so I'll get to the point. I think Lionel had a reason to want Lacie dead."

"Are you talking about your boss? That Lionel?" I didn't see how it could be possible. He had a slight build, and he portrayed an appearance of frailty. Besides, he was the consummate event manager. Nothing ever ruffled him.

"I realize it may sound crazy, but early this morning, I finally got around to listening to and transcribing all the voicemail messages left for him on the day of the murder. There were many complaints about Lacie insulting our clients during the event. The more famous and the more entitled the person, the more adamant they were that they'd never set foot at Oak Creek Inn after this event again." Delaney sighed and rubbed her temples. "When I took the messages to Lionel, he told me to delete all the messages, both voicemail and on my computer, and to shred the printed copy. When I questioned him, he said he'd already spoken to the people in person, first thing on Tuesday. He also had fruit baskets delivered to each of their rooms, at his own expense, to soothe them. Trust me, he hated Lacie with a passion. The reputation of the Inn means everything to him."

"But surely that doesn't mean he killed her. Plenty of other people had reasons to hate her, too." I took a sip of the coffee. It was slightly sweet and creamy, exactly the way I enjoyed drinking my coffee.

Delaney dejectedly pulled a biscotti from the bakery bag I'd been holding, and took a nibble. "That's true, but Lionel did something completely inconsistent with his work ethic. Right after you left Monday night, he asked me to oversee the cocktail and dinner for the playwrights, and then he left. I didn't see or hear from him again until late Tuesday morning."

"He's never done something like that before?"

"Never! Especially not when it's a high-profile forum like this." She handed the bag of biscotti back to me. "Lionel lives and breathes for this event. It's become his most accomplished achievement since he started working here."

"Did you ask him why he skipped the dinner?"

Delaney shook her head. "Definitely not. It's none of my business, plus whatever he told me would probably be a lie anyway."

"Perhaps you should talk to the detectives investigating."

"No!" She glanced behind us, then looked back at me and lowered her voice to a whisper. "I'm telling you in confidence since I know you're looking into Lacie's death. This can't get back to Lionel or anyone else at the Inn. I can't afford to lose my job. If anyone asks about our meeting, you're considering hosting an event here. I'll mail you a packet with rates and meal options to make it seem legit."

"Okay... I'll see what I can find out." Honestly, I didn't think there was much I could do. Lionel's position almost sheltered him from riff raff like me. All my interactions for the opening festivities on Monday had been with Delaney. Lionel was accessible to the famous and VIPs. I didn't qualify.

Delaney thrust her hand into her purse, drew out a white envelope, and handed it to me. Still whispering, she said, "These are the voicemail messages. I printed an extra set before I deleted them. Please don't tell anyone where you got this from."

Once she had my assurance that I'd do my best to protect her identity, she led me to the pool area and pointed out the features that would make it an ideal spot to host a cocktail event. I nodded enthusiastically when a server, dressed in shorts and a polo shirt, passed by on her way to deliver frosty concoctions to two middle-aged women lounging beneath a striped umbrella. After making a circuit around the sparkling turquoise pool and adjacent poolside restaurant, Delaney pointed at the large, adobe-style building.

"Would you like a tour of the spa?"

I couldn't help but notice the poolside bartender

watching us. It was time to let Delaney get back to work. "I think this will do. Send me a quote with some menu options and I'll talk it over with my dad."

She held her hand out to me, and I shook it before she slipped out the pool gate and went back to work. I found a table shaded by an umbrella, as far from the restaurant as I could get, and sat as I mulled over the conversation. I finished the coffee and another piece of biscotti, and watched a mother herd her four young sons and their pool paraphernalia into a blue-striped cabana. The server bustled over to take their order.

I wanted to rip the envelope open and read them right then and there, but worried someone might notice and then Delaney's involvement would be found out. I'd have to wait until I was in my office, where no one was around to observe me.

Making my way back to the self-park lot, I remembered I hadn't asked Delaney about Brett. Turning around, I strode to the entry atrium and found a corner chair to sit on while I called her. Perhaps she'd have a spare moment to give me the information I needed about Lacie's ex-husband. Instead of answering the phone, her voicemail immediately connected. Before I could leave a message, I spied Brett and his companion walking across the reception area, heading toward the Inn's formal seafood restaurant, Waves. While I didn't relish ambushing them in the posh setting, I figured Brett could have avoided it had he not run from me earlier.

Waiting a few minutes until the couple had been shown to a table, I gazed around the atrium to make sure there was no one who would recognize me. The last thing I needed was for word to get back to my dad or the investigating detectives that I was interrogating Brett. When I determined the coast was clear, I nonchalantly strolled to the restaurant. The maître d's station was empty, so I entered the dimly lit interior to look for Brett. Crystal chandeliers, with soft ivory lighting, hung at far-spaced intervals. Etched glass wave sculptures cascaded down the walls while a twelve-foot saltwater aquarium, filled with colorful reef fish, dissected the center of the room.

I spotted Brett and his companion cozied up together on a banquette seat, on the far side of the restaurant. From their demeanor I gathered they were a couple. Using the aquarium as a shield, I tried to get as close to their seating as I could without being detected. When a waiter stood at their table, filling goblets with water, I used him as a distraction to edge even closer. As soon as the waiter departed for the kitchen, Brett looked up and noticed me. His face contorted, and he looked in vain for a way to get away from me. I almost laughed at the absurd position he'd put himself in. Seated on a banquette loveseat, next to a wall and hemmed in by his companion, there wasn't a chance he could get up without shoving the table out of the way. I kept that possibility from happening by sitting down in the royal blue upholstered chair across the table from him.

Brett's eyes blinked rapidly, and his gaze darted to the doorway that the waiter had disappeared through. His companion raised her eyebrows, which made her tawny eyes reflect the candlelight from the votive burning at the center of the table. She looked from me then to Brett before she fixed her gaze back on me.

"Hi. I'm Carissa." I extended my hand to her. "I wanted to introduce myself this morning, but it seemed you were in a hurry."

Her hand felt small and cold, and her grasp was almost non-existent. I removed my hand and wiped my palm down the sides of my pants. She still didn't say anything, so I prompted her. "Brett and I are old classmates. And you are...?"

She turned her head briefly toward Brett, who nodded in response. My irritation ratcheted up. Did she need his permission to speak? What kind of power did he hold over her? And why would she allow it? I tried to quiet the pounding of my heart and bit my tongue before I could say anything rash and ruin my chance to find out about Lacie.

"Tamara." She gulped and looked at Brett, who again nodded. "Tamara Gainsfield."

This was getting weirder by the moment, but I tried to keep the expression on my face neutral.

"It's nice to meet you. Are you enjoying your stay in Oak Creek Valley?"

She nodded and lowered her eyes. I turned and met Brett's gaze. He appeared to have calmed down, except for the muscles in his cheeks and neck that twitched. It made me suspect he was clenching his jaw. "Are you in town for the playwrights' conference or just visiting?"

"I guess you could say both." Brett looked up at the approaching waiter, and I worried he'd have me thrown out. Instead, he motioned to me. "Can you bring another setting? There'll be three of us for lunch."

"You don't have to do that. I need to get back to work soon." I wish I could spare the time, but my responsibilities were calling. I couldn't leave Ashley to shoulder it all for much longer.

Once the waiter had taken their orders—steak and frites for Brett and a salad with scallops for Tamara—I continued with my questions. "Did you know that Lacie was going to be at the opening event?"

"She's the one who gave me the ticket." Brett rubbed his

cheek with pudgy fingers. He lowered his hand to his lap. "Look, I know you're a suspect and that you're investigating. Heck, half the town has tried to warn me about your sleuthing, as if I have something to hide. I don't. And I didn't have anything to do with Lacie's death. It's not much of a surprise she met her demise in a violent, way but I'd never agree with anyone who says she deserved it."

"Can I ask where you went after the event?" I bit the inside of my cheek, anticipating he'd have me thrown out for sure.

Brett closed his eyes for a moment and exhaled, then opened them and looked at Tamara. "Is it okay, babe?"

She nodded but kept her eyes lowered to the brilliant white tablecloth.

"I drove down to Venice Beach to pick Tamara up from her psychologist's appointment. She suffers from agoraphobia, and this is the first outing we've taken together." He reached over and grasped Tamara's hand and glared at me. "She felt a panic attack starting at the patisserie, so I wanted to get her away from people as quickly as possible. It didn't help that you kept staring and then chased us."

I was such a heel, although from what I'd seen of Brett's actions at the patisserie, I was certain there had been anger directed at Tamara. Not compassion or comfort. "I'm so sorry. I didn't know."

"You should leave the investigating to the police. They already know all of this, and I'm not a suspect." Stern Brett was back. "So please leave us alone and stop chasing me."

I apologized again and slunk out of the restaurant like the rat I was. The poor woman had issues, and I made her first trip out miserable. Perhaps I would deliver a gift basket of soothing items like calming essential oils, along with a rose-scented candle and lavender-infused socks. While it wouldn't cure Tamara's issues, it might provide a bit of relaxing comfort. I'd also write an apology note to them both and include some of Jasper's lavender cookies. It was the least I could do to assuage my guilt despite thinking Brett wasn't telling me the entire truth.

CHAPTER TWENTY-SEVEN

Before I started my car, I took a quick peek at the first page of the voicemail messages. Rachel Walton's message was at the top of the page and it was scathing. I flinched reading her rant about Lacie's treatment of her at the event, and her threats to ruin Lionel seemed over the top. Lacie had certainly made herself an enemy. Rachel had been forthcoming about being a suspect with no alibi but had she shared her status to throw off any suspicions I might have had? Given her vitriol, I had to wonder if something else had happened between Rachel and Lacie. I hadn't considered her a likely killer, but now I wasn't so sure. No wonder Lionel wanted the messages destroyed, and no wonder Delaney thought he might have murdered Lacie himself. If Rachel carried through on her threats, his career could be in jeopardy.

Before leaving the parking lot, I called in an order for lunch for Ashley and me, then made my way across town to the deli. When I entered the cool interior of the restaurant, all the tables were filled, despite the place being mostly a takeout service. A group of rowdy teens, dressed in colorful beach attire, crowded around one of the tables. They added to the din of the room but gave me something to watch for entertainment while I waited my turn. A gravelly voice sounded in my ear, and I twirled around to see who it was. My stomach plummeted when I found Detective Raaf standing mere inches from me, arms crossed in front of his barrel chest.

"Ms. Carmichael, we meet again." His smirk made the corner of his full lips twitch, and he studied my face with half-closed eyes.

The skin on my arms prickled, so I took a half step back. "Um, detective. Are you here for lunch?"

"Maybe." He stepped toward me, back into my personal space. "Or maybe I'm checking to see what kind of trouble you're causing today."

Uh-oh. Did he know I'd ramped up my own investigation? Had Brett decided to complain about my behavior? "As you can see, I'm not causing any trouble. I'm merely picking up lunch."

"We'll see about that." He lifted his index finger and thumb, in the shape of a gun, and pointed it at me before clicking his tongue between his teeth. Then he brushed past me and out the door without a backward glance.

"That was weird." The quiet, shaky voice of an elderly woman sounded behind me. "Was that man harassing you? I can call the police and be your witness if you need me to."

Turning, I faced a wrinkled, white-haired woman who barely came up to my shoulder. Her floor-length calico-print dress was faded, and she held a matching bonnet in her hand. She was probably one of the community actresses practicing for an upcoming stage show. "Unfortunately, he is the police."

"That's a shame. They think they can get away with

anything just because they have a badge and a gun." She patted my arm. "If you decide you want to report him for harassment, you just let me know."

I'd like to report him to my dad, but that would be opening up a whole new can of worms, which didn't seem like a good idea. He'd already been told, in no uncertain terms, to stick to working the event. If Dad got in a confrontation with Raaf, I shuddered to think what might happen to his career. "Thanks. I appreciate it, but I'm okay."

The elderly woman turned her attention to the latest iPhone held in her hand, swiping through whatever app she had open. I was relieved when I had my order in hand, and I was safely back in my car without encountering Detective Raaf again. He was going out of his way to make me uncomfortable, and I had to agree with the elderly woman—it was a form of harassment. It reminded me I hadn't heard back from Suzie. I scrolled through my emails but didn't see a response yet, so I sent her another email asking if she'd received my first email. This time, I received an automatic response indicating she was out for the day but would respond as soon as possible.

Aromatherapy Apothecary had several customers, but it wasn't out of control busy. I handed Ashley the bag containing the turkey pita sandwich. "Sorry, I didn't mean to be gone so long. Take a long lunch break. You more than deserve it."

"You know it's not a problem. Besides, Dillon dropped in for a bit to see if we needed any help before he headed to the beach with friends. I told him we were fine." She opened the deli bag and saw the hummus and pita chips I'd included with the order. "Yum! How much do I owe you?"

"Not a penny. It's the least I can do for bailing out of

work... again." I reached into my own bag and plucked out a chip. I'd already eaten half of them on the drive back to the shop. "Is there anything I need to do for tonight?"

"Nope. I've got everything ready to go." She crunched on the extra crispy chip. "I'll pick up the charcuterie board and wine on my break. I made room in the refrigerator for it."

One of the customers walked over to the register and looked our way. I handed Ashley my sandwich bag and asked her to put it in the refrigerator with the hopes I'd be able to finish it before the workshop started. The rest of the afternoon went by in a blur as tourists, sated from lunch, descended on the air-conditioned shops to pick up gifts and souvenirs to take home. I had a couple shoppers complain that they couldn't access our Instagram account. I lied and said we'd had some technical difficulty, although I guess getting hacked could fall under that category. Just one more thing I needed to follow up on.

CHAPTER TWENTY-EIGHT

At six thirty sharp, a rap sounded on the front door. I scurried to let Betty in and gave a sharp inhalation of breath as she walked through the doorway. Her appearance had aged by about twenty years. She wore a curly, platinum-gray wig with eye-watering blue eyeshadow. White, cat-eye framed glasses perched on her nose and magnified the wrinkles around her eyes. That morning, Betty's face had appeared pale and wan. This evening there was a generous sprinkling of freckles with a ruddy complexion. Her makeup skills were phenomenal to make that drastic of a change, and I wondered who the real Betty was. Perhaps I'd never know. Instead of the four-inch wedge sandals from that morning, she now sported white nurse-style orthotic shoes, which seemed out of place with the white culottes and blue tropical print blouse she wore.

"I almost didn't recognize you." I popped my hand over my heart. "You look...."

"Old?" Betty tried to laugh, but it sounded forced.

"No. I was going to say amazing." I studied her face for a moment. "Your makeup skills are spectacular. I'm in awe."

"I used to volunteer at a community theater group in my twenties. You learn a thing or two doing stage productions."

Ashley came into the room and did a double-take. "Whoa. You've got some crazy skill sets, Betty. Awesome!"

"You should see if you can volunteer with some of the student stage productions this weekend. I'm sure they'd love to have you share your expertise." I wanted to finger her wig, but I refrained and kept my hands to myself.

"Maybe one of these days I'll do that again." Her eyebrows drew together, and her light-pink tinted lips sagged. "But for now, the last thing I need to do is draw attention to myself. I can't risk Hank finding me."

"I'm sorry. I hadn't thought of that." Once again, I'd put my foot in my mouth.

She waved away my apology. "It's not your problem. I'm just happy to have the opportunity to work in a place I know he'd never step foot in. It's one of the reasons I couldn't apply for a job at a restaurant or a supermarket."

I left them while Ashley explained the setup and what the workshop entailed, and took Pixie for a quick walk. We strolled by the now closed patisserie and headed for the park. I'd been so busy I hadn't talked to Jasper yet that day, so while Pixie sniffed every single blade of grass and every tree trunk we passed, I called him.

"How are you feeling?" I asked without going through the normal greeting as soon as he answered.

"Hey, Carissa. I've been thinking about you." He paused to cough, and then he gulped down something from a cup that rattled with ice.

It was as I'd expected. He'd been suppressing his body's natural need to cough with medication he shouldn't have been taking. Plus, he'd probably overdone it the day before with houseguests, along with making cookies for me.

"Sorry about that. The cough hits me out of the blue."

"Have you been drinking tea with honey and lemon?"

"Yes, ma'am, although right now I'm drinking some iced water. And I've used your essential oil a couple times, too."

"And you've remembered to take your antibiotics, right?"

"Yes, ma'am." He coughed, but it didn't linger. "Thanks for the soup. I'd love to have the recipe if you don't mind sharing it."

"I'll email it to you later tonight. Ashley's workshop starts soon but I wanted to check on you."

"I appreciate it. It's been a boring day but I know you've got a business to run." He sighed. "The doc says I shouldn't go back to work for another four or five days. Can you come keep me company soon?"

"I promise I'll visit tomorrow, but if you need something tonight, I can swing by around ten."

"Naw. I'm fine, just bored and tired." Jasper yawned. "John and Luke brought me dinner and gossip."

"Oh? Anything good?"

"You mean like did you hear about a certain aromatherapist chasing one of the patisserie's customers out the door?"

"No, I meant was dinner good?" My cheeks were flaming hot. How many people had seen me chase after Brett? It didn't matter. It only took one person to tell another, and then the entire town knew.

"Clam chowder and sourdough bread." Jasper cleared his throat. "I know you've got the workshop starting soon, but if you have time, why don't you bring Pixie over and I'll keep her company while you work."

My heart fluttered, but then I reminded myself that Jasper had mentioned how bored he was. That's all his request meant. I needed to control my expectations. "She'd love the attention. I'm already out walking her, so I'll be at your place in a couple minutes."

"I look forward to seeing you soon, then." Jasper's voice had lowered and sounded husky in my ear. Control of my expectations flew out the window.

I urged Pixie to finish whatever she needed to do, then sped walked to Jasper's apartment. I knocked lightly on the door, which swung open at my touch.

"Come on in." Jasper walked from the kitchen toward us. Clad in blue jeans and a white T-shirt that hugged his torso, he looked like he'd stepped from an Abercrombie ad. He stepped toward me and opened his arms for a hug, and I walked into his embrace. His strong arms encircled me and held me tight until Pixie barked and pawed at my leg. With a quick brush of his lips against my hair, Jasper released me and bent down to scratch beneath Pixie's chin. "Well, hello to you, too."

I handed him the leash. "Thanks for dog sitting."

"Anytime. I'm happy to have you and her here." His dimple deepened with the smile that widened on his face. "Can I offer you something to eat or drink?"

I check the time on my phone. "Sorry. I really have to get back and help Ashley out. I didn't mean to be away from the shop this long."

"Maybe a nightcap when you come back to pick up Pixie?"

"Sure. That sounds great." I smoothed my hair down. "It'll probably be around ten. Is that too late?"

"Nope. We'll be here waiting for you."

I told Pixie to be a good girl. She wagged her tail and licked my hand. Jasper scooped my pup into his arms, then followed me to the door. He watched as I walked down the stairs and reached the corner. I turned and waved goodbye, then headed to the shop.

Upon entering Aromatherapy Apothecary, I stopped to admire the soft classical music Ashley played from hidden speakers and the way she'd spotlighted some of our apothecary jars on display. The calming aroma of lavender emanated from diffusers placed strategically around the room. She had placed two large slow cookers filled with salves on the table, and had heavy-duty disposable cups standing by.

The drool-worthy charcuterie board, the lavender cookies, purple paper plates and napkins were all arranged atop the long marble counter. A copper beverage tub containing ice had carafes of my lavender lemonade and bottles of chardonnay nestled in to keep chilled. Small vases of flowering lavender dotted the surface, adding a touch of elegance and fragrance. The tablescape was Instagram-gorgeous. I hoped Ashley would be able to post photos soon and drum up more customers for future workshop sessions.

"What do you think?" Ashley swept into the room, having changed into skinny white jeans and a short-sleeved tee that showcased a silkscreened cluster of lavender blooms.

"It's beautiful and I'm so proud of you!"

"I'm excited. It's come together even better than I'd imagined." Ashley plucked a purple apron up from one of the chairs. "You'd better put this on. I've got one for each of us, including Betty."

I held the apron up and tears pricked my eyes. Ashley had embroidered my shop's logo on the front pocket. "It's perfect. Thank you."

Betty and I had just slipped on our aprons when the

attendees started arriving. A grandmother with her two teen granddaughters, a retired couple in town for the playwright event, Misty from the flower shop, two elderly sisters who lived in town, and the last two to arrive were none other than Brett and Tamara.

CHAPTER TWENTY-NINE

"Brett! Tamara! What a surprise. I didn't know you'd signed up." I tried to smile instead of allowing my embarrassment to creep in as I remembered, with mortification, how I'd disrupted their first trip together.

"I almost cancelled after the nuisance you caused today." Brett reached over and took Tamara's hand. "But Tamara's been looking forward to this. She's hoping to find natural ways to soothe some of the rashes she gets from stress."

"I'm so glad you came and I hope you find it beneficial." I motioned them away from the door and away from the gathering group surrounding the food and beverages. "I feel the need to apologize again for my inconsiderate actions. I was planning on dropping off a gift basket for you tomorrow morning, but I'll send it home with you tonight."

"That's very kind of you," Tamara said, her eyes still downcast, "but not necessary. I'd be happy to hear your recommendations for products that might be useful for my condition, though."

I had every intention of sending her home with gifts, no

matter what, but now wasn't the time to be insistent. I gestured toward the beverages and food. "Help yourself and find a seat anywhere at the table. I'll pull a few products and set them aside to review with you later."

Brett led Tamara to the table where he sat her on the end, furthest from where Ashley stood with her slow cookers. After Tamara seemed comfortable, Brett went to the marble counter and filled two glasses with chardonnay and placed an assortment of cheese and fruit on a plate. He carried them back to the table and sat next to Tamara. Now that I had a chance to observe them again, I had to wonder about Brett blaming their flight from me this morning on his girlfriend's panic attack. I recalled how he'd sounded angry and jabbed his index finger at her. The way he treated her tonight didn't mesh with the way he'd treated her this morning. I'd definitely be keeping an eye on him and hoped I'd have the opportunity to ask him about Venice Beach. I also needed to find out what his argument with Madame Bonsail was about. Perhaps Betty would know.

Betty came into the room, carrying a tray that held an extra mini slow cooker and a set of ingredients. Ashley pointed to the seat next to the head of the table, and our new employee placed the product on the table, then took a seat. I smiled, realizing Ashley wanted Betty to feel at home and part of the group. From the corner of my eye, I noticed Brett take a second look and stiffen as Betty sat down, but when I turned to look at him, his gaze was fully on Tamara.

Watching Betty, I waited to see how she would react when she noticed Brett and Tamara. Unfortunately, before that happened, one of our attendees asked me to ring up a gift purchase, so I missed out. By the time my attention returned to Betty, her face was a bland mask, and she gave nothing but her utmost attention to Ashley's conversation while she chatted with a few attendees as they sipped wine.

After about thirty minutes of socializing and noshing, Ashley asked everyone to sit, then handed out cups of the warm liquid salve she'd premade. As it cooled, the salve would solidify, thanks to the beeswax. The attendees filled their jars with the salve and then decorated labels to adhere to the lids. Ashley had provided a variety of floral and plant stamps with ink and colored pens for them to use. Betty kept wine goblets and lemonade glasses filled, and cleared away empty plates as needed, in between passing around the cookie platter.

While they worked on filling and labeling, Ashley spoke about the properties of the flora and fauna used in the preparation. She also demonstrated how to make the salve at home with their new mini slow cooker and the measured ingredients they would take with them. Given the nature of the potential mess oil could make, the attendees wouldn't start the process at the workshop. Instead, they had Ashley's finished salve to take home to use until they made their own batch.

As the skin healing salve portion of the workshop ended, Ashley placed a variety of vials of essential oils and sweet almond, coconut, and grapeseed carrier oils in the center of the table. She instructed Betty to hand out three empty vials to each attendee along with lids. She also passed out our printed Basic Care Aromatherapy card, which listed aromatherapy suggestions for ten different ailments.

"Use the guide to make your own blends from the ingredients in front of you to take home. If you have any specific ailments not listed," Ashley paused to look at the two teen girls and then at their grandmother, "like cramps or hot flashes, talk to either me or Carissa, and we'll help you concoct something."

The two girls blushed while their grandmother snorted. "Wish you'd been around ten years ago."

I jumped in with our disclaimer, something that was printed on every receipt, on signs around the shop, and on every piece of paper we handed out. "I need to make sure you fully understand that these products and information are not intended to diagnose, treat, cure, or prevent any disease. Anyone suffering from disease or injury should consult with a physician. If you are currently on medication, please do not stop. Please consult a health care practitioner when making any changes to your medical routine. And please, do not attempt to ingest essential oils. They are for topical use only."

This time it was Brett who snorted, but he cut off any snide remark he was about to make when Tamara elbowed him in the ribs. He mouthed "sorry" toward me, then went back to reading the list handed out.

The group got to work and good-naturedly passed vials of oils back and forth to experiment with and share. The wife of the retired couple poked her husband, then asked if there was a remedy for snoring. He closed his eyes, then started faux snoring, which made the teen girls giggle.

"Let me consult my reference book. I do know there are several essential oils that promote better sleep, so perhaps a combination might help with snoring." I retrieved the reference tome from my office and flipped through the pages until I found the section on sleep. I wrote down the names of essential oils recommended on a pad of paper and placed it in front of the woman.

I spent the next ten minutes helping the couple concoct a blend that they'd want to use on a consistent basis.

Initially, I'd had them add eucalyptus oil, but they both found it disagreeable, so I substituted peppermint and clove oil. With added lavender and thyme oils, they were ready to mix in the carrier oil. They chose the more neutral grapeseed oil, and since the husband wasn't keen on rubbing the oil blend on the soles of his feet, I showed them several diffusers with automated timers and shutoffs that they could use during the night.

As the event wound down, more participants browsed through the merchandise, and I happily rang up the sales, hoping that we'd get some repeat customers in the weeks and months ahead. I tried to catch Tamara's attention so I could talk to her and give her a few products, but she and Brett slipped out the door without giving me even a glance.

After the last guest left, clutching their bags of merchandise and ingredients from the workshop, Ashley, Betty, and I made quick work of cleaning up. As we departed, I was the last to walk through the doorway so I could set the alarm and lock up. Ashley cleared her throat, and when I looked to see what she needed, she jerked her thumb toward the sidewalk. Over her shoulder, I could see Jasper and Pixie waiting for me.

CHAPTER THIRTY

As I secured the lock, Ashley pulled Betty over to Jasper and Pixie. "Jasper, I want to introduce you to our newest employee, Betty. She's Madame Bonsail's sister."

Ashley glanced back at me and smirked before directing her attention to Betty. "Jasper is Carissa's... special friend."

Jasper waved. "It's nice to meet you, Betty. You couldn't ask for a better boss than Carissa."

"I'm happy to meet you, too."

The three of them looked at me expectantly. I wasn't going to give them the satisfaction of seeing me get mushy with Jasper, even if I wanted to gush over him waiting. I'm sure I wasn't fooling anyone though, with the heat that flooded my face. I just hoped it was dark enough that they wouldn't notice.

"Betty, we'll see you at one tomorrow. Thanks for your help tonight." I pointed at the bag she carried. "I'd like your input on your opinion about making the salve at home within the next couple of weeks."

"Gosh, I'd be happy to do that, and thanks for letting me join the workshop. I haven't had that much fun in, well, I don't know how long. Forever it seems." She nodded at us, then made her way toward the parking lot.

"I'd better get home and make sure Hunter is tucked in. He thinks he can wait up for me until I come home, even though he wakes up before dawn every morning." Ashley reached over and hugged me. Before she let go, she whispered in my ear, "I want every single detail tomorrow, and I won't accept any excuses or distractions."

Ashley was luckier than Betty because she'd found curbside parking almost in front of our shop. Jasper thrust Pixie's leash into my hand and rushed to hold the large bags Ashley had been balancing, so she could open the trunk.

"Thanks, Jasper. You're one of the good guys." She climbed in and blew us kisses before driving off into the dark.

Self-conscious, now that we were alone, I didn't know what to say. Did Jasper expect me to come back to his apartment for that drink, or had he met me here so Pixie and I could head to my dad's house?

"Are you up for some hot cocoa and cookies? Or are you too tired? I know you've had a long day." Jasper had his head angled down, as if he were worried I might turn him down.

"That sounds perfect." I couldn't help but grin at the relief I saw in his eyes.

A pickup truck drove up and parked at the curb where we stood. As the window rolled down, my dad's face appeared. He glowered at me. "You haven't answered any of my texts."

"We had a workshop and it just ended." I pulled my phone out of my purse and tapped the screen. "Oops. I have a dead battery, too."

"Climb in and I'll take you to your car and follow you

home." Dad finally seemed to notice Jasper. "Shouldn't you be resting? You don't want to end up back in the hospital."

"Yes, sir. Um, no, sir." Jasper looked from my dad back to me. I shrugged. Dad could be a force of nature.

Realization finally dawned on Dad and a goofy, sheepish look crossed his face. "Err, sorry if I interrupted a date, or something."

"It's okay. I know you're worried about me." I looked at Jasper's crestfallen face. "I'm going to Jasper's for some hot cocoa and cookies. I'll be home in a while."

Dad nodded. "Okay, be safe and turn the alarm on when you get back home."

When my dad pulled away from the curb, Jasper picked Pixie up. She'd lain down and curled around my feet—it was past her bedtime. I couldn't help but smile at the sight of my pup curled up in his arms. "Ready for some hot cocoa? I have peppermint schnapps or chocolate liqueur if you want an adult beverage."

"I think I'd better skip the alcohol. It's been a long day." I suppressed a yawn as I followed him up the stairs and into his apartment.

Jasper tucked a sleepy Pixie into the corner of his couch. "Have a seat, and I'll get the cookies and cocoa."

"I can help."

"All I have to do is pour the hot cocoa into the mugs. Everything else is ready to go." He turned to head to the kitchen. "How many marshmallows do you want? I take five in my drink."

"Sounds perfect." I sat down next to Pixie, and she climbed into my lap for snuggles.

Jasper wasn't kidding when he said he had everything ready to go because he brought out a tray loaded with two oversized red mugs piled high with marshmallows and a plate of assorted cookies. "Luke brought me the cookies. I'm not sure what's all there."

"They look great. Thank you." I plucked one from the plate and took a bite. It was lemon with a crisp exterior and chewy on the inside. Perfection. "Where are John and Luke?"

"They're catching up with some friends at one of the festival events tonight. They promised they wouldn't be home any earlier than midnight when they found out you were coming by." A dimple appeared as he smiled. He handed me a mug and clicked his to mine. "To good health, soon."

We sipped, and then Jasper set his mug down, then brushed his thumb lightly against the side of my mouth. "You have some marshmallow there."

I turned my head and kissed his thumb, where the sticky marshmallow crème was.

Jasper swung his arm around and hugged me. I'd expected a kiss. Had I done something wrong?"

He sighed. "I meant what I said, 'to good health, soon'. I'm not going to kiss you until I'm sure I'm completely well, so please don't think I don't want to."

"I wouldn't mind if you kissed me."

"But I'd feel terrible if you got sick." He playfully nudged my arm. "There'll be plenty of time for that later, if you're interested."

I couldn't help but grin up at him, especially when Pixie took the opportunity to jump up and lick some marsh-mallow crème that had stuck to Jasper's upper lip.

By the time I'd finished most of my hot cocoa and eaten another cookie, Jasper's cough had worsened. I fixed him a cup of tea with lemon and honey, before he walked me and Pixie to the car. He gave me a quick hug, then stepped away when another round of coughing hit him. He waved away my offer of another reflexology session. "It's late, and I think the milk in the cocoa irritated my throat. I'll heat some honey and lemon juice up after I drink the tea if this continues."

"Try adding ten drops of the essential oil blend I gave you to a cup of boiling water. Inhale the steam for about five minutes. If the cough gets worse, let me know and I'll take you to the ER." I'd heard of pneumonia patients cracking ribs from coughing so hard. I'd hate for that to happen to Jasper and hoped the essential oils would soothe his cough.

When Pixie and I returned to my dad's house, all the lights were blazing from the windows on the lower level. Sandy's small SUV, the dark navy shade melting into the night, sat empty at the curb. I parked behind it and carried Pixie to the front door. She must've gotten her second wind because the second I opened the door, she wiggled to get out of my arms, then scampered toward the kitchen. I followed close behind.

Sandy sat at the kitchen table reading a book. A mug of tea sat close by, and a plate of cookies occupied the middle of the table. Fresh-baked peanut butter cookies would be my guess from the sugary and nutty aromas that scented the kitchen. She looked up and smiled at me, then bent down to scratch beneath Pixie's chin.

"Can I make you a cup of tea and offer you some cookies?" Sandy's voice was sweet, just like her personality.

"I'd love a cup of decaf tea, but stay and relax. I can make it for myself." One of the improvements my dad had done to the kitchen was put in an instant hot water spout. While I loved putting a kettle on to boil water when I had time to putter around, nothing beat the convenience of instant hot water and a tea bag. I squeezed a dollop of honey into a mug, tossed in a decaf English Breakfast tea bag, and topped it with hot water. I let it brew for a couple minutes, then discarded the tea bag.

While waiting for the tea to cool enough to sip, I nibbled on a cookie. A rich undertone of warm sweetness balanced the nuttiness of the peanut butter, but I couldn't quite place the flavor. I held up the half cookie remaining in my hand. "I love the flavor and the texture, but there's something different in these cookies. What did you use?"

"I swapped out some of the granulated sugar for brown sugar, then added a bit of molasses."

"Molasses is what I'm tasting. Yum!" I popped the half cookie into my mouth and plucked another cookie from the plate.

"Have you attended any of the events since Monday?" Sandy picked up a cookie and nibbled on it in a much more ladylike manner than I had.

I shook my head as I swallowed. "The shop's kept me really busy. How about you?"

"Not yet. Your dad is hoping to score tickets for a couple of the student stage productions over the weekend."

I remembered that Rachel had planned on giving Ashley and me tickets for her stage show. Jasper obviously wasn't up to going with me, so I decided to offer them to my dad and Sandy. "Do you have any plans for Saturday evening? I might be able to get you tickets to Rachel Walton's show."

"Are you serious? That would be fantastic!" Sandy's face beamed. "How did you manage? I've heard they sold out within three minutes of them going on sale."

"Rachel Walton is comping four tickets for us. Front row seats, even."

"That's so lit! How'd that happen?" It was obvious

Dillon's mom had picked up on some of his teen slang, and I couldn't help but laugh at Sandy's awe and delight.

"She hasn't delivered the tickets yet, but she did promise four. Ashley's going to take Bryon, and I'd love for you and Dad to use the other two."

Sandy's brow furrowed beneath her auburn bangs. "You and Jasper should use the tickets. I don't feel right taking them from you."

I waved off her concern. "Jasper's still pretty sick, and no one in the audience is going to want to worry if he's contagious or not with the way he's still coughing."

"We'd love to go, if you're sure you won't use the tickets." Sandy picked up her mug of tea and cradled it in her hands. I didn't see a single sign of an engagement ring. Had Dillon been mistaken, or had they called off the engagement?

I wanted to ask, but I wasn't comfortable intruding on their relationship. It still seemed so new to me. Perhaps they'd decided to slow down and shelve the huge step of marriage for the time being. But I hoped it didn't mean that their romance was cooling. Sandy was good to my dad.

Dad lumbered into the kitchen and snatched a cookie from the plate. Without taking a breath, he downed the treat in two quick bites. Sandy got up, poured a glass of milk, and handed it to him. There was no doubt about it. She spoiled him.

"Hon, you'll never believe the show tickets Carissa's giving us for Saturday night!" Sandy's smile lit up the entire room as she beamed at my dad.

Dad looked at me and then at Sandy expectantly. "Well? Don't keep me waiting in suspense."

I gestured at Sandy to share the news. She practically

clapped her hands in excitement. "Rachel Walton's show. Front row seats, too!"

His eyebrows shot up toward his hairline. "How'd you manage to score those tickets? That's an extraordinary achievement."

It's not often I can impress my dad, and my smile widened. "Let's just say my wicked-good aromatherapy skills impressed Rachel Walton and she wanted to thank me."

Sandy wanted to hear all the details about meeting Rachel. Her eyes turned into moons when I told her about Lacie's interaction with the playwright. It surprised me that my dad hadn't filled her in on the investigation or, it was entirely possible, he'd skipped over the details and only gave her bare bones.

After eating another cookie, I said good night and shuffled with Pixie for a last-minute walk around the yard and then made our way to my girlhood bedroom. I could barely keep my eyes open. I'd hassle my dad in the morning about scheduling time to go to my farmhouse with me to clean up the huge mess left from the break-in. It would have to be late Sunday afternoon, once the playwright event wrapped up and the tourists fled Oak Creek Valley, back to wherever they called home.

CHAPTER THIRTY-ONE

Luke waited by my shop's front door when I arrived at eight, a pink pastry box in one hand, a to-go coffee in the other. "I'm Jasper's special delivery boy. He thought you'd need this after your late night."

"Thanks. He's right about that." I took the pastry box. "How is he feeling this morning? I sent him a text a bit ago, but haven't heard back."

"I think he's on the mend, but he said the coughing attack he had last night left him exhausted. He got up at o'dark thirty just as I was leaving for the patisserie, to tell me to bring you the pastries. He said he was going back to bed and sleeping in as soon as we left his apartment."

"I hope he manages to get as much rest as possible." I'd been right. He'd overdone it the day before. Cracking open the lid, something chocolatey greeted my senses. I inhaled deeply. I peeked in expecting to find Jasper's Triple Chocolate Rolls, instead, I found chocolate rugelach, a rich, rolled pastry that oozed chocolate filling. "Oh yum! I haven't seen this on the menu before. Is it a new recipe?"

Luke's tinkling laughter filled the quiet street. "It's our

recipe. It was one of our most popular pastries before we sold the patisserie to Jasper."

I unlocked the door and motioned for Luke to follow me in. He set the coffee cup on the marble counter while I disarmed the alarm. Setting myself down on a padded barstool, I opened the pastry box. I couldn't resist the temptation any longer and picked up a rugelach and took a bite. The chocolate filling was tempered with the rich tang of cream cheese. It was swoon-worthy. After swallowing, I offered one to Luke, who shook his head before he scooped Pixie up and cradled her against his chest. He swiveled around on the barstool and took a good look around my shop.

I had sensed that there was some type of good-natured chef rivalry going on between the former owners and Jasper, but I wasn't sure why. These two men were retired, so why would they not want to share recipes with their protégé? I couldn't contain my curiosity any longer. "Why don't you share your recipes with Jasper, and vice versa? You're retired, so does it really matter if he uses them?"

Luke's light blue eyes sparkled. "Oh honey, we may not run the patisserie any more but we are writing a cookbook. We signed with a publisher right before we sold to Jasper and we had to retain the rights to our recipes."

"Congratulations! That's so exciting." I wondered if that had stressed Jasper, knowing he'd have to create his own recipes instead of relying on ones that customers already loved.

Luke must have guessed my thoughts. "From the time Jasper began working with us, we encouraged him to develop his own repertoire of recipes. He's a talented chef in his own right. He doesn't need us and has made the patisserie a success all on his own. I predict he'll have a chance to write a cookbook himself, one of these days."

That was true. And those chocolate rolls of his.... "Jasper won't share his recipes with you. Is that a problem?"

"We give each other a hard time, but don't worry, it's all in jest." Luke patted my arm, then used his index finger to point to the side of his mouth before handing me a napkin.

My face heated. Here I was, talking to a soon-to-be-famous cookbook author with chocolate smeared on my face. My teeth were probably riddled with brown filling, too. I wiped my mouth, then picked up the coffee and took a big swig, only to have coffee spill from the cup and splash down my light green T-shirt. I was mortified.

Luke chuckled and then guffawed. It was contagious, and soon my belly laughs filled the room until tears leaked from my eyes. I swiped the back of my hand across my eye and smears from the dab of mascara I'd whisked on my lashes earlier that morning, streaked my hand black. I used another napkin to wipe my eyes clean.

"Oh, Carissa. You're adorable and absolutely perfect for Jasper."

A blaze ignited my already warm face. "Thank you. He's a pretty terrific guy." While I might look like a wreck, inside I did a happy dance. Jasper's mentors thought I was perfect for the delicious baker.

"I heard some interesting gossip this morning that I think might be of interest to you." Luke leaned against the counter and waggled his eyebrows. "A certain prestigious event manager has been placed on administrative leave."

"What? Why did that happen?" I couldn't even begin to imagine what Lionel could have done to warrant something so drastic while the playwright event was taking place. I wondered who would, or could, take over his job.

"According to my source, two reliable witnesses overheard Lionel threaten Lacie as she left the resort after the event. Yesterday afternoon, the witnesses finally told the detectives what they'd overheard, and since Lionel doesn't have an alibi, the resort decided to place him on leave."

"Do you think he did it?"

He shrugged. "I don't see him throwing away his career and risking spending the rest of his life in prison to kill someone as inconsequential as Lacie. Plus, the ten knives stunt shows someone planned ahead. It wasn't a heat-of-the-moment crime."

"What's the resort going to do about the playwright events going on? Can Delaney step in and do Lionel's job adequately enough?" I took a sip of my coffee after checking to make sure the lid was secure.

"Funny you should mention Delaney. She was one of the witnesses who came forward about Lionel threatening Lacie." He lifted his eyebrows. "And now she's acting manager in his absence. I also heard she gave the detectives some kind of info on guests who were angry at both Lionel and Lacie."

I frowned. Delaney had been at the booth helping to pack everything up since Lacie had left early. Had Delaney made up the threat accusation? Or had she witnessed the threat before returning to help clean up? She'd been eager to make sure I saw the lists of voicemails from all the guests who were angry at Lionel over Lacie's behavior. Had she been gunning for Lionel's job all along and had set the stage for him to become a prime suspect, or could Lionel really be the murderer? I needed to read the entire list soon, even if the detectives now had the contents. "Wait, you said there were two reliable witnesses who heard Lionel threaten Lacie. Who was the other person?"

"Sorry, I can't help you with that name. They chose to remain anonymous, according to my sources."

"Anonymous as in the detectives know who it is, but they don't want the public to know, or anonymous as in they called the station and gave a statement without providing their identity?"

He shook his head. "Your guess is as good as mine. Maybe your dad can find out."

"He's been blocked out of the investigation and is instead focused on the events going on."

"More's the pity." Luke looked at his watch. "I'd better skedaddle or John's going to read me the riot act." And with that, he pecked my cheek and waltzed out the door.

While I should've been concentrating on the new development with Lionel and his threats against Lacie, I was instead thinking about Luke's comments on how I was perfect for Jasper. I hoped I was right in assuming Jasper had been telling the two men about his feelings for me. Feelings I reciprocated.

"Well, well, well. Someone looks like the cat that ate the canary."

And just like that, my mood crashed. Detective Raff stood in the doorway, hands on his hips, and a look of smug satisfaction on his face.

"I don't have any idea what you're talking about." I wiped my hands on a clean napkin and closed the lid of the pastry box. Needing something else to occupy my shaking hands, I tugged at the hem of my T-shirt, then immediately released it when I realized it made my cleavage more noticeable at the V-neck.

"Oh, but I think you do know." Raaf fingered the gold badge attached to his belt. "You're hiding something, and I'm pretty sure I know what it is."

"Well, since I still have no idea what you're talking about, how about you enlighten my attorney?" I pulled my phone out and tapped in Alfred's number. "And while you're explaining that nonsense, why don't you explain to him why you locked me in an interrogation room and then disappeared?"

"You must be mistaken. I didn't lock you in." The sneer that flashed across his face for a brief moment told me he was lying. He strode into my shop and stopped a mere twelve inches from me. He lowered his face until his gaze was even with mine, and his voice turned sing-song. "I visited your so-called crime scene early this morning to make sure the local police didn't botch anything. And lo and behold, what did I find?"

I didn't answer because whatever he was gloating about, couldn't be good news for me.

CHAPTER THIRTY-TWO

I almost burst into tears of relief when my dad poked his head through the doorway. His voice echoed around the room. "Raaf! Just what do you think you're doing to my daughter? Step away from her."

"I was only questioning her about the break-in at her farmhouse." The detective took several steps backward, but still kept his gaze fixed on my face. "I have reason to believe she's hiding evidence pertaining to Ms. Simmons' murder. And I think your officers are assisting her."

Pixie belatedly barked at Raaf, so I picked her up and tried to calm her, then looked at my dad. I'd rarely seen him so angry, and I certainly had never seen his face turn this shade of red. To give him credit, he clenched his jaw and controlled his temper as he moved to stand next to me. He was in pure protective mode. I tried to follow his lead, but I barely managed to keep a string of expletives from bursting from my lips. We both must've realized Raaf was trying to provoke a reaction. But to what purpose? Was he hoping I'd lose control so he could cart me back to the station for assault or harassment?

"If you have evidence, then you need to submit it. Otherwise, what you're doing now is pure provocation." Dad's fists were clenched tight, and his knuckles had turned white. "And from here on out, you'd better not say a word to my daughter without her attorney present."

"Officer Zabor can back up my evidence. He was there when I found it at Ms. Carmichael's house this morning."

"What? Why? Why did you go there today? The forensic team completed their evidence collection yesterday." There was only one reason Raaf would have pulled Bryon into his scheme. He needed my dad's right-hand man to turn off the house alarm without alerting me. "Don't you need a search warrant?"

"Not when you'd already called us to investigate the break-in. We were only following up on that crime."

"That's a technicality and you know it, Detective." My dad's voice had lowered. A sign that his anger was escalating. "You had no right to enter her residence without my daughter's permission."

"A crime was committed there, and I was doing my duty to investigate." Raaf's smirk was back. "Especially when that crime seems to be part of Lacie Simmons' murder investigation."

"Again, Detective Raaf, I have no idea what you're talking about." I crossed my arms in front of my torso and clenched my fists to keep them from shaking.

"Now, I found it quite interesting that this," Raaf pulled a plastic bag from his hip pocket and held up a deck of tarot cards with several identical Death cards visible, "was found at your house. I have to ask myself why? Can you answer that question, Ms. Carmichael?"

The Death card. I hoped to never see another tarot card again for the rest of my life.

"My daughter doesn't have to answer any questions without her attorney present." Dad stepped in front of me, as if to shield me.

"Right." Raaf cocked his head to the side. "You've got yourself quite the convoluted conflict of interest going on, Chief. On one hand, your duty is to uphold law and order. And on the other, a derelict daughter who continually tests the limits of the law."

Dad's entire body tensed, as if ready to spring forward and barrel into the detective.

Placing my hand on his shoulder, I gave him a tight squeeze. "Dad, could you call Alfred? It's past time he got involved in this conversation."

Dad grunted and pulled out his cell phone.

Detective Raaf put up his hand, palm out, as if to stop him from calling. "No need. I'll be on my way. However, I'll expect you down at the station at two this afternoon to explain why you had a pack of Death tarot cards hidden in your pantry." And with that, Raaf did an about-face and strode out of the shop.

I exhaled the breath of air I didn't know I'd been holding. "Whoa. I'm glad you showed up when you did."

Dad nodded but didn't reply. He held his cell phone up to his ear, and I could hear the faint ringing of the call he was placing. As soon as the other person answered, Dad jumped in. "Bryon, can you explain why Raaf took you out to Carissa's and you didn't warn us?"

Bryon's garbled voice answered. Dad grunted a few times, then disconnected. He seemed lost in his own world for a few moments.

"Well? What'd Bryon say?" I offered the last chocolate rugelach to him. He picked it up and took a distracted bite. I took a sip of my now-cooled coffee after making sure the lid was securely attached.

After swallowing, Dad pursed his lips. "Raaf ambushed Bryon at home early this morning and made him drive with him out to your place. Bryon thought something was off, but in his haste, he'd left his cell at home, so he couldn't call me. He promised me that he stood by Raaf the entire time, so he couldn't plant evidence."

"Then how did the deck of tarot cards get in my pantry?" And where would one purchase nothing but a deck of Death cards?

"They were already there. Someone must've planted them during the break-in, and, according to Bryon, an anonymous person called the station and left a message on where they could be found."

"Is Raaf the one who took the supposed anonymous call?" I wouldn't put it past him to be in on this setup.

"Nope. Peg did but couldn't put a trace on the call. Nor could she tell if it was a man or a woman who made the call."

"Somehow Raaf is mixed up in this." I twisted my mouth to the side, deciding how much I should share with my dad. "Um, I've put out some feelers with my San Francisco attorney's office, to see if they had any ideas if Raaf was connected to my, uh, situation up there."

"Do they have anything?" Instead of being upset at my meddling, Dad almost looked relieved.

"Suzie said she'd get back to me, but I haven't heard anything. Plus, she was out of the office yesterday." I twirled a strand of my black curly hair, which had escaped my ponytail scrunchie, around my finger. "I'll call her this morning right after I call Alfred's office. He needs to be available to go with me this afternoon."

Dad finished off the pastry in two quick bites, then brushed off a crumb that had drifted to his navy-colored polo shirt. "Alrighty. I'll meet up with Bryon and see if we can find out anything more about this anonymous caller and how those cards got into your house."

"One more thing, can you lock my new employee's application in your office?" With all that had gone on the day before, the application had sat in my purse. I didn't want to risk betraying Betty's whereabouts by accidentally losing her information.

He lifted an eyebrow. "New employee?"

"It's a long story, but Madame Bonsail asked that we hire her sister." I quickly explained the circumstances and handed him the folded application. The envelope containing Lionel's typed voicemail messages still sat in my purse. I hadn't had a chance to finish reading through them, so I decided to keep them private for now instead of passing them on to my dad. Especially if Delaney had already given the detectives the information, there was no reason to let it slip that I might have been withholding evidence. I could only imagine what Raaf would do should he find out. With the new accusations against Lionel, he'd moved up my list as a murder suspect, and I hoped the detectives honed in on him instead of focusing on me.

My suspicions about Rachel Walton were lessening, although her anger at Lacie and her haste in telling me about her lack of alibi still had me concerned. Had she done so in order to make herself seem innocent? Plus, there were the ten knives at the scene of the crime. It had an air of drama surrounding it, and Rachel would have had access to all the theatrical props assembled for the upcoming productions. I wished I felt comfortable talking to Delaney about Rachel, but with her accusations against Lionel, it was probably best I avoid her for the time being. I couldn't quite shake the feeling that she'd tried to use me in order to push Lionel out of his job, and when I sat on the information she'd provided, she decided to take it to the detectives herself.

"I'll lock it up just as soon as I leave here." Dad folded the application into an even smaller square and tucked it into his hip pocket. "Have Betty give you more information on her husband, especially a photo, and I'll have my guys be on the lookout in case he tracks her here."

Once he'd given me a quick hug and headed out, I securely locked the door and called my attorney. Alfred was busy, so I left a message explaining when and where I needed his services. Despite needing to get the shop ready for opening, I called Suzie instead of sending another email.

"Carissa, I'm so sorry for the wait. I promise I'm looking into it, but I got delayed yesterday with an emergency root canal." Suzie's voice, while cheerful, didn't sound full of her usual bounce. "I'm having to call in a couple favors on leads, but I'm hoping to hear something back later today."

"Ugh. I hope you're feeling okay." While I'd never had the dentistry procedure done, I'd heard it could be painful. "And don't worry about my request. Whenever you can fit it in is fine."

Well, actually, it wasn't fine. Raaf seemed to be ramping up his intimidation tactics. Was he trying to get me to snap or to confess? The sound of ringing phones in the background and Suzie's hurried goodbye brought me back to the here and now. I had a shop to open and run.

Ashley arrived an hour after I'd opened for a scheduled reflexology appointment. Typically, she'd come in around noon, since Friday afternoons were busier than the mornings, and stay through closing. Most visitors drove up from L.A. shortly after lunch to miss rush hour traffic. Tour buses, on the other hand, often left earlier but stopped off along the coast for a seafood lunch before making their way to Oak Creek. Whatever transportation they took, they descended on our town and shops, which made all of the business owners happy.

While busily preparing the reflexology room, Ashley hummed to herself. I wanted to tell her about Raaf's visit, but decided to wait. I didn't need to spoil her mood just before she performed reflexology. She needed to be attuned to the needs of her client and not my drama. When the bells jangled as the door pushed open, I was surprised to see Betty. She wore the same wig as the night before and dressed in the same touristy, older generation style.

"Hi, Betty. Didn't I schedule you to come in at one?" Had my mind been so focused on meeting back up with Jasper last night that I'd gotten the time wrong? "Of course, you're welcome to come in any time."

Ashley appeared in the doorway of the reflexology room. "You did, but I offered to give Betty a short session and introduce her to the services we provide before she starts her shift. Besides, I need the practice hours before classes start next month."

"That's a great idea. I'll prepare some tea for you after the session and show you the scheduling program."

Even with the door closed to the reflexology room, I could hear the women chatting with occasional bursts of laughter. I was glad that Betty seemed to get along so well with Ashley. I was startled when jarring shouts sounded from the Tea Breeze shop next door.

"Where's my wife? I saw her come in here." The man

sounded angry. His voice rose loud enough I could clearly hear each over-enunciated word. "Yvonne! Get out here this second or you'll be sorry!"

CHAPTER THIRTY-THREE

Frozen in place, I worried it was only a matter of time before the man—it had to be Hank—came looking for his wife in my shop. I started for the reflexology room to warn her, then whirled around and ran for my phone to call 9-1-1. As the phone slid into my hand, Tea Breeze's door crashed, slamming into the wall adjoining my shop. Moving, in what felt like molasses, I sprinted toward my glass front door. As my hand twisted the dead bolt into place a scowling, red-faced man popped up in front of me. With meaty fists, he pounded on the glass. It was then that the scores of tattoos covering his forearm, including one very prevalent blue anchor, came into my view.

"I know she's in there! I'll kill you if you don't let me in!" The pounding continued, and I feared he'd break the glass. His red, bloodshot eyes looked unfocused, and spittle flew from his lips as he shouted.

Backing away from the door and the irate man who pounded on the glass, I was brought up short by the counter that ran down the middle of the room. With trembling hands, I fumbled to enter my passcode into my phone. A whimper escaped my lips while I clumsily tried to thumb the emergency call digits. It took three tries before I got it right since I couldn't tear my eyes away from the door. The nine-one-one call finally connected. My knees turned to jelly, and I slid to the floor when Peg answered.

"Carissa, units are already on the way."

"I hear the sirens." I gulped out the words with shaky breaths of air and tried to keep the sobs that bubbled up in my throat at bay. Hank had begun to kick the door, and I saw a spider web of cracks appear. It wouldn't be long before the glass caved in, and then he'd...

"Are you okay or should I send an ambulance?" The crackle of a radio sounded in the background along with the clacking of her keyboard.

"I'm okay, and I don't think there are any injuries. I'll lock myself in my office until he's subdued." My voice sounded calmer than I felt. In reality, I wanted to scream and cry, but instead, I tried to crawl toward my office on my hands and knees. I had to get away from the door, but my sweaty palms slid on the polished concrete floor, and I almost did a faceplant. The phone almost dropped as I cradled the device between my ear and shoulder.

"Do you know who he is?" Peg's voice sounded distant so I sat down and readjusted the phone to my ear. I couldn't tear my gaze away from the widening cracks appearing on the glass.

"His first name is Hank. Last name...." I tried to picture Betty's application but my mind was fuzzy from the terror of the man kicking in my door. The phone dropped with a clatter, sending my heart plummeting. It was a lifeline to safety as the maniac continued his screaming. I snatched the phone back up.

"It's going to be okay, Carissa. Units are less than a

minute away. He hasn't breached the door yet, has he?" Peg's calm voice eased some of my panic.

"No. He's still outside." I gulped in another deep breath of air. "It might be Lakeland. He's the husband of my newest employee. She's been trying to hide from him since he has no regard for the restraining order against him."

Hank must've heard the sirens too, because he turned to look down the street. He took off at a run, and thirty seconds later, a black and white unit followed in the direction he'd taken, sirens still screaming.

"The units just passed the shop and are after him. I think we're safe now."

I disconnected the call, retrieved a barking Pixie, and went to the reflexology room. I gently knocked on the door with a hand that felt like it had been encased in concrete. My limbs felt heavy, and I wasn't sure how long I would remain upright. "Can I come in? He's gone, and the police are after him."

Ashley unbolted the door and swung it open. Betty sat huddled in the reclining massage chair, her arms wrapped tight around her middle. Crumpled tissues littered her lap.

After handing me a box of tissues, Ashley took Pixie from me. It was then that I noticed the wet drips sliding down my cheeks. I wiped my face and eyes and tried to keep my knees from knocking together.

"Can I get you anything? A cup of hot tea or a glass of water?" I felt helpless in the face of this woman's misery.

Betty shook her head, and her voice quavered. "No. I've got to call my sister and warn her. What if Hank goes to her house and does something awful to her since he couldn't get to me?"

I didn't want to offer, but under the circumstances, it

was the least I could do. "Would you like for me to call her?"

Her lips trembled, but she shook her head. "I'd better do it. She won't be satisfied I'm all right until she hears my voice."

Ashley and I exchanged a glance, then we both moved toward the door. I fumbled with the phone still clutched in my hand. "We'll give you some privacy."

After switching the front window sign to 'closed', I made sure the deadbolt was still in place, then put Pixie down. She huddled near my feet. We didn't need customers barging in until the police had a chance to take our statements. I gave Ashley a quick hug, then dimmed the lights. Muffled sobs came from Tea Breeze. I knocked on the locked connecting door separating our shops.

"Are you okay, Fiona? He didn't hurt you, did he?"

She clicked open the deadbolt on her side, and I did the same. The open door revealed Fiona's tear-streaked face. Her iron-gray hair had come loose from the chignon she typically wore, and wispy strands stuck out at odd angles.

"Are you hurt?"

"No. Just terrified." She rubbed a freckled hand across her model-worthy cheekbones that distracted from the lines that framed her gray eyes. I guessed Fiona to be in her early sixties. She still had an elegant grace about her, despite never wearing makeup and dressing herself in what could only be called Laura Ashley vintage styles. The blousy, full dresses disguised her slender body, making her appear squat and matronly at first glimpse. "Do you know who that man is or who he's looking for?"

"He's the husband of my new employee."

"I can't work here or even stay in town now." Betty came into the shop, her arms still wrapped around her middle. Her words, spoken so quietly, made me strain to hear her. "I'm so sorry. I should never have put you or my sister in danger."

Ashley guided the trembling woman to sit at the marble counter, then left. I could hear the gurgle of the electric kettle as she brewed water for tea. Fiona took a seat next to Betty. She'd stopped crying, but the tears had left dried tracks down her face. "He'll be caught, and then you can push for the full extent of the law to punish him. I'll give you the name of an excellent domestic abuse attorney, and she'll walk you through what needs to be done."

I suspected, given Fiona's initial terror at Hank's aggression, that my neighboring shop owner had been a victim in her past. I had a new respect for this quiet, unassuming woman and vowed to get to know her better.

"But I can't afford an attorney." Betty wrung her hands. "And clearly, restraining orders don't mean a thing. This isn't the first time he's tracked me down."

"My friend will work out a payment plan for you, and I promise, she charges fair rates based on each client's capabilities to pay." Fiona grasped Betty's clenched hands. "You can't let monsters like him win."

Betty nodded, then pulled another tissue from the box she'd carried in from the treatment room and dabbed her eyes.

Even though the knock that sounded on my glass door was gentle, the three of us jumped. It was Bryon and my dad. I unlocked the door and they entered, their eyes scanning the room.

"Is everyone okay?" Dad pulled me in for a quick hug, then shuddered when he pointed at my cracked glass door. "Call the glass company and get them out here immediately. If they give you any hassles about not being able to get here within the hour, throw my name at them. They can at least board over the door."

"Okay." Under normal circumstances, I would have thought my dad was blowing a situation out of proportion, but Hank wasn't a normal situation. He was an unhinged maniac, and there'd been too many tragic news stories about what men like him did to their spouses.

The three of us assured him we hadn't been harmed, just as Ashley returned bearing a tray with four cups of hot cinnamon orange tea and lavender shortbread cookies left-over from the previous night's workshop.

"Would you like some tea or coffee, Chief?" She pointed her finger at Bryon. "I know you're always ready for a cup of coffee. It's brewing right now."

"Thanks, Ash." Bryon looked awkward and unable to make eye contact with her. He was the one to do everything by the book, and receiving attention from his girlfriend during an official interview must've made him uncom-fortable.

"I don't need anything, but thanks for asking." Dad swiped his iPad and opened an app. "We'll take your state-ments for the official report."

"Were you able to catch him?" I asked, keeping my gaze on Betty.

She'd shredded the tissues in her hand, a small pile of white fluff now sat on top of the counter, and her breathing had become ragged. I worried she would hyperventilate. I set a cookie on the teacup's plate and pushed the cup of tea into her hands. Her limbs trembled and the tea splashed over the edge. Ashley had just returned with Bryon's mug of coffee. Once it was safely in his hands, she scurried away and came back with a sturdy mug and transferred Betty's tea to it, then gently wrapped the older woman's hand around it.

Dad didn't answer right away, and his heel jiggled up and down. It was apparent he wasn't happy about the answer he had to give. "No. Not yet anyway."

A quiet moan escaped Betty's lips.

"I've got more manpower coming along with a K-9 unit. We'll find him."

CHAPTER THIRTY-FOUR

Given the fragility Betty exhibited after finding out her husband hadn't been caught, Dad agreed that he would take our statements together, instead of individually.

"What's your husband's name?"

Betty still looked shell-shocked, so I answered. "Hank Lakeland."

"No dear. His last name is Simmons." Betty scrunched her nose. "For professional reasons I kept my birth name."

While Dad collected identifying information from Betty—I couldn't bring myself to think of her as Yvonne—my heart raced. Was there a chance that Hank was related to Lacie? It seemed too far-fetched, yet Venice Beach was a connection, however tenuous. I was dying to ask about Lacie, but I didn't want to distract Dad from taking statements, so I didn't say anything. There would be time to talk later.

We each gave our version of the altercation that had transpired and signed our names on the iPad form. Fiona decided she was too unsettled to reopen her shop and offered to drive Betty to Santa Barbara to speak with her attorney friend. I was grateful that this gracious, unassuming woman was willing to step in and offer protection for Betty.

Betty was hesitant at first. "I don't want to leave my sister alone. What if Hank breaks into her house looking for me?"

"She is more than welcome to come with us to Santa Barbara." Fiona had a suggestion for every situation, it seemed. "We can spend the night, too. My apartment has a guestroom if you don't mind sharing a bed with your sister. Hank won't be able to track you down there and you'll at least get a good night's sleep."

Betty thought about it, then called Bertha. After a short discussion, she disconnected the call.

"Bertha's decided she's going to stay here but wants me to go and stay at least overnight, if not longer." Betty wrung her hands together, and her mouth turned downward. "I'm afraid she's putting her life in danger if she doesn't come with me."

"The police will watch over her to make sure Hank can't reach her." I stared pointedly at my dad. "Right?"

He massaged the back of his neck with his opened hand. "I wish I could park a patrol car in front of her house, but with the festival going on and the manhunt for Hank, I'm afraid the best I can do is have officers drive by every hour. I'm sure we'll catch him soon so please don't worry too much."

"Thank you, Chief Carmichael." Betty twisted and tore a tissue, then grabbed a clean square and dabbed at her eyes. "I wish my sister didn't have to be so stubborn. If something happens to her, it will be my fault."

"It's not your fault, Betty." I gripped her hand and gave it a gentle squeeze. "Hank is the only one to blame for all of this. Dad will do everything in his power to keep her safe."

Fiona stood. "Chief Carmichael, perhaps you'll escort us to my car. I think it's best we leave immediately before Hank comes back. We don't want to give him any opportunity to follow us to Santa Barbara."

I could tell my dad had been getting antsy while decisions were being made, and he wholeheartedly agreed, as he ushered the two women to the door. Before he unlocked the door, he looked at me. Worry lined his face.

"We'll be fine. I'll keep the doors locked until the tour buses show up. Get these ladies safely on the road and organize the manhunt." I reached over his arm and clicked the lock open.

"Are you sure? I don't want to worry about him coming back here." He ran fingers through his short-cut hair. "Maybe you should close for the day."

I'd already seen several potential customers come by the shop, look at the closed sign, and walk away. My bottom line couldn't afford to lose that much business. "He's not going to come back if my shop is filled with customers. Would you feel less worried if I asked Jasper to come in for a while?"

"That's an excellent idea, but I want you to swear to me you'll call if there's even a whiff of trouble." Dad held up his pinkie and I connected my pinky to his and shook on it.

Before I had a chance to send Jasper a text, my phone rang.

"Carissa, are you alright? I heard something happened at your shop." Jasper hadn't even waited for me to say hello when I'd connected the call.

"We're okay now, but my new employee's ex-husband tried to break in."

"What can I do to help? Do you want me to come down and make sure he doesn't come back?" His words practically tumbled out of his mouth, and I wondered if he'd had too much caffeine.

"That would be perfect. My dad and I were just talking about asking you to do that." I gave my dad a thumbs-up.

"Give me a few minutes and I'll be there as long as you need me."

True to his word, Jasper arrived four minutes later. His skin tone wasn't so sallow and his voice sounded stronger than it had the night before. He shook my dad's hand—who had waited around until Jasper arrived—then gave me a one-arm hug.

"Thanks for coming in. I hate feeling like it was a traumatic thing, especially since he didn't gain access, but I can barely stop shaking."

Jasper stared pointedly at the fractured glass door. "I'd say it was a pretty serious attack, and I'm happy to help put your mind at ease."

"You can sit in my office or relax in the reflexology room. The chair is really comfy." I pointed at the half-opened reflexology room.

"Naw. I'll hang out here and keep an eye out on things." He ambled over to one of the padded barstools that lined the marble island and sat down.

"Let me know if I can get you anything to drink. I have tea, coffee, or water."

"Just pretend I'm not here. I can help myself if I need anything." He waved me off.

It was impossible to ignore Jasper sitting there since every time I glanced his way, he flashed me a dimpled smile, but I tried anyway to take care of my business and get us back open. Once I'd called the glass company—who promised to send someone out within a couple of hours—I called in a pizza delivery order. Next, I sent Dillon a text begging him to come in. He immediately responded and promised to be there within an hour. That was one employee problem solved. It bugged me that there hadn't been an opportunity to ask Betty about a connection to Lacie. I'd meant to, but once my dad's questions started, I'd forgotten, and then Fiona and Betty were in a rush to leave town before Hank found them again.

With only one bite taken out of my slice of pizza, a group of blue-haired, orthotic-shoe-wearing, bright-pink-lipstick-wearing women, flooded down the arcade sidewalks and stopped in front of my shop. The apparent leader of the group, wearing a banana-yellow tracksuit, banged on the door. I looked longingly at my lunch, then put it down. Wiping my hands right before opening the door, I was almost run over as the group pushed their way into my shop. I took a step back as they practically encircled me and flashbacks of the previous Monday filled me with terror.

"Welcome to Aromatherapy Apothecary. How can we assist you today?" My voice sounded weak, and I hoped it wouldn't give these ladies any ideas that I was a pushover.

"You've got a lot of nerve, young lady." The leader poked her index finger at me. "Fraud is what I call that stunt you pulled earlier this week. How can you live with yourself getting all us seniors living on fixed incomes to come in? We spent our measly social security checks on your product with the promise that one of us would win a thousand bucks."

Jasper stood as if to walk over and intervene, but I waved him back. I needed to assert control over the situation without the seniors feeling like they were being strong-armed.

"My social media accounts were hacked, and an unknown person posted that offer. I apologize for any inconvenience it's caused." Gulping hard, I tried to steady my voice when a couple of the women rolled their eyes and another crossed her arms in front of her and curled her lip. I couldn't blame them for not believing me. "The police are involved, and my accounts are frozen, thanks to the hackers."

A few women standing closer to the door muttered together. Words like liar, fraud, likely story, and investigate floated between them. "The best I can do, since I don't have that kind of cash to honor the prize, is to offer to refund your money for any unopened product."

The leader of the pack snorted. "You know full well we've opened and used everything we bought that day. Your offer is meaningless."

Ashley stepped closer and cleared her throat. "Ladies, would it appease you if we offered five hundred dollars of product or reflexology services to a winner?"

The women turned their backs on me and gave their full attention to Ashley. Their leader spoke up. "What if the winner doesn't live in the area?"

"We can ship." Ashley looked at me as if seeking approval. I gave her a nod, grateful she was thinking clearly. Me? I was in a panic. A deer caught in the headlights analogy came to mind. While giving away five hundred in product wasn't a happy thought, these women, along with all the other seniors who had flocked to my shop on Monday, could very well start a negative social media campaign that would do some serious damage to us.

Being our social media guru, Ashley pointed out the obvious. "Since the hackers have frozen us out of our accounts, we won't be able to draw or announce the winner until it's resolved. We'd like to ask you to be patient with this unfortunate situation we've found ourselves in."

The ladies murmured together, and I took the opportunity to collect a stack of business cards. I handed one to each woman. "Check our website every so often, and we'll make the announcement there in addition to X and Facebook once our sites are back up. I'll also throw in a second-place prize worth one hundred dollars of product as a way of apologizing."

Thankfully, the group seemed to accept our peace offering. Three of them even purchased more product, and I instructed Ashley to give them a twenty percent discount. Before I had a chance to return to my cold piece of pizza, another group of tourists flooded in. The usual Friday afternoon crowds kept us hopping, and I was grateful when Dillon came to help. I sent Ashley on her lunch break, and as soon as she returned, I freshened up. Jasper had remained sitting at the island the entire time, carefully watching each customer as they came in.

"How are you holding up? These chairs aren't the most comfortable." I rested an elbow on the countertop and cradled my cheek with my hand.

"I'm fine, and this has been the perfect vantage point to watch everyone coming and going." He gave me a lopsided grin. "I thought I was going to have to take down that posse of senior ladies and protect your honor."

"I was worried there for a moment. They can be... tenacious." A curl of hair had fallen down over Jasper's eye, and I longed to brush it back. Somehow, I resisted. "I'm heading over to the police station for another round of interrogations. You can head on home now. I'm sure that man isn't coming back."

"Maybe I should go with you and protect your honor at the station." His green eyes twinkled.

"I think my attorney can handle it this time, but thanks for the offer and thanks for coming over this afternoon."

Jasper tipped an imaginary hat. "My pleasure, ma'am."

CHAPTER THIRTY-FIVE

After leaving Pixie with Jasper, at his request, I stood in the entryway of the station, waiting impatiently for Alfred to arrive. Lazy bees buzzed around the eucalyptus trees, their drone making me feel less stressed. Officer Davidson manned the front desk again, and he'd offered to get me a cup of coffee or water while I waited. Apparently, he felt the need to offer the chief's daughter hospitality. I thanked him and declined.

At ten minutes past two and still no Alfred, I called his office and spoke to his assistant, Gabriella. "I'm so sorry, Carissa. He got tied up on a conference call with the mayor and the governor."

"You mean the governor of California?"

"Yes." Her crisp tone made it clear she wouldn't be sharing any details of what they were talking about. "I sent the new attorney, Matt, to fill in, but between you and me, you're probably better off on your own. Didn't he show up?"

"Nope. He hasn't arrived." Obviously, the governor took precedence over me, and I didn't need a bumbling attorney trying to face down Raaf. "Why'd Alfred hire someone who isn't capable?"

Gabriella snorted. "It's his nephew. I think Alfred's sister must've coerced him into giving Matt some job experience, but the guy is more interested in admiring himself in the mirror than in actually doing any work."

I had to wonder how he'd gotten through law school and passed the bar exam. But since he had, maybe Alfred's nephew wasn't that incompetent, but had merely rubbed Gabriella the wrong way. "I'll see if I can reschedule and get back to you with the new time."

Once my cell was tucked back into my purse, I smiled at Officer Davidson. "You wouldn't happen to be able to reschedule my appointment with Detective Raaf, could you?"

"Sorry, Ms. Carmichael. He takes care of his own scheduling." He lifted the receiver to the beige phone sitting on his desk. "I'll let him know you're here."

The elderly officer spoke in a hushed voice, but I could distinctly overhear the detective say 'no' to rescheduling. He hung up the phone, looking none too happy. "I can take you back to the interview room, and he'll be with you shortly."

I wasn't falling for that trick again. "I'll just wait right here until he's ready for me. Besides, I'm still waiting for my attorney."

Officer Davidson seemed nervous. "I have my instructions from the detective so if you'll follow me, I'll take you back."

I huffed out my breath hard enough to make my bangs flop. The attorney, Matt, still hadn't arrived and Raaf's power plays were annoying. Still, it wasn't this man's fault, so I tried not to let my growing resentment show. "Since I'm not under arrest I'll wait right here for my attorney. If Detective Raaf has a problem with that, he can take it up with my attorney when he arrives."

Officer Davidson glanced nervously toward the hallway that led to the offices, but then turned back and nodded at the uncomfortable, plastic molded chairs in the lobby. "If you insist, Ms. Carmichael. Let me know if I can get you anything while you wait."

I thanked him, then set a stopwatch on my phone so I'd know exactly how much time I was going to waste waiting for Raaf while waiting for my attorney to show. It was ridiculous how he wanted to make me sweat it out, knowing full well I wouldn't talk until my attorney was available. I thought any reasonable officer of the law would agree to rescheduling. I played Candy Crush on my phone, although I was distracted by the time adding up on the stopwatch. Where was my attorney? I'd gotten the impression that he'd been on his way when I'd spoken to Gabriella.

After thirty minutes, Officer Davidson picked up the buzzing phone. He listened for a moment and looked decidedly uncomfortable. He placed the receiver down and wouldn't meet my gaze. "Ms. Carmichael? You're, um, free to go."

I had to remind myself that this poor man was only the messenger, so I reigned in my anger. "Did Detective Raaf give you any indication when my interview is to be rescheduled?"

"No, Ms. Carmichael." He scratched his head. "He only said to let you go and you'd be hearing from him soon."

Lucky me. "All right. Thanks for letting me know."

He led the way to the front of the station, and as soon as I was alone, I called Alfred's office again.

Gabriella answered the call, and as soon as I identified

myself, she started in with apologies. "I'm so sorry Carissa. That idiot attorney, wait... you didn't hear me say that... drove to the Ventura PD station. Alfred is going to be livid when he finds out."

"It's okay. Detective Raaf blew me off again after making me wait thirty minutes. I'll let you know when he decides to reschedule."

We disconnected, but not before Gabriella apologized several more times. I tucked the phone back into my purse and made my way back to the shop. There were several customers browsing, and I was relieved none of them were senior citizens waiting for me with pitchforks and torches. I understood their frustration and agreed that it had been a fraud getting them to come to my shop. But it wasn't my fault, and I was suffering the consequences. I wondered what progress had been made on tracking down the hacker.

Surely, Detectives Raaf and Martin had turned it over to whatever department handled these types of cyber-crimes. They wouldn't let my social media sites languish with no resolution, would they? It reminded me that I needed to follow up with each social media security. I'd filled out the online forms reporting the hackers taking over and changing my login information, but so far I hadn't heard back aside from their initial blanket response.

As the day wound down and the customer visits trickled off as they sought out happy hour venues or prepared for local, farm-fresh dinners served at our restaurants, I sent Ashley home. She'd had a long week holding down the shop while I'd been involved in all the drama the murder had caused, plus she'd put in tons of hours organizing the work-shop the evening before. Her son, Hunter, would be missing his mama, and I was certain Dillon wouldn't mind getting a few more hours in before college started.

"Hey, boss." Dillon held up a flyer advertising the upcoming Labor Day fireworks show at the high school stadium. "They're doing vendor tents along with a barbecue and a live band before the fireworks show. Are you interested in participating?"

"Definitely. Is the contact info on the flyer?"

He handed it to me. "Yep. I told Misty, she's the one spearheading the event, to save us a spot."

Raising my eyebrows, I studied the flier. "Will you be able to help out?"

"Count me in." He chuckled. "I know I should've asked you first, but I figured it would be easier to drop out than be put on a waitlist for a spot and not get in."

"That's actually a very good point. Thanks." I looked back up from the flyer. "I'll call Misty next week to solidify."

Dillon looked down at the floor and scuffed his toe back and forth. "Mom stopped by while you were at the station."

"Oh?" Sandy was a sheriff department's bicycle officer. I envied her toned body, but I wouldn't have wanted to be one of those deputies exposed to the hot sun during the summer, nor the cold temperatures that happened once in a while during winter months. Sandy, however, never seemed bothered by it.

"We're invited to meet them at Paco's for dinner as soon as we close up."

By 'them', I took it he meant my dad and his mom. "Okay...."

He looked up from the floor and gazed at me. "Do you think they're going to spring their engagement on us?"

"I think that's a very strong possibility, although your mom wasn't wearing a ring last night."

"It's in her jewelry box." His smile was lopsided. "Please don't tattle that I did a little snooping."

"Will you be okay with this?"

"I think so." He scuffed the toe of his shoe again. "One of my dudes said we could get an apartment together if I need to move out. It'll be a little tight trying to pay for college and make the rent."

"I promise my dad is not going to make you move out." I gave his arm a light punch. "And if it ever gets too weird or uncomfortable, you can stay with me and Pixie. Your education comes first without having to worry about housing."

"Has anyone ever told you you're the best boss ever?" Dillon nudged my arm then jogged to the register to assist a customer.

While Dillon flirted with a girl who'd been in his high school class, I restocked shelves and made a list of essential oils I needed to reorder. I could distill some of the oils we sold, but others used costly ingredients that weren't readily available so an essential oils wholesaler was necessary.

Dillon turned the sign to 'closed' and reconciled the register receipts. While dusting shelves, my phone dinged with an incoming email. It was from Suzie. I swiped it open and quickly scanned the paragraph she had written. My legs felt like noodles, and I slid down the side of the cabinet until I sat on the floor. I reread it. My ex-boyfriend, Vincent, was cousin to Detective Raaf.

"That snake!" Despite the boisterous, margarita-fueled voices that filled the restaurant, several heads whipped around at my exclamation. I lowered my voice and gazed at my dad and Sandy, seated across the table from me and

Dillon. "Vincent said he'd get even with me, so he's using Raaf. Can he be arrested or at least fired for focusing the investigation on me?"

Dad took a huge swig of frosty margarita, then scrunched his eyes together. "Brain freeze. Gimme a second."

I drummed my fingers on the colorful tiled tabletop, then took a tiny sip of my margarita. I didn't need a brain freeze on top of the pain Vincent, the jailbird, was already giving me. Suzie had sent another email a couple minutes after I'd received her bombshell, which contained scans of the birth certificates for the two men. They shared the same maternal grandparents.

While my dad massaged his temples, Sandy reached across the table and gave my hand a quick squeeze. The gentle pressure quieted my thrumming fingers and reminded me to take a deep breath in. "Your dad will have more information than I do, but my bet is Detective Raaf has documented all areas of the investigation he's done so it will appear that he's not targeting you. We know you're innocent, but someone has gone out of their way to plant evidence supporting your role in the murder."

I nodded my agreement. Sandy was right, but that didn't mean I wanted Raaf to escape consequences for his harassment.

Dad pushed his margarita away. "I'll notify Internal Affairs but my guess is Raaf is smart enough to cover his tracks. Maybe they'll reassign him due to a conflict of interest, but even that's doubtful."

"Can you at least warn him that we know about his relationship to that snake?" Vincent was serving an eight-year sentence. I didn't want to contemplate having to look over my shoulder for the rest of my life, worrying about what he'd try next. If Raaf knew we were onto their scheme, perhaps my ex would leave me alone.

"I have every intention of taking him down a few pegs, so email the birth certificates to me." Dad scowled and his cheeks flamed. "I'd like to take him behind the barn and give him a thrashing."

"Now, Rob, there's no need for that kind of talk." Sandy stroked his forearm, then looked around. "Please be careful about anyone overhearing you threatening violence. We don't need to add to Carissa's woes."

"You're right." He gazed first at me then turned his attention to Dillon. "Err, sorry about that. I guess I get protective when it comes to you both."

Which turned out to be the perfect segue for Dad as he took hold of Sandy's hand. "We'd like for you two to be the first to know that this lovely lady has agreed to marry me."

Sandy's beaming smile lit up the room as she gazed at her new fiancé. "I couldn't be happier."

"Congratulations!" Dillon and I chorused in unison.

"Have you set a date yet?" I did my best to act surprised with the news. While I'd initially been uneasy about them rushing into marriage so quickly, seeing my dad happy and well-cared for made it easier for me to be delighted for the couple.

"Not yet." She glanced up at my dad. "We wanted to make certain you both were okay with us moving forward. We know it's a big change for all of us."

"Especially for you, Dillon, since you live at home and still have college ahead of you." Dad leaned in toward the young man. "You'll always have a place with us for as long as you need or want it. I don't want you to ever think that you're unwanted or underfoot."

"Thank you, sir." Dillon blinked rapidly as if to keep

moisture from forming, then leaned across the table and grasped his mother's hand. "I'm really happy for the both of you."

"And Carissa," my dad pointed at me, a twinkle in his eye, "as long as you continue to attract murder, your room will be available."

Dillon poked his elbow into my side and whispered softly enough that only I could hear. "Looks like I'm getting a murder magnet for a sister."

I forced a smile and whispered from the corner of my mouth. "Better watch it, bro, or I'll put you on dog poop duty."

"What are you two whispering about?" Sandy couldn't stop beaming.

"Oh, nothing much. Just shop talk." I jabbed Dillon's leg with my knee, not hard enough to hurt, just enough to surprise him. He managed to keep a straight face, but just barely. So, this was what it was going to be like having a younger brother. Something told me the teasing and good-natured rivalry would be more fun than I'd thought possible. "I can't wait to hear what your wedding plans are."

CHAPTER THIRTY-SIX

The smell of fresh brewed coffee woke me at dawn. My head pounded and my mouth felt as if I'd licked the Saharan desert sands. Celebrating my dad's engagement—or maybe I was trying to forget Vincent the snake—the night before had led me to perhaps consume a couple too many margaritas. Knowing that the day would be busy, I dressed in knit black jeggings and a pastel pink logo tee.

Dad handed me a cup of hot coffee when I entered the kitchen and gestured for me to sit. "I wanted to run a couple things by you before any big decisions are made."

Uh-oh. Did this have to do with the murder investigation? "Okay. What's up?"

"Sandy and I have been talking about where to live. She's in a small rental, so do you mind if she and Dillon move in here?" He lowered his eyes. "I realize this house holds memories of your mother, and I hope you don't feel like I'm rushing to replace her."

"Dad, it's been over four years. Sandy makes you happy, which makes me happy."

"If you're uncomfortable with them moving in, I can sell

this house and move to a different neighborhood if that'll make it easier on you."

"This is a wonderful home and I'd hate to see you sell it. I'll be fine with Sandy and Dillon moving in." While a part of me was sad to see another woman intrude into the space my mom once occupied, I couldn't bear the thought of losing the home that still held those precious memories of her.

"Good. I'd hoped you'd feel that way." Dad took another sip of coffee, then cleared his throat. "I was thinking it might be best for Sandy and Dillon to move in next week."

It was a good thing I hadn't taken a sip of the coffee from the mug that I'd raised to my lips. I was certain I would have choked on the hot liquid. "Isn't that a little quick? You just got engaged."

"Maybe, but we've been dating for seven months now and we were good friends for over a year before I got the nerve to ask her out." He grimaced. "Honey, I know this is springing a lot on you all at once, but with college starting for Dillon, we thought it might be easier on him to get settled in before classes begin. Plus, Sandy's lease is coming up for renewal and, well, I'd just like her to be here all the time."

"I guess that makes sense and the timing is entirely up to you and Sandy, of course. Let me know if there's anything I can do to help with the move." I tried to smile. I wanted to tell him they were taking their relationship too fast. Giving it months, or even a year, for Dillon and I to acclimate to the idea would be better. But, of course, I wouldn't voice my concerns.

Dad and Sandy both seemed elated, and I'd noticed positive changes in my dad. I appreciated, too, that Dad waited until it was only the two of us to ask my opinion about the living arrangements, instead of putting me in an awkward position in front of his new fiancée and Dillon. I suspected Sandy had a lot of input in making sure Dad talked to me in private, so I couldn't help but admire her for that.

"I'll let you know the moving date when it's decided." Dad wouldn't meet my gaze, and I felt bad that I couldn't quite mask my lack of enthusiasm for the looming monumental change.

Dad picked up the newspaper and began reading, our conversation apparently over. Once I'd drained the last drop of coffee from the mug, I rummaged in the fridge for bread and jam, then made toast. Dad grunted his thanks when I set a couple slices in front of him and refilled both our mugs with the black brew.

"Dad?" I waited until he looked up from the newsprint to continue. "Do you know if Hank Simmons has been caught yet?"

"He hasn't. I have no idea how he managed to disappear so quickly, and no eyewitnesses have come forward with information."

My sympathy skyrocketed for Betty. As long as Hank was loose, she'd fear for her life and stay on the run. I made a mental note to look for another part-time employee. If and when Betty came back, I'd figure out a way to keep both part-time employees. "I've been meaning to ask you, do you think it's possible that Hank Simmons and Lacie Simmons are related?"

Dad pursed his lips and bobbed his head back and forth. "Not likely. I think the last name is coincidental. Why do you ask?

"Betty said that she and Hank lived in Venice Beach

and then Brett said he picked up his girlfriend from Venice, which made me think he probably lives in that area as well. With a little imagination, I could see Lacie being connected to the locale before she moved back to Oak Creek."

Dad grunted but didn't say anything, so I pressed on with my questions. "I don't remember Lacie's dad when we were in school together. Could it have been Hank?"

"I really don't know that answer. Ginny Simmons was divorced and raised Lacie on her own." He thought for a moment. "It seems to me she had a boyfriend living with them for a couple of years back when you girls were in elementary school, although I don't recall his name. It definitely got tongues wagging."

"Mrs. Simmons doesn't live around here anymore, does she?"

"I thought you'd heard. She was killed in an accident down in the L.A. area two, or maybe it was three, years ago."

Living in San Francisco, I'd allowed myself to be consumed by the big city glamour and by my hotshot boyfriend, especially after my mom died. I hadn't wanted to know what was going on with anyone outside my immediate family. "I didn't know. Poor Lacie."

"Indeed." Dad lowered his eyes back to his newspaper.

Niggling at the back of my brain was a connection I wanted to make sense of. Was there a link between Lacie, her mother, Hank, and Betty? Hank obviously had homicidal rage. Could he have killed Lacie, if she were his daughter? Betty had indicated that Hank's daughter had caused all sorts of trouble. If Lacie had been the daughter in question, had he killed her mother and she found out? I needed to talk to Betty, and I hoped Madame Bonsail had a phone number where her sister could be reached.

Dad's cell phone emitted a siren wail, and I jumped at

the discordant sound. He snatched up the device and answered before it had a chance to emit another wail.

I watched his face harden as his jaw tensed while the other person spoke in staccato sentences. In response, Dad offered monosyllabic words: where, when, how.

When the call ended, he shot out of the chair and buckled his gun belt on.

"What's going on, Dad?"

With the belt on, he clipped his badge to his pocket and leaned over to kiss the top of my head. "Keep the alarm on, both here and at your store. Someone found Hank Simmons with a bashed-in head out at Wheeler Gorge. It looks like murder."

CHAPTER THIRTY-SEVEN

Following Dad to the door, I made sure it was locked behind him, then reset the alarm. Two murders in one week made my scalp prickle. While Dad might believe there wasn't anything connecting Lacie and Hank, this new development made it seem likely. I wondered if Betty might have returned to town so that she and her sister could have done something drastic in order to protect Betty from her abusive husband. Kind of like the song, "Goodbye Earl", from the band formerly known as Dixie Chicks. Naw. I chided myself for letting my imagination run away from me.

Getting ready in record time, I took Pixie out for a quick stroll down the block and back, pepper spray in hand just in case, then packed us into my car and headed to the Apothecary. The toast I'd had for breakfast wasn't substantial enough, so after placing my pup inside my shop, I headed to the patisserie. Luke waved at me as I came through the door, and I watched as he turned his head and hollered back toward the kitchen. Jasper, face covered with a mask, came through the swinging door and waved. Even from the distance I stood away from the counter, the line was at least twelve people deep. I could see the crinkles at the corners of his green eyes as he smiled.

He reached around Luke and plucked something from the glass case, poured a cup of coffee in a to-go cup with a large splash of milk, then headed my way. *Be still my heart.* The largest triple chocolate roll I'd ever seen sat in an open container. Jasper held it out for me to take. I tried to ignore the jealous expressions from the people in line ahead of me, especially from several of Jasper's female fans who didn't try to hide their crushes on him. Apparently, they'd heard Jasper was back at work and wanted to show their support.

"Thank you." I gratefully took the pastry box and tried to control my pounding heart as his fingers brushed down my arm. Jasper had that effect on me. "You didn't need to serve me ahead of everyone else."

"It's the least I can do after all you did for me while I was sick." He took my elbow in his palm and led me to a table. Three similarly dressed young women were openly glaring at me now as they whispered together.

"You must be feeling better if you're back at work already." Tearing a tiny nibble from the roll, I dipped it into the melty-warm chocolate and popped it into my mouth. I stifled the pleasurable moan that tried to escape.

"Yes. Better, although not one hundred percent." He brushed off a sprinkling of flour that clung to his apron. "Luke said I should ease into coming back in by working a few hours every morning. I picked the time when I thought you'd be around."

My face heated so I bent over and took a sip of the coffee. Jasper had prepared it just the way I liked. "I'm truly happy to see you back up and around, but I probably shouldn't keep you from your other customers."

"You're not intruding, and I'm waiting for dough to rise

before I have to get back to the kitchen." Jasper raised his wrist and looked at his watch. "I have ten minutes. Or do you need to get to work?"

"The shop doesn't open for a while, so I'm free to stay until you need to see to your pastry."

We sat there and gazed into each other's eyes for what seemed a full minute. I, for one, wasn't sure what to say, especially since the other patrons in the patisserie seemed to be trying to eavesdrop.

Jasper cleared his throat. "Did you hear the news that a body was found at Wheeler Gorge?"

I nodded. "Dad's out there right now."

"Oh. Of course." Jasper glanced around, then gazed back at me. "Do you know who it is? Was it murder?"

I looked around and realized practically everyone in the place had their gaze fixated on us. I lowered my voice. "Perhaps this isn't the best place to talk about it."

Jasper finally seemed to notice all the attention we were garnering. "Good point. We can talk in the kitchen."

He picked up the pastry box while I carried my coffee. I could feel the stares of the patrons as we walked behind the counter and entered the kitchen. I found the warmth of the space, along with the fragrance of yeast, cinnamon, and brown sugar, comforting.

"No one can overhear us." Jasper set the pastry box down on a stainless-steel island and pulled two stools out for us to sit.

"It's a long story, but the victim is Madame Bonsail's ex-brother-in-law. He's the one who tried to break down my door yesterday."

His eyes widened. "What happened? Was anyone else injured?"

Since Jasper had already heard the pertinent details of Betty and her abusive ex-husband, I told him my theory about the connection to Lacie. "In all the time she worked for you, did she ever say anything about her father or what she did before moving back to Oak Creek?"

Jasper shook his head. "She was pretty tight-lipped about her past. Once in a while, she'd let something slip about her ex, but clammed up almost immediately, especially if I asked questions. A lot of what I know about Lacie was pieced together over the several months she worked for me."

I fumed. Lacie seemed to have gone out of her way to harass most people and as a result, didn't have anyone she called a friend who could shed light on her life. Brett would be the natural choice to quiz about Lacie's background, but he wasn't willing. And then there was the connection between Lacie, Brett, and Madame Bonsail. Perhaps I'd find some free time to chat with her this afternoon.

Looking at my watch, I realized I'd spent much longer talking with Jasper than I'd intended. "I've got to get to work, and you probably need to get to your dough."

"It'll hold a little longer. Let me walk you to the door." He stood and offered me his hand, which I happily grasped.

"Jasper! I'm so happy you're back." A young woman waylaid us as we headed toward the door. Her overly plump and glossy pink lips pouted as her gaze fixated on our entwined hands. "I've been waiting in line for ages. Can you be a dear and bring me a macchiato?"

Jasper winked at me. "I've got some dough that needs my immediate attention, but tell Luke I said to give you fifty percent off your purchase this morning."

The offer of a discount on her purchase did the trick.

She simpered a moment longer, then moved up to keep her place in line. Jasper sighed, then gave my hand a quick squeeze. "I'd better get back to my dough. Thanks for coming in this morning."

"I'm happy to see you up and around." I lifted the chocolate roll. "And thanks for this. You certainly know how to make my day."

"Would you like to come by my place tomorrow evening for dinner? I'll order tamales from Paco's."

My mouth watered. Jasper certainly knew the way to my heart. "That would be great. Does seven work?"

"Perfect. I'll see you then." He gave my hand another quick squeeze. I watched the muscular backside of Jasper as he walked back to the kitchen, then gathered my belongings, most importantly the chocolate roll and the coffee, and headed to Aromatherapy Apothecary.

With only Dillon to work alongside me, we were busy nonstop. Ashley sent me a text and offered to come in to help. While we wanted her, she'd already worked too many hours this week and her young son needed his mom at home. Besides, she had a date with Bryon, attending Rachel Walton's stage production that evening. Mari dropped by and lent a hand for an hour, but previous commitments meant she wasn't able to pitch in more than that.

The rest of the day went by in a whirl, and I didn't have a chance to mull over the murders. I had hoped I'd be able to track down Madame Bonsail and question her about Lacie, over my lunch break, but it didn't happen. I still hadn't found a spare moment to read through Lionel's remaining voicemail messages either and promised myself I'd go through them that night, no matter how tired I might be.

My curiosity meter was off the charts, wondering how Betty was faring, with Hank dead. Had she returned to Oak Creek yet? Had the detectives questioned her? Could she have been responsible for his murder?

CHAPTER THIRTY-EIGHT

Once I'd locked the shop up tight and made it safely to my car, I sent my dad a text confirming he was still able to take Sandy to the performance. I was somewhat concerned that the new murder would keep him too busy to attend, but in reality, I hoped he'd be able to spill some information on the investigation. It didn't take long to see the three dots appear, indicating he was writing a reply. I started the car, made sure Pixie was secure and comfortable in the seat beside me, and waited.

Raaf pulled me off the investigation and took over. Thanks for tix! Sandy can't wait.

Argh! Hadn't my dad used the information I'd given him on Raaf earlier to kick the detective out of Oak Creek? Where was Detective Martin in all of this? I sat there, fiddling with the radio, hunting for tunes I liked. The playwright event wrapped up tomorrow, and all the attendees would be heading back from whence they came, Brett included. I looked at my watch. It was almost seven. If Brett and Tamara were attending any of the stage productions being showcased, they'd already be at the venue or at least on their way. It would be impossible to track him down right now.

The scene of Brett's argument with Madame Bonsail played in my head. With everything that had happened to her sister and the death of her brother-in-law, I guessed she wouldn't be attending any of the festivities. Now might be the perfect opportunity to talk to her, and if Betty was with her, all the better. I made a quick detour to leave Pixie at my dad's house. After I walked and fed her, I sped off to visit the psychic.

Light filtered from behind the drapes that curtained the front window, and the porch light glowed bright in the evening dusk. Courtesy dictated I should have called ahead, but I didn't want Madame Bonsail to decline my self-invitation to chat. I rang the doorbell, the gong sounding loud in the quiet evening air. I waited a minute, and not hearing a peep, I rang the bell again.

A voice, sounding muffled, called out. "Hold on. I'll be there in a sec."

The supposed *sec* turned into another full two minutes. I tapped my toe, but resisted the urge to ring the doorbell a third time. Finally, the front door opened, and Madame Bonsail filled the doorway. She wore a black flowing caftan and a red turban topped her head. "Carissa? What are you doing here? Did we have an appointment?"

"I'm sorry to drop in like this, but I heard about Hank and wanted to check on Betty." Belatedly, I realized I should have brought some cookies. "Has she returned from Santa Barbara yet?"

"What?" She cocked her head like she was puzzling out something. "Oh. You mean Yvonne."

"Sorry. Of course. Silly me, I keep forgetting that's her

real name." I doubted I'd ever remember that. The name of Betty fit the psychic's sister.

"She's on her way back. Needless to say, she's distraught over the entire tragedy. Thanks for dropping by." She started to close the door.

I hated being pushy, but I couldn't let her dismiss me this way. I'd hoped for an invitation to chat. Inspiration struck on how to keep her from saying 'get lost'. I stuck my foot out to stop the door before it shut in my face. "Do you mind if I come in for a bit before Betty, err, Yvonne returns? I have some questions about the tarot card reading. Perhaps you have time to do another reading for me tonight?"

Madame Bonsail chewed on her lower lip, then heaved a sigh. "I suppose there's time for a quick reading. But once my sister returns, I'll have to ask you to leave. She's been through an ordeal and doesn't need no-, um, visitors."

I mulled over what *no visitors* meant. Was she about to say nosy visitors? Perhaps my conscience heard things that weren't really there.

She opened the door wide and motioned, with nails painted blood-red, for me to step into the hallway. Once she securely locked the door, she led me back down the long hallway and into her cozy sitting room. Motioning me to sit in one of the overstuffed armchairs, she swept from the room, leaving me with my guilt-ridden thoughts of barging in where I wasn't wanted. I worried about what a new reading would reveal. Would the psychic be able to determine I was here to question her and her sister about the murder, or would she tell me I was in danger again and send me on my way?

A few minutes later, Madame Bonsail swept back into the room bearing a tray with a Japanese-style cast-iron black teapot and black handleless teacups. A black plate, rimmed with gold, held light-green and dark-green, leaf and flower-shaped cookies. She set the tray down on the small table separating the two armchairs and pointed to the plate. "You must try these matcha shortbread cookies. Luke highly recommended them."

Plucking one of the light-green leaf cookies from the plate, I broke it in half and took a nibble. The texture was similar to the lavender shortbread cookies, but instead of a floral fragrance, a faint, herbally grass taste, beneath the mild, sweet sugar, hit my tongue. I chewed and swallowed. "These aren't nearly as sweet as the lavender shortbread."

She poured steaming tea into the two cups and handed me one. "Take a few sips of this Japanese green tea and then try the cookie again."

I did as she directed. The cookie tasted sweeter this time, although it was still understated compared to most other cookies I'd had. "This is delicious. It's more refreshing than cloyingly sweet."

"Exactly. I hope Luke and John share the recipe with Jasper."

Not certain if the guys had made their cookbook project public, I decided to keep it to myself and murmured my agreement instead. While I nibbled on a second cookie, Madame Bonsail stood and pulled a TV tray table over to perch in front of us. She retrieved a deck of tarot cards from within the folds of her caftan and began shuffling them.

Swallowing the last bit of cookie and washing it down with the now tepid tea sitting in my cup, I braced myself for what I needed to do. "Excuse me, before we start the reading, can I ask you a few questions?"

She placed the cards on the TV tray, then gazed over at me, brows raised. "You can ask, but I might not answer."

"Fair enough." I gazed up at the ceiling, trying to find

the words that wouldn't make the psychic kick me out. I shook my head. There was no way around it. I had to dive in. "I saw you and Brett having a discussion at the park earlier this week. Do you know him through your sister's connection to Venice Beach?"

"I suppose it's going to come out sooner than later." Madame Bonsail lifted her gaze to the ceiling and let out a long exhalation of breath. "I knew both Brett and Lacie."

I thought back to Lacie, with her insults flying around, at the opening event. While I hadn't seen any interaction between the pair, Delaney had mentioned Lacie had caused a scene with Madame Bonsail. But now that there was a prior acquaintance, I wondered if my hunch had been right all along. "Was Lacie Hank's daughter?"

She whipped her head around to look at me. "Now who's being psychic?"

I took that as a yes. "There were too many coincidences, and it seemed to add up. Why didn't you or Betty, err, Yvonne just say so?"

Madame Bonsail shook her head. "We didn't need the attention of the police after Lacie's murder. Yvonne needed to stay under the radar so Hank couldn't find her."

I plucked another cookie from the plate and took a bite. After swallowing, I said, "Given Lacie and Hank's deaths, shouldn't we be worried that Yvonne might be in danger? What if someone is targeting Hank's entire family?"

CHAPTER THIRTY-NINE

Come to think of it, there was the accident that killed Lacie's mother a few years back. Could that have been a murder? I shook my head, trying to clear the conspiracy theories that threatened to grow. I probably shouldn't share those thoughts with anyone else. They were too far-fetched.

Madame Bonsail remained silent and instead refilled our teacups. The cast-iron teapot had kept the tea steaming, and I gratefully accepted the hot light-green beverage. The cookie felt like it had stuck in my dry throat as I contemplated so many untimely deaths.

After taking a sip of her tea, she cradled the cup between her palms, heaving out another long sigh. "Hank and Lacie were two peas in a pod. Mean-spirited and always dissing one person or another for no good reason. I think they finally crossed the wrong person, and it has absolutely nothing to do with my sister."

"Well, you know best." I shifted in the chair and returned Madame Bonsail's gaze. She seemed to be examining me, and I squirmed a bit beneath her icy-blue eyes. "Of course, you'll need to talk to the detectives first thing in the morning and tell them everything. I'd suggest calling right now, but I doubt anyone's around to take your statement."

"There's no need to do that. My sister doesn't need to have attention drawn to her, especially by the police."

"Why not? Hank isn't around any longer to threaten her." I paused when a scowl appeared on the psychic's face. "Unless there's someone else out there, like Hank and Lacie's killer, who might be hunting for Yvonne?"

"I've told you before that my sister has nothing to do with their deaths." Madame Bonsail's face turned red. "I think now would be a good time for you to leave."

I held my hand up, palm facing outward. "I'm sorry. I didn't mean to offend. It's just that if she were my sister, I'd be concerned for her safety, and the police will know how to protect her if they have all the information."

Despite her size, Madame Bonsail sprang from the cushy chair with surprising speed. Startled, I jumped up too, bumping into the TV tray table, causing the deck of tarot cards to flutter to the carpet.

"I'm so sorry!" Worried I might have bent or damaged the cards in the tumble, I bent down to gather them. My hand stopped in midair, hovering over the Death card. Except it wasn't just one Death card, there were several identical Death cards. I scooped up as many as I could and turned them over, so I could see the face. They were all Death.

"You couldn't just leave well enough alone." Madame Bonsail snatched the cards I held and waved them in my face. "I repeatedly warned you but you had to keep prying."

I stepped back, trying to get away from the cards and from the fury that rolled off the psychic. The back of my knees hit the armchair and I lost my balance. Stumbling backward, the chair stopped my fall, and I landed with a thump onto the soft cushion. Madame Bonsail loomed over me, and I cowered, throwing my hands over my head, as she threw the cards at me. The edge of one card sliced my arm, creating a deep papercut. A trickle of warm blood appeared on my arm, and I watched as it dripped onto the armrest of the overstuffed chair. With the wine-red velvet fabric covering the chair, the drops weren't visible.

"Why are you doing this?" I grabbed a napkin and pressed it to the papercut, not wanting to stain her furniture. "Is it to protect your sister? If you're worried about her, we'll leave the police out of it. They don't need to know her connection to Brett and Lacie."

While my attention was distracted by the bleeding cut, Madame Bonsail bent down and retrieved a length of rope from beneath my chair. Before I could stop what was happening, she'd lassoed me, and even though I tried to twist and turn, she managed to tie me to the back of the armchair. When I struggled to loosen the rope looped around my torso, she picked up a second rope and tied my wrists together. Seemingly content with her knots, she sat down in her armchair, with a thud, and removed her turban. After running her fingers through her short-cropped iron-gray hair, she started unwinding the turban. "It's too late for that, Carissa. You know too much about the deaths."

I watched in horror as the turban became a long, red scarf, and I remembered that Lacie had been strangled. She wrapped the ends of the scarves tightly around her hands and pulled them taut. Imperceptibly, I tried to wiggle the bonds that held my hands, but they remained snug. Unfortunately, it didn't escape the psychic's notice.

"Now, now, you stay right where you're at." She'd released one end of the scarf and wagged her index finger at me. "I need a moment to figure out what to do with you next. I can't have any untoward DNA soiling my home."

Needing time to figure a way out of the deadly situation facing me, I tried to get her talking. Except I couldn't control my quaking voice, so it took several attempts to get the words out. "I understand wanting to protect your sister from Hank, but what did Lacie do to make you kill her?"

"There are so many reasons she needed to die." Madame Bonsail held up one finger at a time as she ticked off the reasons. "One, she tried to end Yvonne's marriage by reconnecting her mom and Hank. Two, she made Yvonne's life a nightmare when she started working for her dad and convinced him that my sister was embezzling. In fact, it was Lacie who was stealing the money. It's what started Hank's pattern of spousal abuse. Three, Lacie is the one who told her dad where Yvonne was hiding out. She tried black-mailing us into paying her to keep quiet. We gave her every spare cent we had, but it was never enough. She kept coming back for more, and when we couldn't pay up, she told Hank."

My mouth dropped open. Lacie had her problems, but this went way beyond rational human behavior. Still, she didn't deserve to die. "That's terrible. I really have a hard time believing someone would be so cruel to your sister."

"Exactly. I got my revenge on her and her horrible father." She wrapped and unwrapped the scarf around her hands.

I shivered, knowing all too soon it was going to wrap around my neck unless I came up with a plan to find a way out. "Obviously, you planned her murder out in great detail, from the tarot cards you gave me to the prop knives."

"Oh heavens, I got a kick out of that. Actually, it couldn't have worked out better with the way you threatened Lacie at the event right after receiving those three cards." Her chuckle sent chills down my spine. "And then the coup de grâce, you finding the body right after the deed!"

Yeah, me and my big mouth. "How did you know I'd go back to the patisserie and find her?"

"I didn't know. It was just luck." She fanned her face. "Everyone in town knows about your longstanding feud with Lacie. It wasn't a stretch of anyone's imagination to think that you'd killed her. It was only a matter of time."

"So, after I found the body, you left Death cards for me to what? Scare me off?" I wiggled my fingers, which were starting to tingle from the tightly tied rope around my wrists. "And why did you have to trash my house? What were you looking for?"

Madame Bonsail cocked her head to the side, her pale eyes blinking rapidly. "Your farmhouse? I didn't break in."

"Then who did?" I had my suspicions it was Raaf, but I didn't think there would be a way to prove it.

She shrugged. "Wasn't me, although I will admit I left you the card on your car the night of Lacie's death and on your dad's screen door. It was a nice, eerie touch, and I'd hoped it would scare you away from nosing around."

Since she seemed so amiable to answering questions, I decided to keep going. At least it delayed, which I was afraid would be inevitable...strangulation. I tried to shove it from my mind and focus on keeping her talking. "And did you hack my shop's social media accounts?"

"Nope. That wasn't me either. You do seem to collect enemies, don't you?"

I wondered if the social media hacks were instigated by Raaf, or I suppose Vincent could have coordinated it from inside prison. I'd probably never know for certain.

She belted out a belly laugh and then abruptly went silent. Once again, she cocked her head to the side. "What was that?"

"I didn't hear anything." Could someone be here to rescue me? I shook those thoughts away. No one knew I'd come to see Madame Bonsail, and most of my friends and family had attended one of the many performances being held tonight. *Think, Cari. How're you going to get yourself out of this mess?*

"No matter. Guess it's time to get the show on the road, as they say." She lumbered to her feet and stretched the scarf between her hands. "I can't tell you how sorry I am to have to do this, Carissa. I really do like you. But it's your own fault for causing me nothing but headaches with your prying."

She stepped in front of me and flung the scarf around my neck. I kicked out, and my foot connected with her knee. I tried to twist away, but the ropes held me firmly in place. Madame Bonsail screeched in pain, then limped to stand behind the chair that held me. She leaned over the back of the chair and wrapped the scarf around my neck once again. I tried rocking side to side, hoping she wouldn't be able to get a good grasp of the scarf, while at the same time, working my fingers between the scarf and my neck. It was no use. Between her bulky strength and the binds that kept me in place, the scarf tightened and cut off my air supply until my vision went black.

CHAPTER FORTY

When I came to, I was lying on the carpet, and a man wearing a paramedic's blue uniform hovered over me. I tried to focus on his face but my throbbing throat and raging headache made me shut my eyes tight.

"Ms. Carmichael? Can you hear me?"

I moaned and managed to whisper a yes.

"Can you tell me where you're hurt?"

This time, I managed to open one eye and raise an eyebrow. I hoped he'd get my message of disdain. Did he not see the scarf still wrapped around my throat? Just in case he thought it was normal to wear a scarf in August, I pointed at my throat, then inched the scarf away.

He sucked in a large breath of air. I guessed I probably had some bruising and abrasions caused by the killer twisting the scarf tighter and tighter.

"I have a bad headache too." My voice was raspy. When I tried to sit up, the paramedic placed a firm hand on my shoulder to keep me in place.

"We need to check out your injuries before you get up."

Someone brought him a medical bag, and he placed a blood pressure cuff on my arm.

I gave one slight nod, then concentrated on keeping the tears at bay. "Can you tell me what happened? I thought I was dead."

"The chief is on the way. He'll let you know." He took my vitals, then shone a light into my eyes for a second. When he touched the side of my head, I flinched, and when he withdrew his hand, there was a spot of blood on his gloved fingers. "I've got another patient to attend to. Stay put until someone tells you otherwise."

I closed my eyes and listened to the murmurs of voices in the room. There was a mix of both male and female voices, along with the crackle of emergency personnel's radios.

"Where is she? Where's my daughter?" My dad was a force to be contended with when he was worried.

"I'm over here." My raspy voice could barely be heard above the other voices, but Dad still heard me.

"Carissa! Thank God!" He crouched down beside me and grasped my hand. "Are you all right? Where are you hurt?"

"I'm alive, so I'll be okay." I blinked hard, trying to hold back the tears that edged my lashes. "What happened? The last thing I remember is being strangled by Madame Bonsail, then everything went black. Did she get away?"

"Her sister got here just in time to stop her from...." Dad gulped. "I can't believe how close I came to losing you tonight."

He wanted to lecture me in the worst way for taking chances and I was grateful he held back. At least for now. But really, no one ever considered Madame Bonsail capable of being a murderous psycho, so I couldn't be blamed. "How did Betty, err, Yvonne stop her?"

"Yvonne hit her over the head with a candlestick. Unfortunately, it slipped out of her hand and the corner caught the side of your head. The paramedic doesn't think you need stitches, but they'll transport you to the hospital to make sure."

That explained the blood and the headache. "I'm sorry I ruined your evening out."

"Oh, Cari-girl, it's not your fault." Again, I sensed he wanted to lecture me, but amazingly, he held back. "Actually, the call came at a good time. I was on the verge of snoring, and I'm sure Sandy would've been mortified."

I giggled. "It must've been a riveting production."

"You know those types of things aren't really my cup of tea." He squeezed my hand. "But I'd much rather sit through that kind of performance than find you in danger."

"I know, and I'm sorry."

Two burly EMTs placed a body board beneath me, then hefted me up and onto the gurney. I was relieved they didn't grunt out loud when they lifted me.

Dad gave my hand another squeeze. "Jasper will meet you at the emergency room and drive you back to my place. I'll see you there later tonight and we'll talk more."

Which was a gentle way to say I'd be interrogated later on.

It turned out that both Jasper and Luke met me at the hospital and then drove me to my dad's house. After the pair fussed over me and got me settled in comfortably, Jasper sent Luke back to his home. Since I'd been diagnosed with a mild concussion, but no stitches required, Jasper slept on the living room couch to be on hand if I needed anything. Even after Dad trudged in at three in the morning, he stayed on so the chief could get some uninterrupted sleep.

The smell of bacon and coffee woke me at eight, so I shuffled down the stairs and into the kitchen. Jasper sat at the table, cradling a mug of coffee between his hands, while Luke tended to sizzling bacon and browning pancakes on the stovetop griddle. Instinctively, my hands flew to my hair to smooth down the curly mass. I hadn't bothered to brush it or even look in the mirror before venturing downstairs, assuming it was only my dad preparing breakfast.

"Good morning!" Jasper sounded chirpy. "How are you feeling this morning?"

"Let the girl sit down and have some breakfast first, dude." Luke poured a glass of orange juice—which looked freshly squeezed—and placed it in front of me. Luke winked at me. "He's already had four cups of java while waiting for you to wake up. He might be a bit wired."

"Ah. That explains the chirpiness." I winked back at Luke and raised my glass of juice to him, while I stroked Pixie's ears with my free hand. She'd pressed her warm body close to my legs the second I'd sat down. "I wouldn't mind having a cup or two of coffee myself."

"Now, Carissa, don't you be going against your doctor's advice. No caffeine, at least for a couple of days." Luke crossed his arms in front of his chest, his voice stern.

"I know." I stuck my lower lip out. "But I need the caffeine to wake up. I'm going to be a zombie all day."

"You're supposed to take it easy for a couple of days at least." Luke turned back to the stove and flipped the pancakes.

Jasper's shoulders were hunched over, and his leg jiggled up and down.

"Are you okay, Jasper?" I pushed the pitcher of orange juice over to him and handed him a clean glass.

"I'm feeling much better aside from being worried about you." His brow wrinkled. "You came so close to being killed last night."

"But I wasn't and aside from a mild headache, I'm fine." I reached over and gripped his hand. "How are you physically feeling? You're still taking your antibiotics, right?"

"Yes, ma'am, I'm still taking them and promise to finish the dose." A small smile appeared on his full lips. He ignored the juice and instead picked up the insulated carafe of coffee. "Actually, this is the first day in over three weeks I've finally felt back to normal."

Luke removed the carafe from Jasper's hand. "No more coffee for you. Your jittery leg is creating a mini-earthquake at the table."

"I was only going to have a little more."

"Uh-hm. I don't think so." Luke pointed at the bacon. "Jasper, make yourself useful and plate the bacon and pancakes. The chief should be down any minute."

Jasper didn't complain and I supposed he was used to obeying orders from Luke after working so long in the patisserie for him. Luke wasn't wrong either. The tromp of boots sounded on the stairway as my dad made his way downstairs. Luke filled a mug with coffee and placed it on the table while Jasper set two plates full of pancakes and bacon down. One in my dad's place and one in front of me. My mouth watered. A pitcher of warm maple syrup materialized by my plate.

"Morning, Chief." Luke's singsong voice filled the kitchen. "There's plenty of hot coffee and breakfast. Jasper and I will make ourselves scarce so you can take down Carissa's report."

"You're a godsend." Dad put his iPad on the table, then shook hands with Jasper and Luke. "Fix yourself a plate and sit with us. There's no need for Carissa to have to repeat this story after I head to the station."

Who was he kidding? I'd be repeating the story at least five hundred times, until every gossipy Oak Creek resident knew it as well as I did.

CHAPTER FORTY-ONE

While we ate, I related everything that had occurred and what Madame Bonsail had confessed to. I'd been a little disappointed that she hadn't cleared up all my questions, but perhaps between Betty, err, Yvonne, and Brett, we'd find more answers. I also made sure Dad understood that Madame Bonsail had not broken into my farmhouse, nor had she hacked into my social media accounts. I placed that all on Detective Raaf and my ex. Dad said he'd pass the information on to Internal Affairs. They had started an investigation into Raaf after Dad had filed a complaint the previous day, but as usual, bureaucracy moved slowly.

"The good news is your social media sites are now back up." Dad forked another bite of maple syrup dripping pancake into his mouth. "I didn't want to tell you before because I wasn't sure it would work, but I have a friend who's been trying to hack into the hacker's password on your accounts. He managed to figure it out. I'll text you the new passwords."

"I'll let Ashley know so she can generate new posts." I

checked the time and stood. "I'd better get ready and head to the shop. Thanks for the breakfast, guys."

Dad motioned for me to sit back down. "Ashley and Dillon will open this morning. You're supposed to take a day or two off, given your head injury."

"I feel fine. I barely have a headache, and I haven't even taken any ibuprofen yet."

"How about I make a deal with you?"

"Okaaay...."

"You promise to stay home and take it easy today, and I'll fill you in on my conversations with Yvonne and Brett."

"You talked to Brett already?" I gripped the edge of the table. "What did he say? How is he involved?"

Dad lowered his head and looked at me expectantly over the bridge of his nose. He twirled his index finger in the air, as if prompting me. "Is it a deal?"

"Oh yeah. I promise I'll stay home and take it easy today."

Luke burst out laughing, then began clearing our empty plates. Jasper stood to help, but Luke motioned him to sit back down. "You're still recovering, too. You'd might as well take advantage of a quiet day and hang out with Carissa."

Jasper's face turned as red as what I assumed my flaming cheeks were.

Dad tried to suppress a smile, but he wasn't successful. "We picked up Brett as he was loading his luggage to head out of town at midnight last night. It's the reason I got home so late, or I guess it was so early this morning."

I waited while Dad took another sip of coffee. My impatience got the better of me. "Oh, c'mon. The suspense is killing me."

"All right, all right. According to Brett, and mostly confirmed by Yvonne, Bertha Bonsail used her gifts for fraudulent purposes. She touted her psychic abilities while finding ways to fleece her customers. She was a small-time operator and didn't swindle huge amounts of money from each client. But a hundred here and a few hundred there starts to add up." He grunted, then took another sip of coffee and watched while the three of us leaned forward in anticipation. "Tamara, Brett's girlfriend, was taken for almost a thousand dollars. He got a private investigator involved, and when Bertha found out, she skipped town, leaving Yvonne behind."

"Was Yvonne involved in the scam?" I remembered Madame Bonsail saying numerous times her sister wasn't involved in the murders, but did she also mean in all her criminal activities?

"She says no, and Bertha says absolutely not." Dad scratched his chin. "We still have more investigating to do."

"So, Madame Bonsail headed to Oak Creek Valley after leaving Venice Beach?" I hoped we'd hear the full story.

"She'd been following Lacie on social media and knew Oak Creek could be a lucrative place to scam wealthy visitors. When Hank escalated his abuse toward Yvonne, Bertha placed all the blame on Lacie, especially when she'd basically accused her stepmother of embezzling from her father. I'm not sure if we'll ever know the truth now that Lacie's deceased, but I could see how it was Lacie doing the embezzling and Yvonne took the blame. Anyway, Bertha wanted Lacie to pay for blaming Yvonne, which caused the spousal abuse to escalate."

"How awful! Why didn't Yvonne leave and move with Bertha in the first place.

"I don't know. Maybe she hoped the marriage would work out when both her stepdaughter and her sister were out of the picture. Unfortunately, it only got worse for her until she felt like she had to flee or lose her life." Dad tapped his iPad open and scrolled through a page before continuing. "Lacie spotted Yvonne, then demanded they pay her or else she'd tell her dad where to find her. They paid Lacie several times, but with Yvonne too frightened to work, their cash ran out."

"Then Madame Bonsail took matters into her own hands and got rid of Lacie." And framed me. It was an unfortunate coincidence that Detective Raaf managed to take on the case with the intent of getting me convicted. Otherwise, I'd have minded my own business and not gotten involved. Probably.

"Yep. And when Hank showed up, she lured him out to Wheeler Gorge and bashed him in the head."

I shuddered. "How does Brett fit in? Dillon and I saw him arguing with Madame Bonsail earlier this week."

"It was strictly a coincidence. Brett and Tamara were here for the event and happened to see Bertha. Brett demanded Tamara's money back, and if she wouldn't refund it, he threatened to go to the police." He took a sip of coffee, then gazed directly at me. "No charges will be filed, but I made him sweat it out. He should have reported it right away, especially since he knew Lacie had been murdered. It might have saved Hank's life and kept you safe."

Jasper kept shaking his head back and forth, while my dad filled in the gaps of the events. "I know that I make an effort to see the best in people and ignore the negative, especially when it comes in the form of gossip, but Lacie sure had me fooled. I can't wrap my head around her actions with the person she led me to believe she was. Do you think she really was abused by Brett or did she make it up to sucker me in?"

"I'm not sure we'll ever know the truth." I bit on my lower lip while I thought about how best to answer. "The Brett I knew never would have abused a woman, and given his tenderness with Tamara and her illness, I think it's safe to say that Lacie brought out the worst in him if anything happened. The only time I saw him angry was when he was around Lacie or when he was talking about her."

With all my questions answered, for now, Dad headed to the station. Luke cleaned up the kitchen and went back to the patisserie. Jasper and I sat at the kitchen table, toying with our now-empty juice glasses. Shy silence lingered in the air. I finally cleared my throat. "Wanna have a couch potato marathon movie day?"

He let out a breath of air, and his shoulders visibly relaxed. "That sounds perfect. Shall I make some hot cocoa while you pick out the movies?"

The sound of the front screen door slamming shut jolted me from slumber. I bolted upright from where I'd been slumped napping, my head resting on Jasper's chest, while Pixie had commandeered his lap. Jasper brushed my wild curly hair from his neck, then smiled down at me. "Hey there."

I smiled back at him. He'd been remarkably amiable watching a sappy rom-com with me, and I tolerated a shoot-em-up thriller that he liked. By the time we'd decided to go for a third movie, we'd found we both loved science fiction and had been too embarrassed to admit it. "Hey there, back."

"How's pizza sound?" Ashley and Dillon bounded into the family room.

"What time is it?" How long had Jasper and I been napping?

"Five thirty. Your dad came by the shop and said to close early. He went to pick up Sandy and pizza, then they'll head here." Ashley plopped herself next to me, looked at my mussed-up hair, and wiggled her eyebrows. "Good day?"

"Umm-humm." I elbowed her. "How was the shop today?"

"Busy, but nothing we couldn't handle. Everyone, and I do mean everyone, wanted to hear what happened last night."

"I'll bet, but it can wait another day."

When Bryon showed up with Hunter, Dillon had the young boy help bring soft drinks into the family room, just as Dad and Sandy arrived with pizza. Jasper and I remained snuggled in together on the couch while we ate. Once Hunter ate a small slice, he and Pixie romped around while the hum of conversation floated around me. As contentment filled me, I realized these people, whether they were blood or not, were my family. I'd found my home.

CHAPTER FORTY-TWO

Ashley and Mari had insisted that I take an afternoon off from the Aromatherapy Apothecary and take myself shopping at the large mall in Thousand Oaks. I'd circled the bottom floor of the shopping center and now worked my way around the top floor, studying window displays that contained dresses. So far, nothing appealed to me, and I'd begun to fret that I'd never find the perfect dress to wear to a fundraising gala that Jasper's mother had invited me to attend with her and Jasper the following weekend.

I gulped hard. The upcoming event and meeting Elaina Whitby for the first time had my stomach tied up in knots. Especially given that my special event dresses no longer fit me, since moving back from San Francisco. I wasn't certain I'd find anything that flattered my current figure. I bypassed a shop that featured rail-thin mannequins wearing skintight, ankle-length dresses that had slits up the legs to the top of thighs. The plunging necklines almost reached the mannequins' navels. Even in my thin days, that style wasn't for me.

The next shop was a sports clothing shop and I longed

to pick out a new pair of stretchy leggings and a loose-fitting yoga top. Fighting the urge, I turned to walk toward the next shop when my gaze swept across Detective Raaf standing next to a rack of T-shirts. His gaze fixated on me, and his mouth formed a thin slash across his scowling face.

Picking up my pace, I thumbed open my phone and hit the record app just in case Raaf decided to create a scene. Shoving the phone into the pocket of my shorts, I practically trotted toward the next shop. With luck, I'd be able to hide out in a dressing room or at least behind a rack of clothes until I could figure out how to leave the mall without him finding me. Before I could reach the entry, strong hands grabbed my shoulders, jerked me to a stop, and spun me around.

"Let go!" Trying to control the quaver in my voice, I reached out and shoved him with my palms against his rock-solid chest. He didn't budge, not even an inch, and he didn't release his hold.

"You and your father are going to pay for what you did to me." His low voice growled close to my ear. "If you thought Vincent was dangerous, you haven't seen anything yet."

I gritted my teeth and shoved harder. "I said, let me go!"

He didn't comply. "Thanks to your meddling, I've had to resign. Even so, Internal Affairs will probably keep investigating me."

"Why'd you hack my accounts and leave Death cards for me?" No one had ever proven it was Raaf, but it only made sense that he was behind the acts that Madame Bonsail hadn't admitted to.

"I wanted to make you afraid and watch you squirm." He tightened his vice-like grip on my arm, and I writhed as his fingers dug into my soft skin. "You'd better always be looking over your shoulder because sooner or later I'll make you wish you'd never been born."

I yelped at the pain, and my stomach plummeted when a look of satisfaction crossed Raaf's face.

"Is there a problem here?" A burly, bald-headed mall security guard walked toward us. His eyes darted between me and Raaf.

Raaf released his hold on my arm and slung his arm around my waist and pulled me close. "No problem at all. Right, sweetie?"

I stomped on his foot, and when his arm relaxed, I pulled away and rushed to stand next to the security guard. "He's threatening me. Can you arrest him?"

Before the security guard could move, Raaf shoved him to the ground, then darted away and charged down the stairs. By the time the guard got to his feet—now that I saw him up close, his wrinkled skin hinted at a much older age than I'd initially thought—Raaf was nowhere in sight.

"Sorry about that, miss. Do you want me to call the police?" He pulled a radio from his utility belt.

"Yes, please. You can let them know that the man is former Detective Erik Raaf." I pulled my cell from the pocket of my shorts and stopped the recording app. "My dad's the chief of police in Oak Creek. I'll call him and let him know what's happened."

He nodded and immediately began barking commands into the radio. Answering squawks came back. He paced back and forth all the while keeping an eye on me.

"Cari-girl! Did you find a dress for Jasper's shindig?" My dad sounded a little too enthusiastic when he answered the phone.

"Not yet." I gulped, knowing he was going to switch gears and go cop mode on me. "I ran into Raaf at the mall.

He threatened me, then got away when security came to see what was going on."

Sure enough, his voice turned brusque. "Are you safe? Is security still around? Did they call the police?"

"Yes, to all three of your questions. I even have a voice recording of Raaf threatening me, so hopefully that'll get him locked up."

"And the security personnel witnessed Raaf with you?"

"He sure did. Raaf knocked the guard down before he ran, so there should be additional charges brought against him."

I heard him murmuring to someone in the background. "Stay at the mall, preferably in the security office. Sandy and I will be there just as soon as we can."

Dead air filled my ears. Dad was on his way to rescue his only child...again. *Whether I needed rescuing or not.*

It didn't take long for a police officer to arrive and escort me to the security office, where he took my statement and listened to the recording. I sent it as an attachment to myself, my dad, and to an email address the officer provided.

By the time I'd given my version of events and signed the iPad report, my dad and Sandy came bursting into the office. Chief Carmichael was a force to be reckoned with, and he had the officer sit back down and go over everything I'd told him.

A squawking radio interrupted my dad's interrogation. I had no idea what was being said, but Dad, Sandy, and the officer all grimaced.

"What's going on?" I hated being the only one not able to understand the radio gibberish.

"Raaf ran a red light and sideswiped a parked car, which made his vehicle roll. He's been caught. He's lucky he didn't injure an innocent bystander." Dad's lips tightened into a grim line. "I think it's safe to say he won't be bothering you or trying to carry out Vincent's threats for a very long time."

I hoped he was right. I was tired of looking over my shoulder.

Once the officer left the office, Sandy took my arm and led me toward the exit. "Let's go shopping. I'll help you find the perfect dress."

I stopped in my tracks and felt my face warm. "You don't need to do that. I really can't impose on your time."

"Are you kidding me? I'd love to help you find a dress for the gala. I have a son and never had the chance to shop for girls' or women's dresses. With my job and lifestyle, I don't even get the chance to shop for myself." Sandy dropped her hand from my arm, and she lowered her gaze to the floor. "Sorry. I don't mean to be pushy. Perhaps you'd be more comfortable shopping on your own?"

"Don't be silly. Carissa wou...." Dad bit off the words he was about to say when Sandy shot him a glance and shook her head.

"Really, Carissa, you won't hurt my feelings if you'd rather shop on your own." Sandy touched her hand briefly to my arm.

I reached out and wrapped my arms around her shoulders, breathing in her jasmine and orange blossom fragrance. "I'd love to shop with you and, more importantly, I'm grateful to have you as my family and my friend."

RECIPE
LAVENDER SHORTBREAD

Jasper shared this recipe with Carissa to serve at her Aromatherapy Apothecary workshop since the cookies complemented the essential oils used in the salve the group made. These lightly lavender-scented cookies have a delicate, sandy texture. Perfect with afternoon tea or an after-dinner treat.

Ingredients
1 cup all-purpose flour
1/4 cup cornstarch
1/4 teaspoon sea salt
1 tablespoon dried culinary lavender*
1 teaspoon vanilla extract
1/3 cup granulated sugar, divided
1/2 cup unsalted butter, room temperature

Optional:
Coarse sparkling sugar for topping cookies
1 teaspoon lemon zest if you'd prefer to make Lavender

Lemon Shortbread Cookies (if using, add to sugar and butter mixture)

Instructions

In a medium-sized bowl, whisk together the flour, cornstarch, and salt. Set aside.

Place 1 tablespoon of granulated sugar, the lavender, and the vanilla extract in a mortar and grind lightly with the pestle. Place the mixture in the bowl of a stand mixer.

Add the butter and the remaining sugar to the lavender mixture and beat on medium-speed for 2 minutes.

Add the flour mixture to the butter mixture and beat on low just until incorporated.

Wrap the dough in plastic wrap and chill for at least 30 minutes.

Preheat the oven to 325 degrees (F). Line 2 baking sheets with parchment paper.

On a lightly floured surface, roll a portion of the dough out to 1/8-inch to 1/4-inch thickness. Cut with cookie-cutter shapes or slice into rectangles. Place on prepared baking sheets and sprinkle each cookie with coarse sparkling sugar if desired.

Refrigerate cookie shapes for 10 minutes before baking.

Bake for 10 – 12 minutes for thinner cookies and 13 – 16 minutes for thicker cut cookies. The edges should barely turn light golden. Don't brown the cookies.

Allow the cookies to rest on the baking sheet for 5 minutes, then transfer to a wire rack to cool completely.

Note:

*You can use dried lavender from your yard as long as

it's pesticide-free. Otherwise, purchase culinary lavender online or from a specialty shop.

Lavender Skin Healing Salve

The following aromatherapy Skin Healing Salve was developed and provided by A.C. Stauble, The Traveling Farmer. This salve is an oil-based moisturizer with skin-soothing herbs and beeswax. Ideal for moisturizing dry skin, first aid applications on cuts, burns, bruises, rashes and bites, and can be used as a moisturizing makeup remover.

<u>Ingredients</u>

3 cups organic extra virgin olive oil
1-1/2 cups organic coconut oil
1 cup dried and garbled comfrey leaf (Symphytum officinale or Symphytum uplandicum)
1 cup dried calendula flowers (Calendula officinales)
1/2 cup to 1-1/2 cups shredded beeswax or beeswax beads (start with less, test, and add more to reach desired consistency)
1-1/2 to 2 tablespoons per 4 cup glass measuring cup of salve (or for smaller batches, use about 2 teaspoons of lavender essential oil per 1-1/2 cups of salve)
2 to 3 tablespoons Vitamin E oil, optional

Supplies

Step 1:

Slow Cooker
2 cheesecloth strips about 8-1/2 x 11 inches
Long-handled metal or silicone mixing spoon (not plastic or rubber)

Step 2:
Mixing bowl
Fine mesh colander
Ladle
Teaspoon

Step 3:
Newspaper
Salve tins or jars
Silicon spatula
Butter knife
Glass liquid measuring cup (2 cup or 4 cup size)
Rags and/or paper towels
Measuring spoons (tablespoon, teaspoon, 1/2 teaspoon)
Labels for finished product
Friends to massage the inevitable excess oil onto

Instructions
Step 1: Infusing

- Add the olive oil and coconut oil to a slow cooker and set the heat to the lowest setting. Oils should not be heated above 120 degrees (F).

- Spread cheesecloth out on a clean surface and add the dried herbs to it. Fold up into a bundle and tie the top off with kitchen twine. Add a second layer of cheesecloth around the bundle and secure with twine.

- Place the herb bundle into the slow cooker and allow 24 – 48 hours of infusing time on low heat. Sometimes the lowest setting is too hot. Use a thermometer every couple of hours to monitor and adjust the temperature as necessary. If your crockpot runs hot, stir the mixture and turn the slow cooker off and on periodically throughout the day. You can turn the slow cooker off during the night and resume heating the next day.

Step 2: Straining Herbs and Adding Beeswax

- After the herbs have infused the oils for a minimum of 24 hours, remove the hot herb bundle and place it into a colander set over a bowl. Allow the oils to drip out and collect in the bowl. When it has cooled enough to touch, press the oil out of the herb bundle and using a spatula, add the oils back to the slow cooker. Alternately, you can bottle the herb-infused oil without adding beeswax (for vegans). Compost the bundle.

- Add the beeswax to the slow cooker and turn the heat up a little so the beeswax will melt. Stir occasionally. If you don't shred the beeswax with a cheese grater or buy the beeswax pellets, you will find that chunks of wax take forever to melt. Batches of beeswax from different apiaries can be different, so start with a half cup of beeswax and more as necessary. While you wait for it to melt, set up your pouring station so you're ready to go (see Step 3).

- Scoop a teaspoon of the salve out as a tester, allowing it to cool (you can pop it in the refrigerator to hasten the cooling process) to see if it is at your desired consistency. You may need to add more beeswax. I like it when I can easily press my fingers into a salve, some prefer a firm salve. Those in hot climates may want to have a firmer salve so that if it is being carried around in a bag, it won't melt. Make a record of what amount of beeswax worked best so you won't have to play around as much next time you make your salve.

- Once the beeswax has melted, turn off the heat

- Add the Vitamin E oil to the slow cooker and stir. Vitamin E is a natural preservative that will extend the life of your salve.

Step 3: Pouring and Labeling

- It is helpful to have your pouring station ready to go, so you can turn the heat off on your salve to add the Vitamin E and lavender essential oil (which are heat-sensitive) and pour before the beeswax firms up the salve.

- Lay out a newspaper on the counter or table. Arrange the tins or jars, with their lids off, nearby.

- Have your lavender essential oil, butter knife, and rags or paper towels nearby.

- Ladle out melted salve into a glass measuring cup to pour.

- Stir in the lavender essential oil: if using a 4-cup glass measuring cup, add about 1-1/2 to 2 tablespoons of lavender essential oil. Stir with a butter knife. If you're using a 2-cup glass measuring cup, add 1-1/2 cups of salve and 2 teaspoons of lavender essential oil and stir. Lid the essential oil bottles immediately after use so their aromas do not dissipate.

- Pour the salve quickly into the containers before it hardens in the measuring cup.

- Allow the salves to cool before you lid them so condensation does not build up inside the tins or jars, which can cause mold.

- Clean up from salve making is messy. Wipe down everything with paper towels or rags that you do not mind composting or throwing out. It seems wasteful but washing these oily containers, utensils and rags in the sink or washing machine will clog up your pipes for a more expensive problem down the line. I've learned the hard way. It is nice to have some friends around to massage the excess oils onto, which also feels less wasteful.

- Once the salve has completely cooled, lid and label your salve with the name, the ingredients, uses, and date made. Salves will usually last 1-3 years.

- Record any notes in your recipe book for future salve-making successes like how many you made, and how much beeswax you ended up using.

ACKNOWLEDGMENTS

It's true, it takes a village to bring a book to life! I'd like to start out by thanking Erica at Harbor Lane Books for taking a chance on me and bringing my story to life. Many, many thanks for working extra hard to make my manuscript the best it could be and for bringing all the small details on the cover to life!

I never would have conceived of the Aromatherapy Apothecary series without the encouragement from my bonus daughter, Briana, who introduced me to the many benefits of aromatherapy. Thank you for your inspiration!

My gratitude to Maggie Stauble for linking me to a variety of aromatherapy Facebook groups and especially for connecting me to A.C. Stauble, Clinical Herbalist and The Traveling Herb Farmer. I am deeply indebted to A.C. for sharing her extensive expertise with me and answering my countless questions. She also graciously allowed me to share her recipe for Lavender Skin Healing Salve. https://www.travelingherbfarmer.com/

To my beta readers, Dan (I never knew how handy it would be to marry an engineer who has both a logical mind and the patience to find the plot holes!), Janet Clause, and Kathleen Costa, I appreciate your time and willingness to read my unpolished manuscripts.

And most of all, thank you to family, friends, and readers who give me the motivation to face a blank page and start writing.

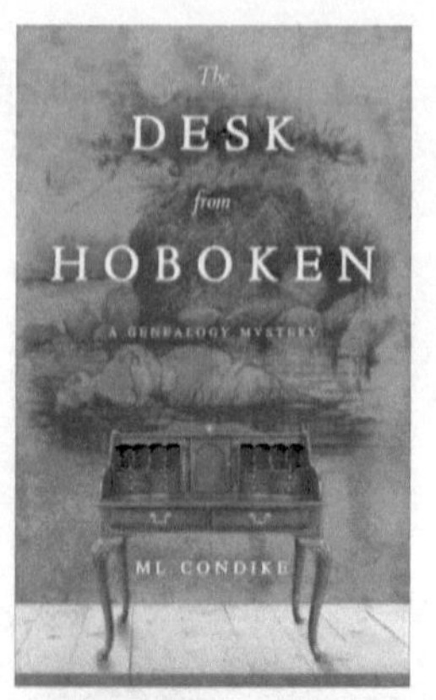
The
DESK
from
HOBOKEN
A GENEALOGY MYSTERY
ML CONDIKE

The
DOLL
from
DUNEDIN
A GENEALOGY MYSTERY
ML CONDIKE
author of The Desk from Hoboken

ESSENTIALS
— OF —
MURDER
KIM DAVIS

MURDEROUS
CONSEQUENCES
USA TODAY BESTSELLING AUTHOR
NICOLE LEIREN

VENGEFUL
CONSPIRACIES
USA TODAY BESTSELLING AUTHOR
NICOLE LEIREN

SHATTERED
SIGHT
THE JACKSON DAVIS MYSTERIES #1
LIZ MILLIRON

ABOUT THE AUTHOR

Kim Davis writes the Aromatherapy Apothecary cozy mystery series, the award-winning Cupcake Catering cozy mystery series, and the middle grade fantasy adventure The Board Game Chronicles series. She has also written several children's nature articles published in a variety of magazines.

Kim Davis is a member of Sisters in Crime, Mystery Writers of America, and Society of Children's Book Writers and Illustrators.

She lives in Southern California with her husband and rambunctious mini Goldendoodle, Missy, who has become an inspiration for several plotlines. When she's not spending time with her granddaughters or chasing Missy around, she can be found either writing on her next book, working on her blog, Cinnamon, Sugar, and a Little Bit of Murder, or in the kitchen baking up yummy treats to share. To learn more, please visit http://kimdavisauthor.com/

ABOUT THE PUBLISHER

Harbor Lane Books, LLC is a US-based independent digital publisher of commercial fiction, non-fiction, and poetry.

Connect with Harbor Lane Books on their website www.harborlanebooks.com and on social media @harborlanebooks.

facebook.com/harborlanebooks

x.com/harborlanebooks

instagram.com/harborlanebooks

threads.com/harborlanebooks

pinterest.com/harborlanebooks